TOO HOT

TO

HANDLE

St. Martin's Titles
by Cheryl Holt

Further Than Passion

More Than Seduction

Deeper Than Desire

Complete Abandon

Absolute Pleasure

Total Surrender

Love Lessons

TOO HOT

～ TO ～

HANDLE

Cheryl Holt

1

"The earl will be with you . . . soon."

The snooty butler, who'd introduced himself as Mr. Fitch, tugged on his vest. Feeling small and out of place, Emily Barnett straightened in her chair.

"Will the wait be awfully long?" she asked.

"I can't say. Lord Winchester is enjoying himself immensely, so he's in no mood to hurry. The *interviews* are progressing slowly."

"I see." A bundle of nerves, she fidgeted. She'd never previously had a job interview, especially one scheduled in the middle of the night, and she was terrified. What sort of eccentric, as Winchester was renowned to be, demanded an appointment at two in the morning?

In a whisper, she dared to pose, "Is His Lordship questioning the applicants?"

The butler gave an undignified snort. "I don't believe there's much *talking* going on in the room."

Emily frowned. Considering the magnitude of the position, that of governess to the earl's new wards—two girls who'd recently been orphaned—she'd expected to be bowled over with inquiries as to her background and experience. Not that she had any true credentials or skills to offer.

Anxiously, she fingered her bag that held the paltry résumé she'd concocted. As part of her pathetic ruse, she'd lied and fictionalized, inventing prior posts and naming imaginary references, from her beloved village of Hailsham. Without a doubt, the document was the most creative piece of writing ever devised.

She'd worried that professionals in the city would be too shrewd to fall for such an evident fabrication, but the gentleman at the employment service had scarcely glanced at the papers before sending her to meet with Lord Winchester. Supposedly, the earl needed someone immediately, and Emily was determined to be that some-one. She absolutely could not fail!

"If Lord Winchester isn't questioning the candidates," she tentatively ventured, "what—precisely—is he doing?"

The butler made a choking sound, and a crimson blush stained his cheeks. "Really, Miss Barnett!"

"Pardon me, sir," she hastened to apologize. "I don't mean to be impertinent, but I'm new to this endeavor. Any suggestions you could share would be greatly appreciated."

His flush deepened. "I hardly think I'm the individual to advise you as to how you should conduct yourself."

She sighed. Amiability was wasted on the man. He had a heart of stone and couldn't be bothered to throw a few crumbs of courtesy her way. He could never com-prehend how frantic she was, how despairing over the future, and she wondered about her competition.

She was positive they were an intimidating group of the

most educated, strict, and cultured females in England. By comparison, she was a dowdy, provincial nobody.

She didn't stand a chance.

Why had she presumed she had the wherewithal to rectify her predicament? What insane folly had driven her to Lord Winchester's door?

"It's so hopeless," she murmured, her head dropping into her hands.

After a lengthy silence, the butler prodded, "What is?"

In her morose condition, she'd forgotten he was lurking. She peeked up, and he was glaring so keenly that she was cowed into commenting. "Well, Mama and Papa passed on within a few months of each other, and there's my widowed sister, Mary. She's blind, and her daughter, Rose, is only nine, so I must watch over them. We came to London so that I could . . . could . . ."

Her voice trailed off. She hadn't intended to explain, but the stress was wearing on her, making her behave stupidly. She was fatigued, petrified, and at her wits' end as to how she should proceed. If the job didn't pan out, she couldn't predict their fate.

They couldn't go home. Her cousin, Reginald, was in Hailsham and ensconced at Barnett Manor. As her father's heir, Reginald was destined to marry her. He wouldn't actually inherit the house, property, or the money necessary to run the tiny estate until he and Emily were wed.

Emily had been resolved to do her duty, to have boring, stuffy Reginald for her husband, as her father had wished. That is, until she'd inadvertently learned of his genuine character. He'd been secretly plotting to commit Mary to an asylum, and the news had sent Emily scrambling to London, with Mary and Rose in tow.

While Reginald frittered away in Hailsham, her pile of precious cash had dwindled, and she was growing desperate.

"So you're contemplating this . . . this outrage to support your family?" The butler was reproachful, condemning.

She bristled. "Yes."

"And your sister is blind?"

"Since she was seven."

"How old is she now?"

"Twenty-eight."

"How old are you?" he asked.

"Twenty-six."

"She knows you're here?"

"Of course."

"Your elder sister condones that you would . . . would . . . *prostitute* yourself merely to earn a few paltry coins?" He wagged a judgmental finger. "For shame, Miss Barnett. For shame!"

"Mr. Fitch!" She stood, pulling herself up to her full height of five feet, four inches. "You've no call to be rude. Good, solid labor never killed anyone. A woman in dire straits must fend for herself."

"There is always other employment." His arrogant nose was stuck up in the air. "Suitable employment."

He certainly had a poor opinion of his boss. She'd heard some appalling stories about Winchester but had chosen to disregard them. No gentleman could be that notorious.

"There's no disgrace in working for a living," she staunchly declared.

He scoffed. "How could you suppose that an innocent

such as yourself would have any talent for pleasing a scoundrel like Lord Winchester?"

"I'm sure he's partial to the more experienced ladies available in the city—"

"Experienced *ladies*!"

"—but I have my own charms and quirks, which I believe he'll find most refreshing. And . . . I've brought numerous references." For emphasis, she showed him her reticule where the *faux* list was discreetly hidden.

"Egad! References!" he grumbled. "Times must have changed in the country since I was a lad. I ought to take a switch to you. I ought to take a switch to your sister."

"Honestly, Mr. Fitch, with your attitude, how will Lord Winchester hire anybody? Who would stay around to be insulted by you?"

She was close to storming out, herself, but her grim prospects kept her feet firmly planted on the floor. Who was Fitch to criticize her simply because circumstances had laid her low? She was doing the best she could.

Her affront was palpable, and it seemed to register with the thick fellow. "I understand your dreadful situation," Fitch claimed, "but I want to confirm that you grasp the consequences of what you're about."

"It's just a job, Mr. Fitch. I'll survive it."

"If you're so determined, at least you could have costumed yourself for the part." He assessed her functional gray gown, with its high neck, long sleeves, and white cuffs. "The earl has instructed everyone to wear red."

"Why?"

"It's his favorite color."

On a governess? "Do I look like the sort of person who would own a red dress?"

"No; that's why I can't fathom your going through with this." He spun away. "I'll fetch you when it's your turn."

He stomped off, and she seethed in the quiet. A table of punch and scones had been arranged, which she deemed touching and odd. She walked over to it and was embarrassed at how her stomach growled. She wolfed down a scone; then, peeking about to guarantee no one was watching, she stuffed more into her purse. In their dismal rented room, food was a scarce commodity, and Mary and Rose would enjoy the treat.

The scone was a tad dry, and she ladled a glass of punch to wash it down. The liquid was bubbly and fruity, and she liked how it tickled her throat, how it heated her cheeks. She had another and another, swilling it so quickly that the sweet concoction made her dizzy.

There was a mirror on the wall, and she stared into it. She'd been reduced to penury, to thieving a rich man's pastries in order to eat. When her entire life had been ripped to shreds, how could she appear so normal?

Her auburn hair was in a tidy bun, the wavy strands meticulously concealed with dozens of pins and combs. Her emerald eyes were expressive, guileless, providing ample evidence that she was the innocent Mr. Fitch had accused her of being. She'd been raised in a quaint village, the daughter of a gentleman, a homebody who'd whiled away the years caring for her aging parents and invalid sister.

She was so far out of her element. How could she hope to convince Lord Winchester that she'd be a proficient governess?

Her nerves frayed, she gulped several more glasses of punch, and the frothy pink mixture had a palliative effect. She slumped down in her chair, her limbs loose and too relaxed to hold her in the seat. If she wasn't vigilant, she'd slide to the rug.

What was in the punch? She hadn't thought to inquire. If she didn't know better, she'd suspect Lord Winchester had spiked it with liquor.

She hiccupped—loudly—as a ruckus erupted in the hall. Another applicant had finished her interview and was leaving. As the woman passed by, Emily was shocked.

The woman was a strumpet! She was attired in a bright crimson dress, the bodice cut so low that it barely covered anything that ought to be covered. She had an enormous bosom, her breasts trying to escape the confines of her corset. Her brows had been plucked, and her lips were painted red, her cheeks, too, and she'd donned an elaborate hat with a feather trailing behind.

This was her competition? What was Lord Winchester thinking? Who would let such an unrestrained trollop in the door? Her confidence soared. Within the hour, she'd have the position; then she'd rush back to Mary with the marvelous news.

The woman halted and bluntly evaluated Emily's conservative outfit.

"Lord, love"—the woman sneered—"what are you pretending to be? The maidenly governess?"

"I'm not *pretending,*" Emily insisted. "I am the ah . . . the ah . . ." Her mind was fuzzy, her tongue tangled.

"I wouldn't count on landing the post," the woman brashly maintained. "Not after how I entertained him."

Emily panicked. What did the hussy know that Emily didn't? What covert deeds was a governess required to perform? "How have you *entertained* him?"

"As if I'd divulge any of my tricks!" She appraised Emily as a rival, then chuckled. "You're too skinny to be a threat."

She strutted out as Mr. Fitch announced, "The earl will see you now, Miss Barnett."

"Fabulous," she replied, but she rose too rapidly. The floor swayed, and she steadied herself by grabbing onto a sofa. She hiccupped again.

Fitch studied her and scowled. "You're sotted."

"I am not," she bravely contended.

He glanced at the punch bowl, which contained much less liquid than it had when she'd arrived. "Miss Barnett, how much punch have you had?"

"Why?"

"Oh, for pity's sake. It was laced with rum! The earl has it shipped in from his plantations in Jamaica."

He clasped her arm and escorted her down the hall, and Emily struggled to keep up. She was disoriented, the corridor an endless gauntlet. Finally, Fitch led her into a candlelit room. Even though it was the middle of June, and a balmy night outside, a fire roared in the grate and, as if she'd been dropped onto a tropical island, she was hit by a blast of humid air.

She squinted into the shadows, stunned to note that the chamber was a virtual den of iniquity, decorated with potted plants, decadent colors, and plush daybeds. Large pillows were scattered about, as if she could plop down anywhere to get comfortable. It was the kind of place one read about in books, a reclusive count's hideaway, or a sheik's refuge in Arabia. If a harem of veiled concubines had flitted by, she wouldn't have been surprised.

A male voice sounded, a deep, sonorous baritone that

tickled her innards and rattled her bones, but she couldn't locate from where it originated.

"Who have we here, Mr. Fitch?"

"Miss Emily Barnett, sir."

"Emily . . ." He spoke her name as if it was honey and he was tasting it.

"She's recently moved to London from the country. To seek employment."

"From the *country*?" the man mused. "Oh, how I love variety."

"She claims she has references, but I feel duty-bound to mention that she may be a tad out of your league."

"But she's managed to snag herself the most lucrative appointment in town. She can't be all that naive."

"She's drunk, sir. She didn't realize there was rum in the punch."

Emily had never imbibed of hard spirits, and truth be told, she was beginning to wonder if she wasn't a bit foxed. There was no other explanation for her wooziness, which had her pondering what type of madhouse she'd entered.

Who would slyly intoxicate a potential governess? Was it a test? If so, she'd failed miserably.

"Be silent, Mr. Fitch," she snapped as she squinted into the gloom, "or I'll tattle as to how much you dislike Lord Winchester. And I'm not drunk."

The curious man barked out a laugh. "Did you hear that, Fitch? She's going to tell the earl how much you despise him."

With no rejoinder, Fitch slinked out. Left alone, her heart pounding, Emily stood her ground.

"Come to me," the man commanded.

She stepped farther into the room, slithering through a gauze curtain, and on the other side, she was face-to-face with the most handsome man she'd ever seen. He lounged on a huge chair that resembled a throne. His hair was black and worn much longer than was fashionable, and his eyes were an intense, mesmerizing shade of blue. He was tall—six feet, at least—and he was lean and fit, as if he practiced fencing or pugilism to keep himself in shape.

Dressed in casual dishabille, he had on a flowing shirt and trousers, the sort she'd expect to witness on a sultan or a pirate. The shirt was loose and open at the neck, baring his chest partway down. She'd never viewed a man's chest before, and amazingly, it was covered with a matting of hair, as black as the hair on his head. She was fascinated and couldn't stop staring.

He hadn't shaved, and his cheeks were darkened with stubble. He looked like a dangerous bandit, capable of any nefarious conduct, and a ripple of trepidation swept over her.

Was she dreaming? She was so exhausted, and it was so late. Had she fallen asleep in the parlor?

Discreetly, she pinched her wrist, but the tweak was discernible.

She approached until she was directly in front of him, and though she had a sinking feeling that she'd already gleaned his identity, she queried, "Who are you?"

"I am Michael Farrow, Lord Winchester."

She winced. "I didn't mean what I said about Mr. Fitch. He thinks you're a splendid emp—"

Lord Winchester cut her off with a wave of his hand. "It's no secret that he loathes me. And with valid reason."

He scrutinized her, taking a slow and inappropriate journey across her bosom, her tummy, her thighs, and he frowned. "I hate your gown."

"I'm sorry." Of her small number of outfits, it was by far the most conservative and unadorned. "I'd thought it would be best for the role I hope to play."

"What role is that? The virtuous governess?"

"Well . . . yes."

"I suppose a fantasy could be amusing"—he shrugged—"although I'm not much for games. I fail to grasp how you'll entice me when you're attired in gray. Do you know anything about masculine inclinations?"

"Of course," which was a blatant fib. Her upbringing had been extremely sheltered, her contact with men garnered through her relationships with her father and Reginald.

"I'd advised the interested candidates to wear red."

"I don't have any clothes that are red."

"Miss Barnett, have you any actual experience at this kind of thing?"

"An ample amount."

"Really?"

"I'm a veritable expert."

"Surely, you jest." He raised a skeptical brow.

"I've had many previous positions."

"And were your prior employers *satisfied* with your performance?"

"Each and every time."

"These references of which you're so proud"—he chuckled—"would your patrons be anyone with whom I'm acquainted?"

"I'm positive they're not." She'd invented the names,

having copied them from gravestones in the Hailsham cemetery.

"Good. I detest having to share my intimate associations with friends."

Rising, he uncurled from his chair and closed the distance between them. He was so near that his feet slipped under the hem of her skirt, his legs tangling with her own. He towered over her, and as she peered up at him, she felt giddy and wild, and she speculated as to what he intended, but she couldn't begin to guess. She'd never met another quite like him.

At the placement agency, there'd been some vague remarks as to his being odd, as to his having irregular habits—hence an interview in the dead of night—but Emily had assumed they'd meant *odd* in a normal way, that he let his dogs run in the mansion, or that he smoked cigars at the table.

None of the ambiguous caveats had prepared her for the reality.

She'd never had a beau, so she hadn't realized that standing next to an adult male could be so invigorating. Her senses reeled; her mind whirred; her pulse hammered with excitement. It was so thrilling to be sequestered with him, to be thrown together in such an unusual setting. She could feel the heat emanating from his skin, could smell the soap with which he'd bathed. There was another scent, too, that was earthy and alluring, and she suspected it was his very essence.

She had the strangest urge to reach out and rest her palm on his chest, and the notion was so bizarre, and so out of character, that she was shocked by her whimsy.

Obviously, her inhibitions were lowered, and she had to proceed cautiously.

"You don't seem the type who would want to do this," he was commenting.

"Oh, I absolutely am," she insisted.

"You'd have to be available at all hours. There's no telling when I might demand your services."

"I'm not afraid of hard work."

"You'd have to do whatever I ask."

"That goes without saying."

"I have some very specific tastes," he asserted.

"Which I'm happy to accommodate."

"How much would you seek as remuneration?"

"Not much. Just enough to pay my bills."

"What?" He was greatly surprised. "No pretty baubles? No gowns from Paris? No house in Mayfair? No private box at the theater?"

For a governess? What peculiar requirements! The other applicants had to be incredibly avaricious. He was wealthy, so perhaps they anticipated they could take advantage of him, or perhaps standards were different in London.

"That would be preposterous. I have very simple needs."

"Ah . . . a thrifty and generous soul. How refreshing."

"What about the girls?" She was curious as to the two orphans who'd been delivered into his care. One was sixteen, and the other nine.

As if he wasn't aware to whom she alluded, he was confused. "What girls?"

"Your new wards."

"My wards? Why would you inquire about them?"

"Would you permit me to meet them, so you can decide if we're compatible?"

Mystified, he assessed her; then he vigorously shook his head. "There's no reason for the three of you to be introduced."

She was crushed. Apparently, she hadn't won the post. How had she disappointed him? With her looks? Her clothes? Her mannerisms? Her . . . her . . . getting drunk on the punch?

She was so distraught that she worried she might burst into tears. Couldn't she succeed at any task? If she couldn't secure a mere job of governess, what would become of Mary and Rose?

He leaned nearer, as she tipped back, which caused her to lose her balance. Her knees were wobbly, her stomach queasy, and she swayed precariously. She was so fatigued, and it would be so marvelous to rest for a while.

He steadied her, latching onto her waist, her hip. "Are you all right?"

"I'm a bit discomfited by the punch," she admitted.

"You definitely are."

"I should go."

The prospect saddened her. Once she departed, she'd never see him again. These few brief minutes were some of the most exhilarating she'd ever spent with another human being.

"I don't think you should," he said, granting her a reprieve. "Not yet anyway."

He was caressing her arm, massaging the soft section above her elbow. The action made it difficult to concentrate, difficult to focus.

"But . . . but . . . it doesn't appear that I'm the person for whom you're searching."

"I disagree. You might be precisely what I need."

Her knees gave out, and he responded immediately, scooping her up so she wouldn't collapse onto the rug.

She was cradled to his chest, and she suffered from an astonishing and capricious impulse to kiss him, which made her conjecture as to whether the punch had addled her. She'd never been kissed before, had never given the deed much thought, but suddenly, it was an endeavor she'd very much like to try. He was staring, too, as if he was considering the same.

Surely, he wasn't a knave who cavorted with his servants. Or was he? The chamber was so dissolutely festooned, the atmosphere so hedonistic, that she had to ponder the possibility of a wicked scheme.

Was he in the habit of luring unsuspecting females into his web by using employment as bait?

She scoffed. No one could be that depraved.

She gazed at him, probing for signs of evil or deceit, but she sensed no treachery. She'd always been a fair judge of character, and she was persuaded that he had a noble heart—despite the image he projected to the world—but how she could be so certain of his stellar traits was a puzzle she was too muddled to solve.

"I hate to impose," she told him, "but could I lie down for a moment? I'm awfully tired."

"An excellent idea. How about if I join you?" He grinned, a dimple creasing his cheek, his blue, blue eyes twinkling with mischief.

"My goodness, no. I'll catch my breath; then I'll be on my way. I promise."

"There's no hurry," he declared. "Take your time."

He moved them behind another curtain and deposited her on a luxurious sofa. As if she were a princess, he tucked a pillow under her head, and arranged a knitted throw over her torso; then he seated himself next to her.

"You're so pretty," he claimed, tracing a finger across her lips.

No man had ever uttered an endearment to her, and though it was wrong for him to have said it, she soared with elation. What a vain creature she was!

"You're a scoundrel," she scolded.

"As I've been informed. On many occasions."

"I like you anyway. In fact, I believe I'm in love with you."

He laughed. "You are, are you?"

"Yes." Why was he so merry? Was she being funny? She was so mixed-up!

"But how could you know so soon?"

"I make up my mind about people very quickly."

"I can tell." He adjusted the blanket. "Have your nap, my sweet Miss Barnett; then we'll see you safely home."

"But what about the position? Did I get it?"

"It's not appropriate for you."

"Please . . . I . . . ."

"Hush. We'll talk about it later."

He brushed his hand over her eyes, so that they drifted shut, and she swiftly slipped into oblivion, but as she floated away, it seemed as if he kissed her—directly on the mouth—although it might have been a dream.

2

Smiling and stretching, Emily stirred. She was warm, cozy, and she wakened slowly, yet as consciousness dawned, she froze and panicked as she tried to recall where she was.

Realization struck with a vengeance.

She was on the sofa where Lord Winchester had placed her, but how long had she lain, oblivious and unaware?

Listening for movement, for voices, she cocked an ear. The only discernible sound was a clock's ticking, but she couldn't see the clock, so it offered no help or reassurance. What time was it? The drapes were pulled, the gauze curtains blocking any light, so it might have been any hour. Was she alone? Had she been left to rest and recover what little dignity she had remaining?

As she lurched to a sitting position, her head pounded with such a violent ache that she worried the top might blow off, and she flopped down onto the pillow. Her stomach roiled, her mouth was dry as dust, and at that instant, she'd have killed for a glass of water.

A flurry of memories assaulted her. It seemed as if she'd flirted with Winchester, had perhaps even babbled that she loved him, and she shuddered with dread. Was it possible? How thoroughly had she embarrassed herself?

She had to escape with the minimal amount of humiliation. If she was lucky—which she hadn't been so far— she'd sneak out without encountering anyone. If she had the horrid misfortune of stumbling upon Mr. Fitch or Winchester, she couldn't conceive of what she should say. There was no way to muster any aplomb.

Ignoring her nausea, she stood and took a faltering step, then another, when feminine laughter stopped her in her tracks. It was an alluring titter that emanated from the direction of Winchester's fancy throne.

Oh gad! A woman was in the room. What were the chances? Couldn't anything go right?

She needed to learn what was happening so that she could plot her exit and slip away undetected. On tiptoe, she went to the curtain and peered around the edge.

The woman was buxom, shapely, with blond locks curling to her hips. She was attired in a silky red robe, and as Emily spied on her, she slithered out of it. From the waist up, she was naked, her breasts exposed, her nipples jutting out. Her bottom was outlined in a pair of frilly drawers that dropped below her knees, her calves covered in lace stockings, her dainty feet balanced on spiky heels.

Emily was transfixed by the sight. She hadn't known that a female might prance about in the nude. Nor had she grasped that there were such outrageous undergarments in existence. She hadn't thought that unmentionables had any purpose beyond modesty and functionality.

She couldn't quit staring.

The woman was sipping on a glass of wine, and she dipped her finger into the liquid and dabbed some onto her nipple. Emily was so shocked that, lest she gasp aloud, she clapped a hand over her mouth.

The woman thrust her bosom up and out, and she inquired over her shoulder, "Would you like a taste?"

"No," a man answered.

Winchester! He was lounging on his throne, drinking wine, too, and peevishly assessing the woman. His shirt was off, his chest bare, and Emily could view the matting of hair that she'd glimpsed previously. It was thick across the top; then it thinned and descended into his trousers, disappearing to points Emily couldn't imagine.

"Not even a nibble?" the woman asked. "Are you sure?"

"Very."

She dipped into the wine again and slathered her other nipple. "Take a good look, darling. I know how you like to watch."

"I like to *watch*," he replied, "if there's anything worth seeing."

"Don't be surly," the woman pouted. "I said I was sorry."

"You have no idea how to be sorry."

"Oh, I do," she cooed. "I really do." She climbed onto his lap. Her thighs were spread, her knees perched on either side of his, and she caressed him between their bodies in a manner that made him squirm and writhe. "You can't pretend you're not interested. I know you too well. You're glad I came."

"Don't be so smug, Amanda," he cautioned. "An anonymous whore could arouse me as easily as you."

Emily gaped at them. Lord Winchester wasn't married, so Amanda had to be his mistress. Emily had never met anyone quite so notorious, and she was fascinated. As she had been raised in a rural village, there hadn't been many courtesans parading around in men's parlors. Amanda earned her living by providing Lord Winchester with feminine favors, but Emily was curious as to what those *favors* entailed. What services could Amanda offer to Winchester for which he was eager to pay?

Evidently, they'd had a spat and Amanda was hoping to reconcile, but Emily couldn't stay around to observe how the tryst ended. There was no telling what she might witness.

How had she landed herself in such a wretched predicament? And how was she to get herself out of it? The door was so far away that it might as well have been across the ocean. She couldn't creep out without being spotted.

A vision of Winchester's two wards popped into her mind, and she wondered how he could bring the girls into such a foul environment. Were they already in London? Were they residing in the house? What if one of them wandered in while he was philandering?

The notion had her so angry that she considered rushing out, scolding the couple for their reprehensible behavior, then stomping off in an insulted huff, but she was too much of a coward. Winchester must have forgotten that she was dozing on his sofa, or perhaps he presumed she'd gone, and she couldn't figure out how to make her presence known.

Amanda began a calculated seduction, but she wasn't

having much success. He was furious with her and not inclined to participate. Yet the more he ignored her, the harder she tried to entice. She snuggled and nestled, and when he didn't react, she placed his hand on her breast. For a moment, he relented and squeezed the nipple.

The gesture had an intriguing effect on Emily's anatomy. It felt as if he were stroking her *own* breasts, as if he were pinching her *own* nipples, and they ached and throbbed with each beat of her heart. She was hot, dizzy with excitement. The mysterious woman's spot between her legs grew moist, and her womb seemed to shift and stir.

Emily was stunned. Was this typical conduct among men and women? Did they regularly engage in such antics? This had to be the secret of the marital bed. How could she be twenty-six years old and not have learned about it?

If she'd wed Reginald, would she have been required to flaunt herself before him? She shivered with dread. The thought of Reginald touching her so intimately was disgusting.

But I could do it for Lord Winchester. . . .

The naughty concept whizzed past, leaping into her head so quickly and with such vehemence that she frightened herself. Was there a lusty side to her character of which she wasn't aware? Had she been furtively pining away for a man's physical attention? How could she have been when she wasn't cognizant of what the attention entailed? Reginald always claimed that she'd been a spinster too long. Was he correct?

"You're very tense," Amanda was commenting. "How about if I relax you?"

"It won't do you any good. I'm not taking you back."

"So you've insisted before."

"This time I mean it," he declared.

"No, you don't."

Amanda was so confident, so assured, and she blazed a trail of kisses down his stomach, to his navel and lower. She slid to the floor and knelt, as she untied his trousers and reached inside, which finally produced a response.

Winchester fidgeted, his fingers gripping the arms of the chair. He appeared stressed, yet pleased, and Emily strained on tiptoe, anxious to see what Amanda was doing.

Amanda smirked. "You never could resist me."

"Like I said," he told her, "any whore will suffice."

She halted and scowled. "You're being cruel."

"Did I ask you to stop by?"

"No, and now that I have, I'm not certain why I bothered."

"Maybe because you're worried about how you'll afford your town house if I toss you over?"

Apparently, he'd pushed her too far, and Emily was positive Amanda would slap him.

"You callous beast!" Amanda snapped. "Be my guest! Choose some cheap doxy over me! As if I care. I hope you come down with a virulent case of the pox."

She whipped away, prepared to tramp out, but before she could, Winchester seized her and pulled her to him so that she was, once again, hovering over his lap. While she put up a struggle, it was obvious she was pretending, that she had no intention of fleeing. He knew it, and she knew it, and it was part of an odd game they enjoyed.

Emily was confused. When it was clear that they abhorred each other, why keep on?

Winchester was rich and powerful, so he could have any woman he wanted, and Emily suffered from the strongest urge to march out, to grab him by the shoulders and shake some sense into him. Didn't he realize that he could do better?

"I suddenly find myself in the mood," he informed Amanda. "Finish what you started."

"No."

"Last I checked, I hadn't ceased paying you. I suggest you earn your salary."

"I'm worth every penny you give me."

"You're entitled to your opinion." He shrugged. "I'm entitled to mine."

"I'm the best you've ever had!"

"You have a bad habit of overestimating your value."

"And you constantly misjudge how much you need me."

"Then I should be reminded," he stated. "Get down on your knees and make yourself useful."

"Bastard!" she cursed.

"Now, now, you shouldn't question my antecedents. My parents were married a full six months before I was born."

He dipped down and latched onto her nipple, sucking hard, nipping at it in a way that had Amanda sighing with pleasure. He grew impatient and ripped off her drawers, and he massaged her between her legs, his fingers working in a slow rhythm until she was quivering with ecstasy.

"I love it when you do that," she groaned.

"Shut up," he chided. "I'm sick of listening to you."

He clasped her thighs and widened them; then he lurched against her. She let out a cry of either pain or delight—Emily couldn't decide which—and they began moving together, rocking in a peculiar sort of dance.

Emily was mesmerized, so swept up that she couldn't breathe. Amanda was noticeably thrilled, but how was Winchester spurring her to such rapture?

Their motions increased, Winchester flexing methodically with his hips, and Emily strove to ascertain what was driving him, but peeking through the curtain made it difficult. She leaned in, her hand balanced on a wobbly decorative table, when, without warning, it collapsed and tipped over with a loud crash. She had no time to right herself, and she tumbled into the room, materializing so swiftly and so completely that she might have been a sorceress.

Amanda squealed with affront, as Winchester said, "What the devil?"

Amanda jumped away from him to frantically scoop up her robe and tug it on, while Winchester yanked at his trousers. If it hadn't been the most humiliating episode of Emily's life, their frenzied ruckus might have been comical.

She was mortified to her very core and determined to talk herself out of the mess. What would Winchester say? What would he do? What was the penalty for spying on an aristocrat while he was in the throes of passion with his mistress?

"Who the hell are you?" Amanda demanded.

"Emily Barnett." Longingly, she studied the door. She considered racing for it, but she didn't imagine they'd permit her to escape so easily.

"Miss . . . Miss Barnett?" Winchester was aghast. "How dare you interrupt. What were you thinking?"

"I . . . I fell asleep."

"But that was last night. Why are you still here?"

"I apologize. I just woke up."

Her malice palpable, Amanda snarled at Winchester, "You know this . . . this . . . interloper?"

"She's one of the top candidates."

Amanda was incensed. "What's she supposed to be? The innocent governess?"

"Yes," Winchester retorted. "She likes to play games."

"You detest games."

"No. I detest *you*."

Amanda glared at him. "If you take her out in public, you'll be a laughingstock."

"I doubt it," he said. "Picture her in a stylish gown. She'll be stunning, and every man of my acquaintance will be green with envy."

"You're a dreamer."

"You wouldn't believe how *satisfied* I was during our interview."

"You wretch!" Amanda seethed.

"I so enjoy a pretty face."

"She's not *that* fetching," Amanda insisted.

"Plus she's a naïve lass, straight from the country, who's practically begging to be debauched."

"Debauched?" Emily interjected, though neither of them paid her any heed.

"You perverted beast!" Amanda reprimanded. "You'd lie down with a barnyard animal."

"After the fare upon which I'm used to dining," he rejoined, "I'm sure she'll be most appetizing. I can't wait to commence."

Emily fumed. Clearly, he had designs on her that went

far beyond what she would agree to as his servant. Though she was fearful for his wards, and the future they'd have under his roof, no force in the world was strong enough to compel her to accept the position.

"Actually, I've changed my mind," she stated. "I'm not interested."

"Of course you are," Winchester asserted in a tone that brooked no argument. "And the job is yours."

He was wealthy and omnipotent. Could he order her to work for him? She wasn't certain, but she sidled toward the door. "No, thank you. I don't want it."

"But I've picked you, and my decision is final."

"I won't. I can't."

"You have no choice in the matter."

"Oh, yes, I do!" Her knees were quaking. Was a commoner allowed to refuse a peer of the realm?

Amanda took a menacing step toward her. "Be off, you little harlot, before I tear your hair out by the roots!"

Terrified that Amanda might carry out her threat, Emily stumbled away.

"I'm going; I'm going." Emily peeked about for her reticule, which was nowhere in sight.

"This position is filled," Amanda claimed. "By me— as it has been for years. So don't come sniffing around again, or you'll be sorry."

"The position is *not* filled," Winchester contended to Amanda. "We're finished. When will you get it through your thick head?"

"You can't be serious." Amanda gestured at Emily's drab costume. "Look at her. You'd toss me over for that?"

"Miss Barnett will be a fine substitute. I won't miss your dubious companionship for a single second."

Emily was puzzled. Amanda was the governess? But wasn't she the mistress? Was she both governess and mistress?

What a sordid scheme! How horrid for the two children who would be thrust into this cauldron of lust and loathing.

She'd always heard that the lives of the Quality were too bizarre to fathom, and she wouldn't delve into the convoluted relationship between Winchester and Amanda. Whatever was transpiring was beyond her ken, and if the true details were ever disclosed, it would be more than she could abide. It was best to depart and forget about them and what she'd witnessed.

"No, I shan't return," she vowed as she hurried out, mumbling to herself, "I never really wanted to be a governess anyway."

There was a startled silence; then Lord Winchester hollered after her, "What did you say?"

Emily halted and explained, "I'm not cut out to be a governess. I shouldn't have bothered you."

"A governess? You're here because you're hoping to be my governess?"

"Yes." What had the impossible dolt presumed?

"But I thought you wished to be my new mistress."

"Your . . . your mistress? Are you mad?" With each passing minute, it was more obvious that the man was a lunatic.

"Who sent you to me?" he asked.

"The placement agency you hired."

"Are you telling me they arranged an interview in the middle of the night? That's idiotic."

"They said you're an idle sluggard who sleeps all

day," she rudely mentioned, "and you weren't ever available at a decent hour."

He stood, unfolding from his fancy chair like a graceful African cat, and he stalked toward her. She had no idea what he planned, and she wasn't about to wait around and find out. She whirled and darted away.

"Miss Barnett!" he yelled. "Hold it right there!"

She careened down the hall, out the front door, and into the street, where she was dismayed to discover that it had to be noon or later. For the briefest instant, she paused to get her bearings; then she ran toward her rented room without stopping or glancing back.

3

Michael Farrow gazed around the seedy parlor of the boardinghouse where Emily Barnett rented lodgings.

Though he usually went out of his way to offend, and could not care less for the opinion of others, he had a conscience—a buried, ignored, rarely used one—and he felt awful about what had happened.

The placement agency, with which he'd promptly severed his business connection, had given him her address, and he'd sent a footman with a note, which hadn't been answered. A second footman had gone, with orders to obtain a response, but he'd waited in vain. Then Fitch had been dispatched, with instructions not to return without her, but the intrepid fellow hadn't brought her back.

So Michael had lowered himself to visiting, certain that she couldn't refuse to speak with him.

If he had to grovel, if it cost him every penny he possessed, the obstinate female would be his employee. Like it or no.

He abhorred that he'd been reduced to pleading, but

Pamela and Margaret Martin—his two wards, whom he scarcely knew and had no desire to assist—were about to arrive, and he had to have a governess hired.

He understood nothing about children, had none of his own, and never intended to have any. Eighteen years earlier, when Michael had been twelve, his father had killed Michael's mother in a jealous rage by tossing her off a balcony. Then he'd killed himself with a pistol shot to the head. Michael was terrified that their insanity ran in his veins, and he wouldn't risk passing on his tainted blood to any unsuspecting offspring, so he was in desperate need of guidance and advice.

He simply couldn't watch over the Martin girls, and why their father—his main partner in a decade of depravity and vice—had deemed Michael a suitable guardian was a mystery. His reputation for corruption was so low that no other woman had had the courage to apply to be his governess. Emily had been the only one with the gumption to seek the position, but without his realizing her purpose, she'd foolishly plopped herself in the middle of his search for a new mistress.

Amanda had been his consort for ages, having weaved her greedy presence through every facet of his life, until it was difficult to split with her. Their public fighting, their breakups and reconciliations, were legendary, but lately, she'd grown too sure of her relationship with him, so he'd decided to solicit for a different paramour. In hopes of wresting the spot away from her, the courtesans of the demimonde were flaunting their sexual prowess.

All of London was aware that he was conducting his outrageous interviews, so how had Miss Barnett stumbled into the despicable carnal foray? She truly was the virtuous country maiden she'd professed herself to be, and when he thought of what she'd seen and heard in his home, he rippled with an unaccustomed wave of shame.

He and his younger brother, Alex, were renowned scapegraces. They philandered and gambled and drank with a reckless abandon. What sensible female would work for them? How could he convince Miss Barnett that what she'd observed was an aberration when everything she'd witnessed was a factual rendering of how he carried on?

Footsteps sounded, and he rose, anticipating Miss Barnett, but it was the landlady.

"Beg pardon, milord," the woman started, "but Miss Barnett insists that she's unavailable."

"Unavailable?" he sputtered.

"That's what she claims."

"Have you apprised her that I'm downstairs?"

"Yes." The woman nodded, edgy as a dog about to be beaten. "May I apologize for her rudeness?"

"You may."

How dare the little nymph decline to attend him! Obviously, she had no idea with whom she was dealing. No one denied him. No one snubbed him or failed to do his bidding. He told others to jump, and they asked, *how high?* She had no say in how the situation would be resolved.

"For how long a period has she paid her rent?" he questioned.

"It was due last Saturday. She's behind."

He opened his purse and proffered a few gold coins. "Should Miss Barnett inquire, you won't accept a late payment, and her apartment has been let to another.

Beginning tomorrow." He marched toward the stairs. "Which room is hers?"

"You can't go up! This is a feminine establishment. No gentlemen are permitted. Not even an exalted one such as yourself."

"Which room, madam?" He slipped another coin into her avaricious hand.

"Third on the left," she mentioned without hesitation.

He climbed the dank, narrow stairwell, crinkling his nose at the odors. It was a dismal abode, and it bothered him that Miss Barnett was reduced to residing in such squalor.

In her rush to flee his mansion, she'd forgotten her reticule, and when he'd peeked into it, it had been stuffed with scones she'd pilfered from his parlor. Was she starving, too?

He'd listened to stories about what befell young women when they moved to the city, but he'd never pondered the social problem. He made it a point to remain detached, yet Miss Barnett had crossed his path in an unexpected way, and for no reason he could specify, he liked her very much. She'd become a real person who was in trouble. If she didn't find a post, and soon, there weren't many rungs to the bottom of the ladder, and he couldn't stand to consider what dire fate loomed.

Outside her door, he paused and rapped once, and it was yanked open.

"Mrs. Smith, you may tell Lord Winchester that I—" Appearing as if she'd seen a ghost, Emily Barnett halted in mid-sentence.

In the stark morning light filtering through the lone window, she was prettier than he recollected. Her auburn

hair was down and brushed out, the curled tresses re-
strained by a single ribbon.

Instead of gray, she was attired in a fetching gown of
green muslin, with a scooped neckline and puffed sleeves
that accented her thin figure, her pert bosom and tiny
waist. The color of the dress set off the emerald in her
eyes and the pink in her cheeks.

He shifted, uncomfortable with how attractive he
found her, and he masked his reaction. His parents' scandals had hardened him, so he was a master at covering up
his emotions. He'd never allow her to discern any heightened sentiment.

"Hello, Miss Barnett."

"Lord Winchester?" She gulped with dismay.

"We meet again."

Before she could slam the door in his face, he strolled
past her.

"Wait a minute," she scolded. "You can't barge in."

"I already have."

As he assessed her pitiful surroundings, he wondered
what abominable predicament had delivered her to such
a juncture. From her demeanor and speech it was clear
she'd been raised in a good family, that she was educated
and cultured.

What catastrophe had transpired?

Another woman sat on the bed, as well as a girl of
eight or nine. There were three of them living in the di-
lapidated space! How wretched!

"Who is it, Emily?" the other woman queried.

As she turned toward him, Michael concluded that she
was Miss Barnett's sister. Her hair was darker, and her
eyes more hazel, but the resemblance was unmistakable.

From how she blankly stared, he was stunned to acknowledge that she was very likely blind.

"It's no one, Mary," Miss Barnett interjected. She urged him toward the door, saying, "If you'll excuse us, sir, it's a violation of the rules to have male visitors."

She gave him a heartrending look—beseechment coupled with fury—but he ignored her and approached her sister.

"I am Michael Farrow, Earl of Winchester."

"Oh my!"

When she started to rise, he added, "Don't get up."

She stood anyway and curtsied, which was awkward in the cramped area. The girl stood, too, and joined her. "I am Mrs. Mary Livingston," the woman announced, "Emily's elder sister. This is my daughter, Rose."

"How do you do, Mrs. Livingston? How do you do, Rose?"

"Very well, thank you," Rose answered politely.

He glanced around again, trying not to gawk, determined not to be affected by their plight, but he couldn't help himself. "Are you a widow, Mrs. Livingston?"

"Why, yes. I have been for several years now."

So . . . there was no man in the picture. Just the three females. On their own. One a child, and one disabled.

Miss Barnett had to locate a salary that would support them, but how could she? They'd never make it. What would happen to Mrs. Livingston? To Rose?

He fought off a shudder of dread. Except for his constant struggles to aid his brother, Alex, he never immersed himself in others' difficulties, yet he was horribly concerned over this trio's dilemma and suffering from the worst need to save them.

What was he? Some bloody knight-of-old out to rescue damsels in distress? He hadn't a benevolent bone in his body, yet he was scared to peek down, lest he suddenly find himself decked out in shining armor.

"It's kind of you to stop by," Mrs. Livingston was commenting. "We're very honored. I wish we were at home in Hailsham, where we'd have had more suitable environs in which to receive you."

"I had to call on you." He perceived a rational soul in Mrs. Livingston. Plus, her civility indicated that Miss Barnett had not discussed the sordid events she'd witnessed. "Your sister applied to be my governess. We had a misunderstanding"—Miss Barnett swallowed down a choking sound—"and I feel awful about the confusion, so I thought it best to personally offer her the job."

"I don't want it!" Miss Barnett vehemently declared.

"Emily!" Mrs. Livingston admonished. "Mind your manners. The earl has journeyed all this way to see you."

Emily scowled. "Mary, I must speak with Lord Winchester. Alone."

She grabbed his arm and dragged him into the hall, closing their door with a sharp click; then she whipped around. "Are you insane?" she hissed. "How dare you come here!"

"My wards will arrive Wednesday afternoon. You begin today."

"I most certainly will not."

"You'll travel to my residence with me in my carriage, and I'll send a wagon for your things."

"I wouldn't work for you if you were the last man on earth!"

"You have no choice."

"I'm not a slave. I'm not in bondage. I'm not indentured to you. You can't force me."

"Actually, I can."

She wagged a reproaching finger. "I realize you have a high opinion of your importance, and you're used to lording yourself over others, but you'll have no success with me. You're like a big, spoiled baby. You think you can act however you please."

"What's the advantage of being an earl if you can't have your own way?"

"You're likely to get me evicted."

"It's a definite worry," he said, "but you can't blame me."

"What do you mean?"

"Your rent is overdue, and your landlady has let the room to someone else. They're moving in tomorrow. She's about to notify you to vacate the premises."

"You're lying, you despicable swine."

"Shall we go down and ask her?" She studied him, searching for evidence of deceit, but he kept his expression carefully blank. "You're about to be tossed out on the street. When you are, what will become of your sister and niece?"

The terror of the prospect gripped her. Her knees grew weak, and she collapsed against the wall. He reached out to steady her, holding her up lest she slide to the floor. They were thrown into an intimate position, their legs tangled, their torsos melded. Quietly, he advised her, "You don't have an alternative, Emily."

"Don't call me that."

Her nearness elated him. His senses reeled; his pulse pounded. Idiotic as it sounded, he was happy, merely from being around her. He couldn't fathom why, but he intended to exploit the impression whenever he had the chance.

"Look, about the other night—"

"Don't remind me." Mortified, she glanced away, and he was chagrined anew.

It was disgraceful that he'd exposed her to his brand of dissipation. There'd been a time in his life when he'd had principles and standards, when he'd abided by the tenets that guided others. When had he drifted from the straight and narrow? He'd wandered so far past the bounds of civilized behavior that he no longer recognized when he was being an ass.

"I was interviewing for a . . . a . . . mistress." He had sufficient conscience left to blush with embarrassment.

"Which is the most contemptible thing I ever heard."

"I didn't know you wanted to be my governess. I assumed you were there to . . . to . . ."

His voice trailed off. He couldn't utter the word *fornicate* in her presence, and his inane need to clarify such a ghastly error was proof that he'd spent entirely too many years wallowing in sin.

"Is your confession supposed to make me feel better?"

"You deserved an explanation."

"Thank you for supplying it. Now go."

"What you saw . . . that's not the kind of man I am." A huge fib, but he hoped it would suffice.

"Hah! It's *precisely* the kind of man you are. You're a lecher. A reprobate."

"I am not!"

"Have you no shame? No morals? How could you bring your wards into such a den of iniquity? Have you no decency remaining?"

"None of that twaddle will be occurring once they arrive," he asserted. "My brother, Alex, and I are bachelors, and we've carried on as bachelors, but that's about to change. The house has been cleaned and tidied. The . . . the women are gone, and they won't be invited back."

"Where will you entertain them? At your club? At your country estate?"

As that had been his exact plan, he gnashed his teeth, hating that she could read him so well. "I'm resolved to be the perfect guardian."

"Bully for you."

He'd never encountered anyone who was so unimpressed by his rank and title. Her disregard was so aggravating, yet so invigorating. He wanted to shake her; he wanted to hug her.

"Emily . . ."

"It is *Miss Barnett* to you."

"Emily," he sweetly coaxed, "would you be my governess? Please?"

"No."

She stepped away, into a darkened corner, and he stepped with her. He relished how he felt when he was around her. She was like a bracing tonic, a fortifying dip into brisk ocean waves, and he had to stay close so that he could bask in the sensations she produced.

"I reviewed your references."

"You snooped in my reticule. How crass!"

"The list is remarkable."

"It's fabricated," she contended. "I invented every single name. I copied them off gravestones in the Hailsham cemetery."

Curious if it was true, he chuckled. "You have the qualities I'm seeking. You're educated, refined, genteel."

"I have no skills, I have no previous experience. I was taught by my mother at her dining table. I've never been a governess, and I have no aptitude for such a post."

"You'll be ideal."

"While visiting your home, I got drunk. You're too polite to say that I passed out, but I did. You're a fool to ask me, so by refusing, I'm saving you from yourself."

Unnerved by how he towered over her, she tried to shove him away but couldn't. As if they were adolescent sweethearts, he clasped their hands and linked their fingers, and he bent down and buried his face in her hair. The soft curls tickled his nose and chin.

"I like you when you're drunk."

"You're the sole man in the kingdom who would be charmed by such appalling conduct."

She edged herself farther into the corner, and he followed, needing to touch her, to be as near as he was able. "Before you fell asleep, you claimed that you're an excellent judge of character. You even insisted that you love me."

"Aah!" she shrieked. "I was intoxicated! I didn't mean what I said, and you're a beast to mention it."

"Do it for me, Emily," he whispered in her ear.

She peered up at him, her eyes wide and trusting, and she was nettled by his earnest request. She was a compassionate individual, and she wanted to stand firm, but she grasped how much he craved her assistance.

Though he couldn't deduce how or why, she made him yearn to be someone else, someone respected and admired, a man worthy of her esteem. She was unsullied, pure, as far removed as could be from his dishonorable acquaintances and sordid amusements. He was eager to spend time in her cheery company. If he were lucky, some of her integrity and propriety might rub off.

She was so close, her ruby lips inches away, and without thinking, he kissed her. In the history of kisses, it wasn't much, but it seemed natural to attempt. In his convoluted swirl of absurd logic, he felt as if she belonged to him, as if she were his.

For a few brief seconds, his mouth was lightly melded to hers, and he was jolted by the contact. He lusted after her in a fashion he hadn't in years, hungering for those heady days when desire had been so exhilarating.

At first, she was amenable. As if holding on for dear life, she gripped his jacket and leaned into him, but sanity swiftly returned, and she lurched away.

"Lord Winchester!" She was stunned, accusing. "What on earth are you doing?"

"Pardon me," he murmured, though he wasn't sorry in the least. He lied, "I don't know what came over me."

"My goodness. I don't know, either."

"You bring out the worst in me."

"I have that effect on people."

They were both embarrassed, gazing anywhere but at each other, while anxious to gracefully end the discussion that he'd thoroughly mucked up, but he couldn't depart without obtaining her consent.

"I need your help, Emily," he stated. "With the girls. No one else has evinced the slightest interest. Only you."

"Well, that certainly has me flattered."

He'd tried commanding, then pleading, but with no success. Perhaps the answer was to be brutally frank.

"They're afraid of my reputation. They're afraid to work for me."

"With valid reason," she scolded, though without her prior fervor.

"My father killed my mother." He wasn't sure why he'd alluded to the incident—he hadn't planned to—but he was desperate. "They all maintain that his insane blood flows through my veins. They stay away because of it."

"You? Insane?"

"Yes."

"That's poppycock. You're not mad. A tad too salacious maybe, but definitely not mad."

"See? You comprehend what sort of man I am deep down. I'll treat you well, and I'll strive to do what's best for the girls."

She studied the floor, his admission weighing on her. Their short kiss had altered their relationship, had lowered barriers and created a novel bond.

Could they be friends? With her a female, how peculiar it would be!

"I believe you're a decent person," she finally concurred, "but you struggle so hard to hide it, and I can't figure out why."

They were the truest, kindest words anyone had ever spoken to him. "I'll pay you whatever you demand. What is your price?"

"It's not the money."

"What, then? I'm rich and powerful. Tell me what you want, and it's yours."

She paused, considering. "So maybe it is the money. You couldn't pay me enough."

"Five hundred pounds."

"A year?"

"Seven hundred fifty."

"An entire family could gambol on that much."

"A thousand."

"Stop it!"

"I need you. Badly. I wasn't joking."

"You're not being serious," she argued. "I couldn't possibly merit such an enormous amount, and I wouldn't allow you to waste so much on me."

"You'd be surprised at how much I deem you to be worth." He assessed her, astounded that he'd offered her a small fortune, with her in dire straits, but she'd been totally unmoved. She was the sole individual he'd ever met who hadn't greedily clutched at his purse.

He grinned, more positive than ever that he was doing the right thing. "Plus room and board."

"That goes without saying."

"For you, but for Mary and Rose, too."

"I couldn't let you."

"Why not? I own a drafty, huge mansion, with just me and my brother lumbering around. There's plenty of space."

"But such an arrangement would be outrageous. What would your servants think?"

"Do I look as if I care?" That wrangled the first smile he'd managed to garner from her. "Rose would be a great help to me, too."

"Rose? How could she be?"

"My wards, Pamela and Margaret, are sixteen and nine. Rose could be a companion for Margaret." They stared at each other, the silence lengthening and settling around them. "Emily, I saw the scones you'd stuffed in your bag. I appreciate how grave your circumstances are, and I won't leave the three of you here."

"I can't decide . . ." As if she had a terrible headache, she rubbed her temples.

"It's for the best, Emily."

Transfixed by nothing, she scrutinized the floor again, as she mentally debated the issue. Ultimately, she muttered, "There couldn't be any inappropriate behavior."

"Meaning?"

She glared at him. "You know precisely to what I refer."

"Not even with you?"

"Especially not with me."

He mulled it over, convinced that if he agreed, he'd be giving up something wonderful. With a sigh, he said, "As you wish."

"And I don't want your lady friend, Amanda, skulking around. I won't have her dropping by, I can't be running into her in your vestibule; I won't have her hallooing us when we're walking down the street." She hesitated. "Swear to me that she's out of your life."

It was an easy vow to make. "She's gone. You'll never have to worry about her."

"Then I'll try it. For three months, which will put us through the summer and into the autumn. After that, we'll discuss the situation to determine if I should continue."

"You'll all come to live at my town house?"

"Yes."

"Today?"

"Yes," she repeated.

"How much will you require as remuneration?"

"When the three months have ended, you can pick the sum, depending on how valuable a service you feel I've rendered."

He scoffed at her naïveté. "You should have lessons in how to negotiate. What if I take advantage and never compensate you?"

"You won't."

He was thrilled by how well she understood him. "No, I won't."

In complete accord, they went to share the news with Mary and Rose.

4

"Let me get this straight." Alex Farrow glared at his older brother. "We're about to be overrun by women."

Michael hemmed and hawed, then admitted, "I guess you could look at it that way."

"You know how I feel about the Martin girls living with us."

"You've been extremely vocal in your objections."

"Any sane man would have sent them directly to boarding school, with the annual letter inquiring after their welfare. But not magnanimous, wonderful you! Oh, no!" Contemptuous of the bloody business, he waved his hand as if the topic were a foul odor he couldn't bear. "By all means. Move them in! Let them have keys to the place! Why set any limits? Why keep our own routines intact?"

"I've merely requested that you not drink in front of them. Or invite any prostitutes over. I'm positive you'll survive."

"You can amuse yourself at your country properties and your club. What am I to do?"

Since Alex's return from his insane stint in the army, their disparate fiscal stations were a constant source of strife. Michael was wealthy and had his fingers in every pie that made up the Winchester coffers, while Alex was reduced to barely subsisting on an allowance that never went far enough.

Alex hated to be envious, to incessantly harp, but his jaunt to the Continent had left him bitter and resentful, and anymore, he couldn't talk to Michael without complaining.

"When the mood for companionship overtakes you," Michael said, "you may use either one," which was an easy boon to grant when Alex wouldn't avail himself of a public haunt. His pride guaranteed that he couldn't tolerate the stares or whispers.

"You're too, too generous," he sarcastically griped. He sounded like a nagging fishwife, but he couldn't stop. "When will the governess arrive?"

"She's already here."

"With her whole damned family! Are we operating a pauper's haven for every unemployed female in London? What were you thinking?"

Michael sighed with exasperation. "Alex, we have a huge mansion, and these destitute women need somewhere to stay. We'll sort it out. Give me the summer to have things settled. That's all I'm asking. It won't kill you to be flexible."

Absently, Alex rubbed the horrendous scar that had ruined his face, detesting—as always—to be reminded of the marring an enemy's sword had inflicted in Portugal. Once, he'd been as handsome as Michael, with the customary Farrow black hair and blue eyes. Now, even his prior fiancée avoided him, and his vanity couldn't abide the derision he experienced from those who were supposed to be his friends. Bit by bit, their veiled pity was destroying him.

"I don't want these strangers poking about," he grumbled.

"I know you don't," Michael kindly concurred, which made Alex even more irascible. Did Michael have to be so understanding?

"Then why are you doing this to me?"

"I am not doing it *to* you. I simply need to deal with this new situation and, hopefully, to resolve it in a fashion that works for everyone."

"Aren't you the empathetic arbiter?"

In a fit of temper, he whirled away and hurried to the stairs, marching up to the seclusion of his bedchamber.

How dare Michael institute so many changes without discussion or consultation! Yes, it was Michael's house. Yes, he owned every knickknack and bauble, but the accursed dwelling was Alex's home, too.

Michael had welcomed guests, hired employees, and rearranged sleeping quarters, without soliciting Alex's opinion. There were so many people joining them, the floor piled high with their luggage, that the main foyer resembled a coaching inn.

Where was he to hide? How was he to have any peace?

He was hurt, despairing, and wanting Michael to . . . to . . .

He couldn't decide what he wanted from his brother. Michael had been naught but attentive and considerate about the maiming, but every word spewed from his mouth was like salt on a wound.

Michael seemed to have everything, while Alex had nothing. He was wretched, pessimistic, deplorable in his drive to wallow in misery.

What abominable fortune had conspired to lay him low? Others had endured worse fates, had died, sacrificed limbs, or grown crazed from war madness, but his arrogance had slain him with the humiliation of his disfigurement.

Why me? he woefully, disgustedly, mourned for the thousandth time.

Stomping into his room, he slammed the door, as a feminine gasp froze him in his tracks. He whipped around to see an unfamiliar woman hovering in the threshold to his dressing chamber. Close to his own age of twenty-six, she was exceptionally pretty. She had brunette hair, worn in a fetching chignon, big green eyes, and a mature, curvaceous body that was rounded where it should be, and thin where it should be, too.

His loud entrance had startled her, and her fist was clutched to her splendid bosom. She was winsome, alluring, but overtly befuddled, and during any other period of his life, he'd have acted the part of the gentleman he'd been raised to be.

"Who the hell are you," he crudely demanded, "and what are you doing?"

"I most humbly beg your pardon," she responded in a steady, soothing voice. "I believe I'm lost. I'm so dreadfully sorry."

She reached out and groped for purchase, and he was shocked to discover that she was blind as a bat. She had to be a member of the governess's family, which meant that Michael had failed to divulge the relevant details.

A blind woman? Living with them? What next! He was trapped in a madhouse, against his will, and without the financial wherewithal to flee!

"You most certainly *are* lost. Have you no better sense than to inflict yourself where you don't belong?"

Astonished by his rudeness, she bristled but hastily stifled the reaction. "It was an innocent mistake. There's no cause for discourtesy."

"Don't let it happen again. I don't care to have outsiders invading my privacy."

"Of course you don't."

"It's quite uncivil of you to be wandering around where you're not wanted."

A scarlet wave of embarrassment washed over her. "It was an accident."

"A pitiful excuse." She possessed the regalness of a queen, which had him feeling petty and small, and he wished he could bite off his impolite tongue, yet he kept berating her.

"I'll be going," she snapped, "and whilst I'm on the premises, I shall guarantee that our paths don't cross."

"I would appreciate it."

"So would I."

She'd told him, hadn't she? It was his turn to blush, but with shame.

In recent months, he couldn't calculate how often he'd rebuked acquaintances, or chastised the servants, many of whom had worked for the family since before he was born. Nary a one had commented. Not even Michael. As though Alex were made of glass, others tiptoed around him, anxious about his mental state, and worried about his delicate sensibilities.

She was the sole individual who'd been brave enough to suffer his disrespect, then toss it back. He was mortified. To what a filthy trough he'd descended! When had he become the sort of villain who'd abuse a blind woman?

She hadn't mentioned her disability, hadn't used it as a justification for her blunder, and he could tell that she was too proud to cite it as a defense. She took several halting steps, her arm furtively searching for an exit.

As she was disoriented, her stealthy fumbling was fruitless, and she tripped over a pair of his boots. With a soft wail of dismay, she pitched forward and smacked onto the rug.

Dumbstruck, he rushed forward and lifted her to her feet. "Are you all right?"

"I'm perfectly fine." She yanked away, even as she surreptitiously massaged her wrist, and he was furious to note that there were tears in her eyes.

He couldn't abide a display of histrionics! "For God's sake, don't cry."

"I'm not," she insisted as she swiped her hand across her cheeks. "If you'd be so kind as to point me toward the hall, and the stairs to the third floor, I would be much obliged."

It galled her, having to ask for directions, and her palpable wrath cooled his own, restoring his manners to an appropriate level.

"Sit for a minute. Please."

"I'd rather walk across a bed of hot coals."

"A thoroughly warranted reprimand." He eased her toward a nearby chair. She felt it brush her legs but wouldn't slip into it, so they dawdled, awkward and much too close together. To break the thorny silence, he declared, "I apologize for my boorish behavior. I've had a terrible day."

"So have I." She was in a temper, which he suspected was out of character. She was trembling, upset by the fall and he couldn't guess what else.

"I'd say we were even."

"I doubt it. I resided in the same locale for twenty-eight years, and now, I'm a vagabond. Have you any notion of how awful it is to be accustomed to routine, to know where every little item is placed, and then to be thrust into this monstrosity of a house?"

"No, I can't imagine."

"Suddenly, I'm relying on the benevolence of strangers; I'm praying for charity, and hoping there'll be food for supper to feed my daughter. Can you envision how hideous it is to be helpless? To be dependent? To be in such dire straits, and incapable of assisting in any worthwhile fashion?"

"No," he repeated, discomfited by the information.

"Then don't insult me by pretending our situations are the same."

He was unsure of how to respond, and her anger had him fascinated and wary.

"Hello." He clasped her hand and bowed over it. "I'm Alex Farrow."

On learning his name, she blanched. "So, I've offended the earl's brother, and I haven't been here an hour. Isn't that the icing on the cake?"

Charmed by her pique, he chuckled. "And you are?"

"No one of any consequence, at all."

She moved away, and he almost went after her, but he was positive that any aid would be rebuffed. When she detected the door frame, she paused, her confusion evident.

"The rear stairs are about eight paces to your right," he murmured. "There are two flights, of ten steps each, with a landing in the middle. You'll be at the third floor."

"Thank you." Her reply was short, bitter. She started off, and he listened; then he tiptoed after her and watched as she disappeared.

Soon, he could hear her overhead, and apparently, she was lodged in the bedchamber above his own. When she'd erroneously stumbled into his room, she'd likely miscounted and presumed herself to be on the third floor when, in reality, she was on the second.

"A harmless and interesting mistake," he mused to himself.

The stairway was a convenient route between the two rooms. Not that he'd ever have occasion to climb them and speak with her. Not that he'd ever have a reason to go up and knock.

He contemplated their peculiar conversation. She couldn't see him, so she was the first person in ages who'd stared at his face without revulsion, who'd talked without flinching, gawking in horror, or wrenching away in disgust.

Intrigued, he retreated, even as he conjectured as to how he might contrive to parlay with her again.

Nervous and excited, Emily tarried in the foyer. Through the opened front door, she could view the Winchester coach that had delivered Pamela and Margaret Martin to

London. The luggage was being unloaded, the girls about to be handed down.

Her heart pounded with anticipation and dread. What would she think of them? What would they think of her?

Too much had happened too quickly, and she was having a difficult time absorbing it all. She was stunned to find that despite rumors as to Lord Winchester being a ne'er-do-well, when he wanted something badly enough, he was a veritable whirlwind of activity.

With a snap of his fingers, he'd had them transferred from their despicable accommodations and ensconced in his own. Rose had a cheery spot in the nursery, while Emily and Mary had been given spacious guest suites. They hadn't been boarded with the servants, an honor and distinction about which she'd complained, but he'd been adamant, and as she was discovering, when Michael Farrow made a decision, it was impossible to oppose him.

He was more stubborn than any individual she'd ever known.

Alert and vigilant, he stood beside her. If he was nervous, too, he hid it well.

He'd sworn that there'd be nothing improper between them, and so far, he'd kept his word, but her meeting him, her observing his carnal antics, had rattled loose her inhibitions. Restless, edgy, she was disturbed in ways she couldn't define, which had her absurdly eager to race to perdition. It was torture, loitering next to him, and she was mortified to admit that with the slightest encouragement, she'd leap into his arms and beg him to corrupt her.

"How old are they?" she questioned, anxious to break

the tension that sizzled whenever she and the earl were together.

"Pamela is sixteen, and Margaret is nine," he answered.

"How long has it been since you've seen them?"

"I don't believe I ever have."

"Then why would their father entrust them to you?"

"I haven't the foggiest idea," he bluntly claimed.

He glanced away from the carriage and focused on her, leaning in so that their bodies were nearly touching. Sparks erupted; the air crackled and heated.

She was swept up in the blue of his eyes, and she hated how easily he overwhelmed her. Anyone watching would conclude that they were involved in a torrid affair, which was the last assumption she needed to have drawn. There were servants everywhere and she jumped away from him, but—knave that he was—he moved with her so that the strident stimulation continued. She was convinced that he recognized how thoroughly he unsettled her and he received an enormous kick out of having her so flustered.

He whispered, "Tell me the truth: Would you consign your children to such a dubious fate as having me for their guardian?"

"Never in a thousand years, you bounder."

He chuckled, then sobered. "I'm glad you're here."

From how he was gazing at her, she was certain he was recollecting their kiss, that he might actually be speculating as to whether he could get away with doing it again. The notion terrified her. Would he dare such a thing, with the majority of the staff hovering about?

At the idiotic caprice, she scoffed. It was preposterous to imagine that he was attracted to her, and she had to remember that he was an insatiable libertine. He thrived on flirtation and worse, and any attention he paid her was feigned.

She scowled, which had him chuckling again, and she whipped away as the girls left the carriage. They proceeded inside, and Emily evaluated them.

They were both fetching, with blond hair and blue eyes. Margaret appeared smart and shy, but also melancholy, which was to be expected after having been orphaned and uprooted.

Pamela was a shock. Everyone referred to her as a *girl,* so Emily had a picture in her mind of her being youthful and in need of supervision, but Pamela was definitely an adult. She was taller than Emily, and more feminine, with a curvaceous figure, ample bosom, and shapely hips. Her corset was laced too tightly, and her gown cut much too low for the modesty Emily would demand.

Seeming crafty and cunning, Pamela turned toward them, and she appraised the mansion as though calculating its value.

Here comes trouble.

The impression flitted past, and Emily tamped it down. She was determined to befriend them, and she wouldn't make any hasty judgments.

Pamela entered, sauntered over, and snuggled herself to Winchester. Being the unbearable cad that he was, he let her.

Emily was aghast, but as it was their initial introduction, she was perplexed as to what she should say about the conduct of either.

"Hello, Michael." Pamela was brash, shameless, stroking her hand across his chest. "We meet again."

"Yes, we do," Winchester fairly cooed, "and you're all grown-up."

Pamela was acting like a harlot, and Emily foresaw months of misery, with the two of them constantly at loggerheads.

"Lord Winchester," Emily interrupted, barely able to keep from reaching over and yanking Pamela away from their cozy tête-à-tête, "I thought you hadn't met Miss Martin previously."

"I'd forgotten," he insisted.

He was fixated on Pamela, giving her the rapt consideration he often focused on Emily, and if Emily hadn't known better, she'd have sworn she was jealous. Which was ridiculous.

How could she be covetous of Winchester? How could she be jealous of a sixteen-year-old child?

"Who is this?" Pamela asked, as she rudely studied Emily's clothes.

"This is Miss Barnett," he explained. "I've retained her as your governess."

Pamela laughed. "Surely, you intend her for Margaret. You can't think that *I* need her."

"I'm afraid so."

He was fawning, obsequious, and practically leering down Pamela's dress, and Emily wanted to hit him.

"Miss Pamela," Emily interjected, her patience exhausted, "let's get you up to your room. You can relax and rest; then I've arranged for tea so we can become acquainted."

"I can hardly wait," the snooty termagant remarked; then she batted her lashes at Winchester. "Will you join us, Michael?"

"Probably not."

"Pity."

She strolled by and started up the grand staircase, exacerbating the swish of her skirt. Like a dog at a bone, Winchester's eyes followed, and Emily elbowed him in the ribs.

"Pretty girl," he murmured.

"Shut up," she hissed.

Quiet and demure, Margaret trailed behind her sister, and it was instantly obvious that they were as different as night and day.

"Hello, Lord Winchester." She curtsied as a young lady ought when in Winchester's presence.

"Hello, Miss Margaret."

"How do you do, Miss Barnett?"

"Very well, thank you."

Margaret analyzed Winchester, searching for something, which she apparently didn't find. "You don't remember us, do you? I heard you talking to Pamela, but you don't really recollect."

He shifted uncomfortably, then admitted, "No, I don't. I'm sorry."

"It's all right. It was a long time ago. I hope you don't mind terribly that we've come."

"How could I?"

"When Father was ill, he didn't know where he should send us after he . . ." She swallowed twice. "Well, after. I told him that you'd be the best choice."

"Me? But why?"

"Because you helped me."

"I did?"

She gazed at Emily. "My father was prone to heavy

drink. It was a weakness he had. He'd fallen and couldn't get up. It was very late. Lord Winchester was visiting, and he assisted me in putting Father to bed."

An awkward silence ensued, and finally, Winchester broke it. "I do recall."

"It meant very much to me. I never forgot."

What a lonely life she must have led! A drunkard for a father. Men like Winchester as his associates. Winchester was the only one who'd been kind. Emily couldn't conceive of what Margaret must have endured.

Winchester was shaken by the story and embarrassed that Margaret still had such a high opinion of him. "Gad, you couldn't have been more than three or four."

"Like I said, it was ages ago." She stifled a yawn and peered at Emily. "I'm awfully weary. Would you be upset if I went directly to my room?"

"No, darling." It took every ounce of strength Emily possessed not to reach out and hug her. "Let me show you where it is."

"Don't put yourself out on my account. The maids can guide me." She climbed a few steps, then stopped. "Don't worry about Pamela. She can be vain and bossy, but I'll keep her in line. I promise we won't be any trouble."

"I know you won't," Winchester agreed, and he gave her an encouraging nod.

She trudged up and out of sight, a cadre of servants bustling with her, lugging trunks and boxes. As she disappeared, Emily realized she was trembling.

"My Lord, but that was horrid." How had she allowed Winchester to dump her in such a mess? She'd envisioned sweet girls, pleasant afternoon outings, and scholarly classroom discussions. Not trauma, not distress. Not a vamping, overdeveloped adolescent, or an anguished, suffering child in desperate need of mothering.

"I'm going to want daily reports." Winchester stated. "At least in the beginning."

"Of course."

He stared up the stairs, frowning as if he were about to utter a profound comment, but what emerged was, "I need a drink. A very stiff one."

He walked down the hall and vanished, leaving Emily to pick up the pieces of the Martins' complex, disturbing arrival.

5

"You're two hours late, Emily."

"I know. I apologize."

"You *know,* you apologize, and that's supposed to make it all right?"

Michael sipped his whiskey, one of too many he'd already enjoyed. He was much more irritated than he should have been. After all, he'd hired her to tend the girls, not to be his leisurely handmaiden, but she took her job seriously, so he rarely saw her. He hated being ignored, and he wasn't about to be relegated to second place merely because she had more important things to do.

"I asked you to attend me at nine," he griped.

"I realize that."

There were dark circles under her eyes, a testament to her exhaustion. The day had been extremely vexing for her, and she'd worked hard, so he should have let her head for her bed, but he seemed bent on tormenting her.

"It's nearly eleven," he pointed out.

He was trying her patience, but she managed to refrain

from snapping her reply. "I understand that you've not had much contact with children, but I feel I must explain again that you now have two nine-year-olds living under your roof."

She was constantly busy, constantly minding the girls, and he was so irked by her diligence. "And their presence would induce you to disobey a direct instruction from me because . . . ?"

"They've been thrust into strange circumstances," she added as if he were an imbecile.

"So?" he immaturely countered. "They've had almost three weeks to adjust."

"Which is a very short interval, considering what they've been through. It took an enormous amount of effort to calm them so that they could fall asleep. Then, of course, Pamela was angry and demanding to know when I'll let her paint up the town." She scowled. "You might have warned me what she was like."

"You think I had any idea?"

"Yes, actually, and you deliberately kept it from me."

"It *is* amusing to aggravate you."

"Lord Winchester . . ." she started, when he cut her off.

"Michael."

"What?"

"When we're alone, you know you're to call me Michael." He told her as much every evening, but she refused to join him in taking their relationship to a higher level.

"I most certainly will not," she retorted as usual.

He was exasperated with her independence. He didn't like women to be autonomous, didn't deem it proper for them to exhibit such self-sufficiency. Every female of his acquaintance was positively thrilled to rely on him, to have him lead and control. Even Amanda, with her domineering temperament, comprehended who was boss.

Emily Barnett hadn't a clue.

"Come here," he ordered, and without argument—praise be!—she walked across the library and halted at the sofa where he'd been hiding, tippling and pondering the recent changes to his life.

As Alex had grumpily indicated, there could be no bachelor activities, no raucous parties or carnal gamboling. His abode had been transformed as thoroughly as if a group of nuns had moved in.

"Are you drunk, milord?"

"Not as drunk as I intend to be."

"You can't be inebriated. What if we needed you? What if one of the girls were ill or injured? What then?"

"With your competent administration, I'm convinced everyone would survive."

"But what of Margaret's past? Her father's vulnerability to alcohol has had a horrendous impact on her, and she worships you as a sort of savior. Would you dash her veneration by having her detect the same failings in yourself?"

He was furious that she'd remark. He'd been whiling away, ruminating over the paths he'd selected, but he wasn't about to have her discover how he was fretting. She was much too astute as to his faults and flaws, and she would presume that she was having a beneficial effect on his character.

In his estimation, nothing was more annoying than a female attempting to rid a man of his imperfections, and if Emily had the slightest inkling that she was having an affirmative influence, there'd be no living with her.

"Emily," he scolded, "despite how foul you find my personal habits, it's not your place to comment."

She recognized that she'd crossed the line. "You're correct. I apologize again."

Wasn't she a veritable fount of contrition?

"Stop it," he growled.

"Stop what?"

"Stop being so bloody sorry."

"Don't curse at me."

"It's my own house, and you are my employee. I'll speak however I damned well choose."

"Yes, you may, but I don't have to listen."

She whipped around, prepared to stomp out, when he couldn't bear to have her depart. Much as he loathed acknowledging it, he'd been so forlorn before she arrived, had been anxiously awaiting her, and he couldn't stand to contemplate how quiet it would be once she left.

He grabbed her wrist, and they engaged in a tug-of-war she couldn't win.

"Let me go," she insisted, furious with him.

"No."

He dragged her onto the sofa, so that her body was draped across his. Through several layers of gown and petticoat, he could feel her stomach, her mons, her thighs, and his cock leapt to attention with an urgency it hadn't shown in years.

There was something about her that provoked him, that spurred him to behave as he oughtn't, and though he'd pledged that he wouldn't trifle with her, he couldn't remember why he'd offered such an idiotic vow.

"I didn't mean what I said," he claimed.

"Yes, you did!"

"I'm just tired."

"So am I."

She glanced away, and there were tears in her eyes, which tore at his conscience. He was eager to make amends, but he wasn't sure how. He wasn't used to begging for forgiveness.

"I've had a lousy day," he endeavored to explain. "I'm irritable, and I shouldn't be taking it out on you."

"My day hasn't been so grand, either."

"I can tell."

"Then quit picking away at me."

"I'm an ungrateful wretch," he admitted.

"Yes, you are; now let me up."

"No." He planted his hand on her lovely bottom, and his phallus was ecstatic.

"You're being a bully."

"My normal state."

"I can't abide your acting like a tyrant."

"I don't know how to carry on any other way," he asserted.

"You could learn another way."

"Why would I want to?"

"Because your manners are atrocious."

"We'll get along better once you grasp that my every wish should be granted."

"Despot."

"Emily?"

"Yes."

"You talk too much."

"So I've been told." She shifted about, trying to

dislodge his hand, and the motion was tremendously stimulating. "Lord Winchester?"

"If you call me Michael, I'll release you."

She studied him, expecting a trick. "Swear it to me."

"I swear," he fibbed.

"Michael," she intoned, "will you please let me up?"

"No."

"Ooh! You despicable, lying rat!"

She started to wrestle in earnest, grappling and shoving at him, but to no avail. It was becoming difficult to hold on to her, so he rolled them, pinning her to the back of the sofa, with himself stretched in front to block any escape.

"Emily?"

"What?"

"Hush."

She went still but watched him warily. She was nervous as to his intentions—and her own—and she confessed, "You make it impossible to behave."

"Have I asked you to behave?"

"No, but one of us needs to keep a clear head."

"Why?"

"So we don't . . . don't . . ."

He wiggled his brows in naughty invitation. "Succumb to ardor?"

"Well . . . yes."

It was a nightly game they played, with both of them tiptoeing around their obvious attraction. He flirted and cajoled, while she would nearly relent, then panic and flee, so they hadn't been able to move from the spot where they were entrenched.

"Have I furnished you with any indication," he queried, "that I want you to be strong and resist me?"

"No."

"Then why persist?"

"We can't keep doing this," she said. "It's sinful."

"According to whom?"

"To everyone that matters."

"Not to me, and I'm the most important person of all." He assessed her, his heart pounding with excitement and anticipation. "Give over, Emily. You want this to happen as much as I do."

"How could I *want* it," she inquired, "when I don't have any idea of what you mean to do?"

"Your body knows. Let me show you what you need."

Though he was eager to forge on, he wasn't positive what he planned. She was a respectable gentlewoman, with whom he dare not romp lest he had marriage in mind, which he didn't. Was he set to ruin her? Could he?

The blatant answer was no.

Though his reputation was the worst in London, he never dabbled with innocents. There were too many wicked, willing courtesans who would perform any deed for a price, so there was no need to expend the effort or create the scandal that would arise should he cavort with the wrong female.

He couldn't decide what was best, but he wasn't about to let her loose, so he kissed her. She was too shocked to object, and he seized the advantage. His lips were melded to hers, her soft breath coursing across his cheek, his tongue in her mouth. Initially, she was stunned by the intimate contact, but as his arms folded around her, she shook off her stupor and joined in the embrace, kissing him back with a relish and exhilaration he'd not imagined before meeting her.

The moment was thrilling and exotic. Instantly, he craved more from her than she could ever confer. An absurd swirl of yearning rushed through him—for camaraderie, caring, and companionship, but sex, too. Sex that was so stirring he couldn't fathom what it would be like.

Why was he so attracted to her? With each passing minute, his fascination was more extreme. Why couldn't he curb the reckless infatuation? She incited him beyond all sane reflection, and he was overcome by the notion that if he bonded with her physically, he would gain a peace and solace for which he'd been searching without even realizing he was.

With her, everything seemed attainable. Even happiness. Even contentment.

He pulled away, and she gazed at him, disquieted by her response.

"You always push me farther than I intend to go," she chided. "Why do I let you?"

"I told you: You're so ready for the kind of pleasure I can bestow. It's futile to fight your temptation."

"But you promised we wouldn't dally."

"I guess I lied."

"Is fabrication a trait for which you're notorious?"

"Not usually."

"Except perhaps in your amorous conquests?"

"Perhaps," he allowed.

"Why do I have the feeling that you'll say anything to get what you want?"

"Because I'm a cad?"

"Precisely my worry."

"Has there ever been any doubt as to my having dastardly tendencies?"

"No, but I'm an optimist," she said. "I continue to hope for better behavior."

"Don't grow too sanguine in your aspirations for my improvement," he cautioned. "I'll constantly disappoint you."

"Hardly. I have a much loftier opinion of you than you have of yourself."

"Really?"

"Yes."

On hearing that she held him in elevated esteem, his heart raced like a silly lad's. He was desperate to have her see him as the man he wished to be, rather than the man he was.

"How can I foster this wave of confidence?" he asked.

"We can begin by your not lying to me. I can tell when you are."

"Can you? How?"

"You look so guilty," she maintained.

"I must be out of practice at hiding my thoughts."

"Actually, you're quite adept, but where you're concerned, I have a second sense. Why is that?"

There were many plausible answers to her question. He could have talked about sexual magnetism, when there was no reason for any appeal, or how the universe worked mysteriously and some things were meant to be. But if he voiced any of the drivel, he'd sound like a fool-ish romantic, who believed in such folly as love at first sight, which he most categorically did not. Passion and unchecked ardor had destroyed his family, so he would disavow their power at every turn. He wouldn't be so id-iotic as to fancy himself in *love* with Emily Barnett, so he would never be so stupid as to suggest the possibility.

He settled for a simpler clarification. "It occurs because you're wild about me."

"You are so vain."

"Being vain and correct are not mutually exclusive."

"Are you so conceited that you presume every woman is bowled over by your pretty face?"

"Of course," he replied.

"Then I expect you suppose that every woman in London is dying to snuggle on this cushy sofa and be kissed to high heaven by you."

"What could be more enticing?"

"You can't continue to accost me," she scolded.

"Why shouldn't I?"

"Because it's . . . it's . . . unbearable."

"Unbearable!"

"It makes me yearn to have a different relationship with you, but I can't ever forget that I am your employee."

"You're more than that."

"No, I'm not."

He should have apprised her of what prominent position he felt her to occupy, but he couldn't describe it. Yes, she was his governess, but she was becoming a friend and confidante, a guide and counselor, and eventually, he'd have her as a lover. No other conclusion seemed likely or acceptable.

It wasn't in his nature to deny himself, and he wanted her more than he'd wanted anything in such a long, long time, yet he was loathe to picture himself seducing her like some aging, dissipated reprobate. It was such a trite, pathetic story: the lord of the manor inflicting himself on an unsuspecting girl.

Wasn't he mulling a deed that inexcusable? When had his moral state been reduced to such a disgraceful level?

"It's just kissing, Emily," he contended, though he was desirous of doing so much more. "There's no harm in it."

"Not to you, you seasoned libertine."

"And not to you, my little beauty."

She scowled and blurted out, "Have you any idea of how much I enjoy being with you like this? Or how anxiously I'd hoped you would kiss me again?"

So . . . she'd been pining away, had she? He laughed. "You're a veritable slattern."

She punched him on the shoulder. "Don't make fun of me."

"I'm not."

"You assume that I'm loose."

He was surprised that her assessment was so off the mark. "You're wrong. I think you're very fine. *Too* fine for the likes of me."

"It's so difficult to be here in your home, to be around you, and to . . . to . . ."

He silenced her by resting a finger on her lips. He couldn't tolerate her protests, not when he was aware of how horridly he was transgressing. Nor could he listen to her objections, for he respected her very much. She could easily discourage him, when he wouldn't be dissuaded.

"I want to know you this way," he told her. "Give this part of yourself to me."

"You make it so hard to say no."

"Good."

"Especially when I like everything you do to me! I'd have to be a saint to resist."

"And you're not one—you're very human—so it's a waste of energy to try."

He bestowed another kiss, quickly leaping far beyond where they'd journeyed previously. She'd admitted to being eager for a repeat of their madness, so he intended to show her how it could be between them. He would have her so overwhelmed that she'd never hesitate to philander.

He shifted them so that she was beneath him, and he was struck by how perfectly she fit. Her breasts were pressed to his chest, and her legs had widened so that his torso fell between her lush thighs.

He fussed with the pins in her hair, yanking them out and tossing them on the floor. The luxuriant auburn tresses flowed free, and his lust spiraled higher. He was so desperate for her!

"I'm going to touch you," he advised.

"Where?"

"Under your dress."

"You shouldn't."

"I have to."

"Oh, I can't refuse," she wailed. "I really *am* a slattern."

"I see nothing wrong with engaging in a bit of wicked conduct every so often." He grinned. "It builds character."

His naughty hand wandered down to dip inside her bodice, to cradle her breast. It was soft, supple, and he caressed and petted it. She did nothing to hinder him, but even if she'd complained, he wouldn't have halted. He pinched the nipple, which sent her into a dither of squirming and exacerbated the pleasure for his phallus. He was so close to dragging up her skirt and deflowering her that he scared himself.

Of what might he be capable? She drove him to new

heights of licentiousness. Any appalling peccadillo might be committed.

He tugged at the front of her gown, drawing it down so that her breast popped from corset and chemise. The silky mound was creamy white, the nipple a delightful shade of rose, and he licked his tongue across it.

"Oh, oh my." Panting, breathless, she arched up. "What are you doing?"

"I'm making love to you."

"Well, stop it! I can't abide this . . . this . . ."

As a maiden, she had no vocabulary to convey her titillation, and he chuckled, then wrapped his lips around the tempting bud and sucked it into his mouth. The effect was abrupt and potent, as she gripped his neck and jerked him nearer, urging him to feast. He was tickled by her response, elated by her sexual nature, by her willingness to allow it to flourish.

He kept on as long as he dared, until he was too inundated by desire. With great reluctance, he eased away, taking a last, covetous glance at her nipple, and vowing to himself that he'd see it again very soon. He wouldn't let her avoid him.

She frowned. "Are we finished?"

"For now." As if in farewell, he placed a kiss at the center of her cleavage.

"But . . . but . . . you can't leave me like this."

"It can't be helped."

"I feel all ragged inside," she grumbled. "I'm in misery!"

"I'm sure you are."

"Is there a cure for what ails me?"

"A most dramatic one."

"Then I demand you initiate it. At once."

He sat up, his cock an uncomfortable rod between his legs. He pulled her up, too, so that she was facing him. With her hair spread across her shoulders, her cheeks flushed, and her lips swollen from his kisses, she looked adorable.

And all mine. The greedy, satisfying message shot through his head.

"I'm a man, Emily."

She batted her lashes. "I noticed."

"You arouse me beyond any circumspection."

"I do?" Amazed by his admission, she smiled.

"So we have to quit."

"But I have no wish to quit."

"That's why I'm deciding for you."

"Arrogant beast."

"It's very late. Let's get you up to bed."

"To bed?" She stared as if he were deranged. "Just like that?"

"Yes."

"What are you? A spigot that can be turned off and on at the drop of a hat?"

"No." He assessed her in a crude and chilling carnal fashion, meant to alarm and disturb. "I want you so badly, in such a thoroughly masculine way, that if you don't depart—immediately—I can't predict what might transpire."

She gulped in dismay. "Would this, by any chance, involve the loss of my virginity?"

"Absolutely."

She fidgeted, then asked, "Could you enlighten me as to what that might entail?"

"No, but imagine that it would have been entirely wonderful, but utterly reckless." He stood and hauled her up with him. "Now go, before I'm not quite so chivalrous."

She studied him, the door, him again. "Will I . . . will I . . . see you tomorrow?"

"Definitely, my dearest Emily. You most definitely will."

She dawdled, clearly yearning to say more, but better sense prevailed. She spun away and fled.

Pamela Martin tiptoed into Michael's library, peeked around, then rushed to the sideboard. She retrieved a silver flask from her reticule and filled it with brandy. Every now and then, she liked to have a nip, especially at bedtime, so it was important to keep a hidden stash.

With the snooty, puritanical Miss Barnett constantly lurking, it was growing more and more difficult to indulge in her favorite amusements.

For years, she'd been free to gad about in whatever manner she chose. With her mother deceased and her father a wastrel, she'd had a liberal upbringing, with few restraints or restrictions, so it was aggravating to have Miss Barnett setting limits.

Barnett actually believed she should act as a governess ought, and Pamela was tired of the interference. From long experience, Pamela knew how easy it was to dispense with an irritating servant, and should Miss Barnett become too bothersome, Pamela would get rid of her. Michael Farrow was a typical male, as malleable as her father had been, so it would be simple to trick him into doing what was necessary.

From down the hall, Margaret yelled to announce that they were ready to depart. Miss Barnett insisted that they engage in tedious rounds of afternoon visiting, and the notion of sitting and chatting in all those stuffy drawing rooms made Pamela ill. She needed a restorative, so she grabbed the whiskey decanter and downed several hefty swigs. The liquor, coupled with the amount she'd imbibed earlier, was immediately soothing.

To conceal the odor on her breath, she popped a minted candy into her mouth, then headed into the corridor.

"Yes, Margaret," she called. "Be silent. I'm coming."

She strolled to the foyer, where Margaret was on tiptoe, eager to race off on another adventure. In contrast to herself, Margaret was the perfect child, and Pamela couldn't wait to be mistress of her own home so she could be shed of the little angel.

Margaret studied her gown, then scolded, "Miss Barnett will never let you wear that."

Pamela had deliberately donned her most shocking dress. The red color was much too bright, the neckline much too low, but the maids had been gossiping as to how Michael loved red, and while he was usually absent during the day, there was always a chance she might run into him.

"How I attire myself is none of Miss Barnett's business."

"*She* thinks it's her business."

"Well, she's wrong."

"She'll be upset," Margaret whined.

"So?" Pamela shrugged. "Why would you assume that Miss Barnett's opinion matters to me in the slightest?"

"And why must you be so awful to her? You go out of your way to be disagreeable."

"Have we asked for Miss Barnett to be thrust into our lives?"

"I find her to be very pleasant."

"I find her to be extremely annoying."

Further comment was cut off as Barnett tromped down the stairs. She was tying her bonnet and straightening her shawl, so she didn't glance up till the last moment, and when she did, her vexation was obvious.

"My, what a pretty . . . outfit," she began, "but I'm not certain it's appropriate for what we have planned."

"Will we bump into Michael?" Pamela queried. "I selected it for him. I hear tell that he adores red on a beautiful woman." The remark had a peculiar effect on Miss Barnett. She blushed so hotly that Pamela was surprised she didn't ignite.

"We're not out to impress Lord Winchester," Barnett asserted, "and no, I'm positive we won't see him."

"Where do you suppose he goes all day?" Pamela prodded.

"His whereabouts are none of our concern."

"I bet he's with Amanda. Have you met her?"

Pamela garnered another strident reaction, and she was tickled. Clearly, Barnett was familiar with the infamous mistress. Wasn't this interesting?

"I'm not acquainted with any of his lordship's associates," Barnett staunchly declared.

A blatant lie, Pamela was sure, so she dug the knife in deeper. "Father used to bring Amanda by the house. He claimed she was the best. The absolute best."

"The best what?" Margaret innocently inquired.

Pamela chuckled, while Miss Barnett stewed, and it was evident that, for once, Pamela had pushed her too far.

"Change your clothes, Pamela." Barnett's eyes were shooting daggers. "Right now."

Margaret—ever the mediator—discerned that they were fighting, though she couldn't understand why. "Don't listen to her, Miss Barnett. Father never had a visitor named Amanda."

"How would you know?" Pamela chided. "You can't say who stopped by after you were asleep."

"Neither can you," Margaret retorted.

"Go!" Barnett snapped.

Pamela flashed a cunning smile, meant to notify Barnett that Pamela was privy to much secret information, the likes of which would probably send Barnett into a swoon.

"I'll help her, Miss Barnett," Margaret said. "I know what's in her wardrobe."

"It would be easier to choose something suitable," Pamela complained, "if we could buy the new gowns I've been requesting."

"I've explained about your funds," Miss Barnett responded. "Your father left many debts. After Lord Winchester and the solicitors have sorted through them, we'll discuss the items you feel you require."

Pamela was furious that Barnett would denigrate her father, but she had no reply. Her father had led an extravagant existence, but she had no idea how much he'd spent or from where he'd obtained his cash.

"In the interim," Pamela jeered, "am I to prance about looking like a pauper?"

Barnett rudely evaluated Pamela's stylish garment. "You definitely appear as if you're on your last penny. You poor thing! From where will your next meal come?"

Pamela stomped off, fuming at Barnett having the final word, but Pamela was unable to devise an insulting rejoinder. Well, she'd get even with Barnett. All in good time. The woman would be so bloody sorry.

Like an irritating gnat, Margaret flitted up the stairs ahead of her, while Pamela marched up at a stately, regal pace. As she reached the landing and rounded the corner, the front door was opened, without announcement as to who'd arrived, and Michael entered. Margaret had vanished, leaving Pamela alone, and she hid and spied on him.

"Hello, Miss Barnett," he grinned and greeted much too gallantly.

"Lord Winchester." Barnett made no deferential curtsy, which, given her lowly post, was deplorable.

"Fancy meeting you here."

"I work for you, remember? I'm always here."

He peeked down the hallways. Not seeing any servants, he stepped closer, approaching until they were toe-to-toe. "What's wrong?"

He improperly placed his hand on her waist that could only indicate a heightened relationship of which others were ignorant.

"I lost my temper," she confessed, and he laughed.

"You? The most docile person in the world? I can't imagine it."

"It's true."

"And who threw you into this frenzy of rage?"

"Miss Pamela."

"You unfortunate creature," he crooned sympatheti-
cally, and Pamela bristled, realizing that they'd parleyed
over her, and that their comments hadn't been kind.

"She goads me relentlessly, and I broke down and
voiced some of my exasperation." She sighed. "I'm so
ill-equipped for dealing with her."

In a loving gesture, he stroked her nape. "You're doing fine. Don't be so hard on yourself."

"You haven't watched us together. She has such an intense dislike for me, but I'm not certain how I incurred
her wrath."

"Would you like me to speak with her?"

"That's all I need."

"It's been said"—he preened arrogantly—"that I have
a way with the ladies. I could talk some sense into her."

"Hah! You unrepentant bounder, you wouldn't know
sense if it sneaked up and bit you on the bottom."

"Miss Barnett, I'm shocked! Totally shocked at such
language! What's happened to you? It must be a result of
the company you've been keeping."

He caressed a thumb across her mouth, looking very
much as if he might kiss her, and Pamela's heart skipped
a beat as she wondered if he would, but he pulled away
and toyed with a ringlet in her hair.

"The quality of my *company* has deteriorated," she
concurred, glaring at him. "Why are you at home? I
thought you were busy."

"I just stopped by for a moment; then I'm off to another conference."

"About Mr. Martin's finances?"

"Yes, but I'll return later, and I'll expect my nightly
briefing."

"A briefing? Is that what you call it?"

He leaned in and whispered a remark Pamela couldn't decipher, and Barnett squealed and pretended to be offended.

"Aah! You cad! Get out of here before the girls come down."

"I'm gone; I'm gone."

He walked toward his library, but he halted to peer over his shoulder, and he gazed at her with such longing and affection that it hurt to observe him. As smitten as he, Barnett mirrored the gaze, then he disappeared from view, and Barnett went onto the stoop to collect herself in the outside air.

"Isn't this fascinating?" Pamela mused to herself.

They had to be lovers. There was no other explanation. Pamela had witnessed enough of her father's shenanigans to have some notion of how adults behaved. Michael and Miss Barnett were exhibiting all the classic signs.

How delicious! How droll! How scandalous! There had to be a mode of utilizing the discovery to maximum advantage, but what would it be?

Obviously, Amanda would have to be enlightened. Despite Margaret's mewling, Pamela really had met Amanda, and she was in awe of the rich, unconventional older woman. Rumor had it that Amanda and Michael had had another spat, so perhaps Amanda wasn't aware of how Barnett had usurped her position.

Wouldn't Amanda die when she learned of how she'd been tossed over?

Her pulse racing with excitement, Pamela rushed for her room, suddenly eager to change as rapidly as she was able. She couldn't wait to be shut up in the carriage with Miss Barnett. What an amusing afternoon it was destined to be!

"Are you sure Lord Winchester had no response?"

"Absolutely, ma'am."

Amanda Lambert sat at the writing desk in her elaborate boudoir, tapping a perfectly manicured nail against the wood. Her footman shifted nervously.

"Were you granted an audience?"

"No," he replied.

"I explicitly advised you to ask for one."

"Mr. Fitch had me tarry in the foyer while he spoke with the earl."

Fitch! The pompous bastard! Amanda loathed him and, on numerous instances, had pleaded with Michael to fire him, but Michael wouldn't. While he had many faults, Michael could be extremely loyal. Fitch was so embedded at Michael's side that a shovel would be required to dig him loose.

"Are you positive you heard Fitch correctly?" she questioned.

"I'm sorry, but there was no mistaking his answer."

Amanda frowned, her temper spiking. It was simply inconceivable that she could swallow her pride and send a conciliatory note to Michael, but he would refuse to accept it. They were like an old, married couple who had a rhythm to their relationship. They coasted, they fought, they reconciled, then the cycle started over again. They were volatile individuals, with strong personalities and passionate natures, so from the first, they'd carried on outrageously.

She'd been his mistress for nearly a decade, and at this juncture, he couldn't break the chain of how they interacted. How dare he decline to cooperate with her attempt at a compromise!

"That will be all," she said, and he bowed but didn't leave, so she queried, "Was there something else?"

"Yes, Miss Amanda." He gulped with trepidation. "The staff was curious . . . that is . . . they wanted me to . . . well . . ."

"Spit it out, James."

He squared his shoulders. "We were wondering if Lord Winchester will be coming back."

She carefully shielded any reaction. Her employees weren't stupid. They comprehended that their salaries were dependent on her keeping Michael happy. Previously, their quarrels were resolved within days, yet this rift had continued for weeks. The servants had to be growing concerned, as was she.

"Don't be silly." Feigning nonchalance, she chuckled. "Of course he'll be back. You may notify everyone that the situation will be remedied shortly. Today was just a . . . a misunderstanding. In fact, the earl and I have a rendezvous scheduled for tonight."

It was a huge but effective lie. He was desperate to be reassured and was visibly relieved by the news. She flashed a confident smile that masked her apprehension, and he turned and departed.

As his boots clicked down the hall, she huffed out a heavy breath. She didn't know how long she could sustain the ruse that all was fine. With Michael's rejection of her message, she was terrified that he might sever their association.

If he tossed her over, what would she do?

While she'd saved a few pennies, her tastes were voracious, her style of living expensive, and she didn't have any cash put away. She'd be forced to find another benefactor, but at thirty-two, she was far beyond the age when another man of means might be interested.

She intended to remain with Michael well into her middle years, after which he'd be so grateful he'd pension her off. She'd been his consort forever, and she knew more about him than anyone. She made his life so easy! She jumped through hoops to please him, to coddle him, to arrange his affairs so that he was content.

How could he contemplate splitting with her? Didn't he grasp how much he needed her? They were salt and pepper, paint and brush, two peas in a pod. It would be impossible for people in London to imagine one of them without the other. He'd be wretched, lost, without her, but he was too thick to realize it.

An odd event must have transpired to have him behaving so abnormally, and she had to learn what it was. Once she'd uncovered the mystery, she could reverse his path, could coax and cajole him until he forgave her.

She struggled to recollect any alteration to his circumstances, but the sole modification she could conjure was his hiring the governess.

She scoffed. As if that frumpy piece of baggage could have wreaked such a disaster!

Pamela Martin was ensconced in the mansion, too, and Amanda pondered whether Pamela might have enticed him, but ultimately, she discounted the prospect. Michael hated virgins and detested the chatter of young girls, so he wouldn't have given her a second look. However, she could be useful.

Amanda had known Pamela's father intimately, had reveled with him on many debauched occasions. From her innocuous discussions with Pamela, Amanda had been left with the impression that Pamela shared most of her father's worst traits. Plus, she wasn't very bright.

"Yes," Amanda reflected, "Pamela might be the key."

Pamela was gullible and greedy, fascinated by vice and profligacy, so she could provide tons of information, could be bribed with all manner of depraved boons into spying and eavesdropping. With Pamela having such close access to Michael, who could say what details might be gleaned? There was no telling what she might be prompted to reveal or attempt.

Amanda relaxed, much less distressed than she'd been.

Pamela Martin was about to have a secret friend.

Reginald Barnett dawdled in his parlor. A large stack of unopened bills taunted him, and he shoved them away. As there was no money to disburse, what was to be gained by bothering with them?

From the time he was a lad, he'd been the Barnett heir, had recognized that he would grow up to own the property and marry one of the daughters. Originally, his spouse was to have been Mary, but after she'd been struck blind, his parents had insisted on Emily being the fiancée, so the change had been made. Reginald hadn't cared which sister was selected. He'd merely wanted to garner his rightful place.

When Emily's father had passed on, Reginald had been so excited. He'd waited three decades for his future to culminate, so he might have been a tad too enthused over his inheritance. He'd purchased some items on credit, and now, he had to pay the piper, yet due to Emily's stubbornness, his coffers were bare. His small estate, and the funds necessary to run it, were still held in the trust that had been created at her father's death, and neither title nor cash would be released until Emily became his bride. The lawyers claimed that if the match was never brought to fruition, the entirety would revert to the Crown. The King would have it to waste!

It had never occurred to Reginald that she would spurn him, that she'd renounce her heritage and decline to do her duty, that she would leave him destitute. At remembering how she'd shamed him, his temper flared.

He glanced at the letter he'd received from her, and he was goaded to recklessness. Since she'd hied herself off to London, it was her only correspondence, so he assumed it was meant as a further insult.

She was proud of her exploits, utterly chatty in bragging about her new job. Her employer was the Earl of Winchester, and as he thought of Emily residing with Winchester, he felt ill. Even in his rural section of the country, he'd heard tales of the Farrow brothers and their disgusting antics.

Why would she willingly subject herself to such iniquity?

At age forty, he was a virgin. He was overtly frustrated by the situation, and impatient to make Emily his own so that he could utilize his male power to subjugate her. She'd never appreciated that—as a female—she should be subservient and beholden, and he was determined to grind her under his heel.

Years earlier, he'd begun buying erotic French picture books from a traveling peddler, and his collection was enormous. The tomes showed how a man could force a woman to obey, even if she didn't wish to yield. The books were sinful and foul, but he never tired of studying them.

Every night, he would shut his eyes, would touch himself and visualize Emily—naked and tied to his bed. He would torment her until she pleaded and begged for mercy, until she finally acknowledged his authority over her.

He considered Mary, as well. With her blank stares and silent wanderings, she gave him eerie shivers. He dreamed of her being bound and gagged, too, perhaps the two sisters manacled together and compelled to do his bidding. He had no doubt that Mary had encouraged Emily to flee, and once he succeeded in returning them to Hailsham, he would be avenged.

He would have Mary for his own before he shipped her to Bedlam, where she belonged; then Emily would pay and pay and pay. If she lived to be a hundred, she could never fully compensate him for the dishonor she'd inflicted.

In his fantasies, she was sweet and chaste. But what if she was tainted in London? She had chosen to cast her lot with Farrow, so any calamity could befall her. She might succumb to temptation, might start drinking or carousing, might be seduced by Winchester or his brother.

Emily was a fool to risk so much, and Reginald couldn't allow her to offer to Winchester what was rightfully Reginald's. He had to stop her.

There was no hope for it. He'd have to journey to

London and reason with her, although he wasn't optimistic. Emily was too arrogant, smarter and more intractable than any female ought to be, but if he couldn't get through to her, there was always Winchester.

Reginald wouldn't hesitate to spew any falsehood, so Emily's post was about to be lost to her. After all, who would permit a slattern to tend children? When Reginald was finished, after his malicious gossip was spread throughout the city, Winchester would have to fire her.

Emily's reputation would be ruined. She'd be unemployable. What would she do then?

He smiled. She'd have to come home, where Reginald would be more than happy to take her in.

Oh yes, Emily's little jaunt was about to end.

7

Mary moved toward her room, counting her steps as was her habit. It was very late, and she liked to practice walking at night, when there was no one about to witness her mistakes. After that first, humiliating afternoon, when she'd wound up in Mr. Farrow's private suite, she'd been studying the layout of the large mansion, and she was finally beginning to be confident as to her location.

She was determined never to make a fool of herself or to wander in where she wasn't wanted. She was desperate for Emily's position to work out, so she couldn't have anyone complaining. If Emily lost her job because Mary had displeased someone, Mary would never forgive herself.

How she hated being beholden! As a girl, she'd contracted a virulent case of the measles and gone blind, so the majority of her life had been a long trial of dependence and reliance. People treated her as if she were demented, as if she were retarded and mute, as well, though she'd been luckier than most who found themselves in a similar situation. She'd had a comfortable home, loving parents, a kindly sister, and a complacent husband, but with their hovering, sometimes she felt as if she might start screaming and never stop. She'd give anything to be able to care for herself, to earn a salary and live on her own, to be free of the prison that her disability had created. While Emily was the best sibling in the world, it was degrading to sit back, year after year, doing nothing as Emily toiled away on Mary's behalf.

She reached her door and entered, and the instant she was inside, she halted and frowned. Though she couldn't see, her other senses were extremely sharp. She could ascertain so much about what was transpiring, and at that very moment, she was positive Alex Farrow was lounging on her bed. It had to be Farrow, yet the possibility was so bizarre that she couldn't process it. So many mixed messages were being sent to her brain that she was dizzy.

Since their ignominious meeting, she hadn't run into him, but she'd often perceived him watching her from a distance. When he was lurking, it was easy to distinguish his surly presence. He was an angry, bitter man, and his antipathy rolled off him like a malodorous cloud.

She didn't know why he was so dour, and she didn't want to know, but she had to tread cautiously, lest she have him racing to his brother with a demand that they be evicted.

"What do you want?" she asked without preamble, and she could tell that she'd surprised him. Others regularly assumed that she was an imbecile. He bathed with sandalwood soap, and he'd been drinking brandy. Didn't he realize that she could smell him?

"I wish to speak with you."

"Now you have. Why don't you go?"

"Do you always sneak about the halls in the middle of the night?"

"Yes, as a matter of fact."

"Why?"

"I haven't been pilfering the silver, if that's what has you worried." She held out her arms, and spun in a circle, showing him that she had no silverware shielded in the folds of her skirt.

He sat up, the bed frame creaking with his weight, as he planted his feet on the floor. Curiously, he was in his stockings, his boots disposed of before he'd crept up the stairs. Obviously, this was a furtive outing, and there was only one reason she could think of that he'd intrude.

Had he ravagement in mind? Would he behave so despicably?

She'd listened to many tales about the Farrow brothers, but she hadn't heard that they were rapists.

Of course, she'd been in residence for such a short period. There was much she couldn't yet have gleaned. What was his intent?

He stood, and she braced, utilizing her acuity to assess his purpose, and to her great relief, she felt no menace. She relaxed. Whatever his scheme, whatever misguided, peculiar urge had driven him to visit, it wasn't malicious.

He approached until he was very near, and he scrutinized her face, her hair, her figure.

"Were you born blind?" he queried.

"No."

"How did it occur?"

"I fell ill. When I was a child."

"Can you see anything, at all?"

"No."

He waved his palm before her eyes, as she sniffed his skin. He had a warm, masculine scent that thrilled her, that had her wanting to lean in and rub herself against him, and the notion stunned her. Having been married, she was no innocent. She recognized that she was experiencing desire, and she was flabbergasted.

In the decade that she'd been a widow, she hadn't once craved a man's touch, hadn't fretted over what she was missing, or waxed nostalgic for past delights.

Her husband had been a subdued, modest fellow, who had worked for her father, and her father had paid him to wed her. Not that Mary had had an inkling of the financial transaction that had inspired the sudden proposal.

They'd had a tepid, congenial relationship, but he wasn't a particularly physical individual, and amorous endeavor had usually been beyond him. Being virgins when they'd tied the knot, they hadn't known much about sex, but he'd been too shy to experiment or learn. Rumor had it that the marital act could be very rousing and passionate, and she'd waited for an ember to ignite, but it never had.

To this day, she wondered how they'd managed to have Rose. Their conjugal mating had been so intermittent that she considered Rose to be a miracle baby.

After his health had deteriorated, their intimacy had ceased altogether, so it had been quite a while since her interest had been piqued, and she couldn't discern why it was transpiring. Especially with Mr. Farrow.

What did it portend?

He noted the strange electricity, too. He hesitated,

halting the movement of his hand so that he could revel in the sparks that flew between them.

"You're a widow?" he asked.

"Yes."

"At what age were you wed?"

"Sixteen."

"To whom?"

"One of my father's employees."

"How long were you married?" he probed.

"Two years."

"What happened to him?"

"He died of a lung fever. He never was very hale."

"Were you happy?"

She bristled. "How rude of you to inquire."

"Were you?"

"I suppose." As happy as a woman could be when the union was formed out of pity, obligation, and duty.

"Your sight vanished and never came back?"

"Yes."

"Can you detect light or shapes?"

"No."

"Is there any hope of it returning?"

"No. There's no hope." She paused, then added, "I'm resigned to my fate."

"I'm trying to decide," he said, "what would be worse: to never have seen at all, or to have had it snatched away."

"I would deem it to be fairly horrendous either way."

He chuckled, a low, pleasing rumble that tickled her stomach and rattled her nerves, as he asserted, "You don't strike me as an invalid."

"I hate being a burden."

"I've watched you walking, exploring the house."

"I know."

"You do?"

"I can tell when you're close by." She shrugged. "To accommodate for the loss of my vision, my other senses are stronger than the average person's. I can fathom many details that others can't."

"How fascinating."

He circled around her, evaluating her as one might a horse at an auction. What was he thinking? What was his objective?

She still couldn't determine what had brought him upstairs.

Perhaps it was simple curiosity about the new boarder. Or perhaps he was intrigued by her infirmity. Or maybe this was his method of apologizing for his initial anger, but she doubted it.

Though he perceived their affinity, he couldn't plan to act on it. Could he? What if he meant to dally? Could she? Should she? She'd been lonely for ages, but Mr. Farrow wasn't the cure for what ailed her.

He'd completed the journey around her body, and she risked prying. "What color is your hair?"

"Black."

"And your eyes?"

"Blue."

"As the sky?" she prodded. "As an icy lake? As the Mediterranean sea?"

He pondered, then said, "The sky."

"May I . . . may I . . . touch your face?"

"My face? Hmm. . . ." He was silent for a lengthy interval; then he agreed. "I guess that would be all right."

Tentatively, she rested her palm on his cheek. She massaged across bone and flesh, ridge and valley. He had striking features, and she imagined he was very handsome, which made her regret her lack of sight in a fashion she hadn't previously. What she wouldn't give to be able to see him! To judge for certain rather than to speculate!

She investigated the other cheek, where she was amazed to find a rough, terrible scar. She traced over it, starting at the base under his jaw and traveling up to his hairline. He was tense, apparently anticipating a comment that he was positive would be derogatory.

She wanted to laugh. Could he really presume that *she* would chastise over a little scar?

Foolish, vain man!

"What happened to you?" she inquired.

"I was in the army. I fought in Spain and Portugal."

A wounded soldier! The information clarified much about his curt temperament.

"Does it hurt?"

"No," he claimed, but she didn't believe him. There were many kinds of *hurt*.

He'd asked her what it had been like to become blind so suddenly, but she could ask him the same sort of question. By all accounts, he'd been dashing and attractive, but his military service had altered him, and he'd been thrust into high society appearing very diverse from how he'd left it. From his attitude, it was evident that his peers hadn't been gracious in accepting the changes.

He was different from everyone else, on the outside

looking in—as was she. She smiled. She'd erroneously assumed that they had naught in common when, in reality, their situations were very similar.

"What is your opinion?" he queried.

"Tall, broad, fit." When he relaxed, she adjoined, "Arrogant, conceited, bossy."

He harrumphed. "You can gather that much?"

"And a good deal more." She smirked. "How did I do? Was I on the mark?"

"You're a nosy, meddlesome mind reader, and thus, I shall guard my thoughts around you, lest you glean much more than you ought."

"A wise course. I'm not a woman to be underestimated, though I usually am."

"I can see that. Now, why are you grinning?" He was suspicious and wary, expecting her to mention his disfigurement, which she would never do. Between the two of them, how could it possibly signify?

"Because we're going to be great friends," she maintained.

"We are, are we?"

"I'm convinced of it."

Her hand dropped away, and he clasped it and linked their fingers so that he could lead her toward the bed. She trudged after him, not helping, but not resisting, either. She was in turmoil, struggling to deduce what she wanted to occur.

By visiting her room, he'd been administering a test, which she'd passed, though she wasn't aware of how she'd pleased him. Perhaps it was no more complicated than her being blasé about his deformity.

He was bent on seduction, but she was confused as to

what would be best. She was an adult, a widow, with no one and nothing to stop any misconduct, but for her ingrained sense of morals. Fornication would be wrong, a sin she must not commit, yet she was intrigued by him.

Was she wishing to philander? Dare she?

Throughout her marriage, she'd been disappointed by the absence of raw excitement, and trifling with Alex Farrow would be an astounding event. He was raging on the inside, driven by an anguish and torment she didn't fully comprehend, and in a libidinous relationship his agony would metamorphose into potent, powerful emotion.

She'd lived a sheltered life, surrounded by ordinary, contented people, and she was captivated by the opportunity for titillation, for turbulent passion and uncontrolled ardor. Could she frolic with abandon? Could she set loose her unrestrained character?

He wasn't a villain. She could tell him to desist and he would, but for some absurd reason, she couldn't force the command from her lips. Her torso had made the choice that her mind couldn't render, a nagging fascination overriding her better judgment.

A giddy impression of freedom washed over her. She—plain, unpretentious Mary Barnett Livingston— was about to misbehave with complex, sophisticated Alex Farrow. What were the odds?

He lay down and stretched out, and he pulled her on top of him. Down below, she was comfortably snuggled, and there was no mistaking the bulge in his trousers.

"Mr. Farrow, what do you intend?"

"I'm not sure," he answered candidly.

"You must have some idea. Why are you here?"

"I'm still trying to decide."

"Are we to be lovers?"

"It seems that we are."

He was as bewildered as she. What was their goal? Would they rut for sport, like beasts in a field? Would she enjoy such a cold coupling?

He'd view any exchange as a simple, straightforward romp and naught more. Could she participate without letting her feelings become involved? If she succumbed, how would she face him later on?

In an instant, before she could rationalize further, he kissed her, his hand on her neck, his tongue in her mouth.

For a moment, she was so stunned that she froze. Her husband had never kissed her in such a way, so she hadn't realized that kissing could be so wild and uninhibited. She jerked out of her stupor and joined in, holding him tight, euphoric at being able to explore. She trailed across his shoulders and arms, his head and back, even bravely dipping down to squeeze his buttocks, which definitely thrilled him.

He groaned and deepened the kiss.

She reeled, responding to his slightest caress. While she'd recognized that she was lonely, it had never dawned on her that she'd been so starved for affection. She felt as if she'd been lost in the desert and stumbled upon an oasis.

He rolled them, so that she was on the bottom and he was on top. As he was a big man, his weight pushed her down in a manner she liked very much. Like an old pair of slippers, he was extremely familiar, and her body welcomed him, her legs widening of their own accord. He slid between her thighs, his phallus pressed to her privates and rubbing where it should. She was breathless, overwhelmed, nearly paralyzed by the expectation he induced.

They fit perfectly, and she was elated to note that he was acquainted with the female anatomy and exceedingly cognizant of what he ought to do with it.

He knew precisely how to touch her, what would spur the encounter to a higher level. In fact, he understood more about her preferences than she did, herself. Not that she was an expert. Her husband should have taught her, but he hadn't liked the sweating and effort that fornication required, and if she was honest, she'd have to admit that he'd been revolted by the whole sordid exploit.

Impatient for more, she was eager to go where she'd never had the chance to travel. She tugged at his shirt, yanking it off and tossing it on the floor.

While her husband's chest had been smooth, Farrow's was muscled and covered with a thick matting of hair. Anxious to investigate, she burrowed down to nestle through it.

He was rigid with desire, and he wrenched at her dress, ripping the fabric in his haste to bare her bosom; then his fingers were inside the bodice and roughly massaging her breasts.

He grabbed her nipples, squeezing so hard that it hurt, but it felt so good! She was on fire, every nerve tingling, until she couldn't tolerate much more.

Just when she thought she'd burst, that it couldn't possibly get any better, he latched onto her nipple. She'd speculated as to whether such sucking wasn't supposed to have been part of the mating ritual. With her husband, her nipples would be so tender that she'd cry out in frustration, but the sole time she'd asked him to stroke them, he'd been so appalled that she'd never subsequently made the request.

Farrow grasped how to manipulate them, how to nip and play until she was writhing in agony. When would it stop? How would it conclude? Did he know what could happen to a woman? How she could shatter in ecstasy?

The wave had crept over her sporadically with her husband. The first occasion, she'd been so astounded that she'd been very loud, which had resulted in his chastising her for being loose and wicked.

After that, whenever the feelings rushed over her, she'd stifled her reaction. If she was swept away, would Farrow be shocked? Would he be repulsed?

He was drawing up her skirt, fussing with his trousers, and she was aware that this was the last spot where she could reverse their course. But she said nothing. She did nothing.

Clasping her legs, he spread them and prodded in, the blunt crown stretching her. Then, with a swift lunge, he drove in, his phallus filling her to her womb, and she arched up in exultation.

He started thrusting, penetrating all the way, then retreating to the tip, and the motion was so fabulous that pleasure seized her in its vehement grip. The stimulation was so strong that she couldn't hide it, and she called out.

He kissed her again, swallowing the sound of her joy, and he was goaded to his own swift end. He spilled himself inside her, and their combined passion went on and on, the deluge never seeming to crest. She savored every second, cataloging the details so that she would remember them after he'd gone.

Finally, the apex was achieved, and they floated down together. They were very still, and he was studying her and frowning, though she couldn't figure out why.

Was he horrified by her response? Was he aghast to learn that she was so lusty?

Her temper ignited. Had she invited him to her room? Had she given him any indication that she'd wanted this to transpire?

If he was disappointed, she cared not, and she wouldn't disgrace herself by trying to explain her wanton nature. She'd wandered down that fruitless road during her marriage, and she wouldn't humiliate herself.

If he wasn't happy, he could leave, and though it pained her to conceive of this being their only tryst, so be it. She was a grown woman. She'd agreed to the fling of her own free will. There was no reason to lament.

She looked away, staring at the wall, providing him with an unqualified signal that she considered the rendezvous to be over. As if he might say something, he tarried, and she prayed that he'd be silent. What could they have to discuss?

Without a word, he pulled out of her, and as soon as he moved, she rolled away and showed him her back. Though she couldn't see him, she could picture him rising, stuffing his privy parts into his pants, straightening his hair and clothing.

For another moment, he dawdled, his perplexity and embarrassment billowing out, and, as if he might pat her shoulder, he reached out. She stiffened, letting him know that the gesture wouldn't be welcome.

He left, and she lay quietly, listening as he walked to the stairs, as he sneaked down. Her hearing was exceptionally acute, so she could perceive him entering his bedchamber, pacing the floor. Her imagination supplied the rest, his ultimately shedding his clothes and climbing into bed.

Unblinking, she gazed at nothing. A candle was burning, and she stayed awake till it petered out. Then, feeling more alone than ever, she sighed and drifted off.

"Lock the door."

"I most certainly will not."

"I intend to ravish you," Michael announced. "If you don't care whether someone walks in on us, that's fine with me. I don't mind an audience."

Emily whirled around and turned the key in the lock, sealing them in the library. It was very late, the entire house abed, but she couldn't risk being discovered. He'd been eager to receive his daily briefing, so he'd commanded her presence, and she'd obliged him, though she couldn't figure out why she had. She should have insisted on an innocuous morning appointment, and the fact that he was dressed in the flowing pants and shirt he'd been wearing when they met only underscored how wrong she'd been to come.

She had to keep her wits about her, had to give him her report, then depart before she landed herself in another imprudent predicament.

"What's this nonsense about ravishing me?" She

scowled. "You're not going to, are you? Because tonight, I'm not about to allow any mischief."

"You're not?"

"I let you get the better of me once, but now that I grasp your wicked ways, I'm prepared to fend you off."

He was walking toward her, taking slow, casual steps, and with each stride he advanced, she retreated twice as far.

"Have you brought a club?" he asked. "Or a pistol?"

"Hardly."

"Then how will you keep me at bay?"

"I plan to remember my morals and upbringing. Just because you tempt me to all manner of indiscretion doesn't mean I have to succumb."

"I loathe your high standards."

"You would," she said. "You're a libertine, so it would never occur to you that I might be able to control my base inclinations."

"Why would you wish to control them?"

"Because I'm not like you."

He chuckled. "You're more like me than you want to admit."

"I am not!" she was honor-bound to declare, although she couldn't help worrying that he was correct.

He made her feel free and unencumbered, as if she could attempt any loose deed that tickled her fancy. Her body was inflamed, with various spots irritating her in a fashion she'd never noticed. Her breasts were fuller, her nipples constantly rubbing her corset so that she had no surcease from the torture he'd instigated.

She was so anxious for relief that on one desperate occasion, she'd sought to alleviate the pressure by massaging them, but she set off such a flurry of sensation that she'd frightened herself and hadn't tried it again.

"It's all right to indulge yourself," he contended. "There's no harm in having a bit of fun."

She bumped into his desk. "There is when the amusement you seek leads to folly and ruin."

"Do I look as if I'm bent on ruining you?" He was all innocence, all sweet, decadent resolve.

"Yes, and don't you dare. You won't find the easy mark you encountered prior."

"Are you sure about that?"

"Absolutely."

In a swift move, he lunged forward and pinned her to the desktop, his arms on either side of her so that she was trapped. He leaned in, and she was terrified. If he snuggled himself to her, she couldn't resist him.

"I've missed you," he claimed, and her idiotic heart soared.

"Don't say such a thing to me."

"Why not? It's true."

"It is not, but I'm foolish enough to believe you."

He was urging her down when she was determined to remain vertical.

"Have you missed me?" His expression was peculiar, as if he was genuinely curious.

"No," she lied. "Now, behave yourself."

"I have no desire to."

"Stand away so that we can chat."

"I'm not about to speak with you from across the room."

"I insist."

"And I'm ignoring you."

"Talking to you is like talking to a wall."

"So I've been told." His hand was between her shoulder blades, and she was a palm's width from being prone.

"Do you ever listen to what anyone says?"

"Yes, if what they're telling me is worth hearing."

"Wouldn't you like to know about your wards?"

"My wards?" He seemed confused by the question.

"That's what we're here to discuss."

"I don't think so."

He dipped under her chin and bit at her nape, the attention giving her goose bumps. She hadn't realized the area was so sensitive, and she shivered with delight, which made him laugh. The sound was like a splash of cold water on her burgeoning passion.

She would not yield!

"Margaret had a wonderful day," she commented, pretending he wasn't seducing her. "She's assimilating quickly, and she's becoming fast friends with my niece, Rose."

"Is she?" He nibbled down her arm. "I'm so glad."

"Pamela, on the other hand"—he buried his face in her cleavage, which made it difficult to focus—"is a problem. When we were shopping, she wandered off, and I couldn't locate her for many minutes."

"Yet she returned unscathed?"

"Eventually."

"So you're informing me of this because . . . ?"

"You're their guardian, and this is your daily report."

He glanced up. "Have I asked you for a daily report?"

"Yes."

"You're positive?"

"Completely."

"I've changed my mind," he said. "I don't care to be apprised of these trivial details."

"Lord Winchester . . ."

He slipped his fingers inside her dress and slithered across to grab and pinch her nipple. Her anatomy reacted with a gleeful vigor, her pulse pounding, her womb in spasms, her womanly core weeping. In an instant, she'd tumbled into another mess, when she hadn't intended any rash conduct.

How did he overcome her better judgment? He was a master at coaxing her to iniquity. Why was she so weak? Why couldn't she say no and mean it?

"We're beyond *Lord Winchester*, remember? It's Michael now."

"It is not." She attempted to push him away. "And stop that."

He tugged on the bodice of her gown, and her breasts popped from their confines. Smiling at the sight, he clasped both nipples.

"You have the most fabulous breasts," he remarked, and he bent down and sucked on one of them.

She arched up, not sure if she was shoving him away or dragging him nearer. "Lord Winchester . . . milord . . . Michael . . ."

Grinning, he halted his torment. "Yes?"

"I really, really can't do this with you."

"Yes, you can."

"Michael . . . I . . ."

He wrapped his lips around her nipple again, and whatever complaint she might have registered was lost. It was simply impossible to protest when he was feasting like a starved man at a banquet. His actions were too thrilling, and deep down, she didn't want him to cease.

Oh, she was so spineless! So irresolute!

Was this why she'd visited? Had she been hoping that another tryst would transpire? Perhaps she had the soul of a slattern but had never recognized it.

"Have you discovered how a female is pleasured?" He cupped her between her legs.

"No, no . . ."

He was inching up her skirt, easing the hem out of his way. His hand was on her knee, her thigh, roving higher and higher in slow, agonizing circles. "I'm going to touch you, Emily."

If he would grant her a reprieve from her misery, she'd let him try anything.

"Where?"

"You know where."

"You mustn't."

"It will be like nothing you've ever imagined."

He slid his fingers into her mysterious feminine sheath, and he stroked them in a languid, tantalizing motion that rocked her world and altered her view of life as she'd known it. She felt as if she'd been waiting forever for him to caress her so intimately. It was heaven; it was bliss. Her agitation increased, her tension spiraling to a hazardous level. She was about to explode, to shatter into a thousand pieces.

"What's happening to me?" she managed to ask.

"This is sexual desire, Emily."

"I don't want it," she asserted. "I can't stand any more."

"Of course you can."

"You're killing me!"

"Almost finished," he soothed.

His thumb flicked out and prodded at a spot she'd never before noted. It seemed as if all the sensation in the universe was centered there. He jabbed at it, as he sucked on her nipple, and she leapt over a precipice, her body in free fall, and she blindly careened through space and time as if she were being hurled across the sky.

She cried out, and he captured her lips in a torrid kiss, silencing the sound. The commotion went on and on, until she began to worry that it would never end, then gradually, she floated to earth, and she was cradled to him. She blinked and blinked, peeking around to get her bearings, but everything was different, as if reality had been transformed.

He kissed her, sweetly, tenderly. "You are such a gem."

She struggled to push him off, to sit up and right herself, but her arms had turned to rubber, her torso a limp rag. Dazzled by new perceptions, she demanded, "What was that?"

"The French call it the *petite mort*."

"Don't spew foreign phrases," she snapped. "Speak to me in English."

"The little death," he whispered.

"Can it occur more than once?"

"Definitely."

She quivered with excitement, and she was alarmed by her response. Was the exploit habit-forming? Could one become obsessed, like an opium addict to his drug? Had she already started down the path to destruction? What if she developed into an uncontrollable amorous fiend?

She had a vision of herself, old and aged, and sneaking down the hallways in his house, desperate to catch him alone. She was blatantly fascinated. Who wouldn't be? The bounder was irresistible. What if she'd joined herself to him in a way she couldn't sever?

He was gazing at her, a look of gentle speculation in his eye, and she couldn't abide it.

Was he growing fond? More than fond?

The exhilarating, absurd prospect had her scoffing. She had to recollect how they'd met, what he'd been doing. He was the type who would cavort with anyone, and when she jumped into these ridiculous situations, she was only torturing herself.

He wasn't like the men from Hailsham, and any fantasies she might have to the contrary were folly. The ordinary man of her acquaintance never trifled with a woman unless marriage was the ultimate goal. The ordinary *woman* never permitted liberties unless she had a ring on her finger.

Why was she misbehaving? What was she striving to achieve? He wasn't a marrying sort of fellow, and though his position required that he wed someday, she would never be in contention for the role of bride.

He would toy with her until he tired of the chase; then he'd move on. No other result was possible, so why persist? Why attend him, without a chaperon, when she was powerless to refuse his advances?

With the cooling of her ardor, she felt like a trollop. She was sprawled on the desk, her bosom exposed, her hair down, her legs wrapped around him. What must he think!

The answer was obvious: He presumed she was loose, that she would engage in whatever licentious conduct he suggested, and why shouldn't he have a low opinion? From the first, she'd continually disgraced herself.

"How do you do that to me?" she asked.

"Do what?" Pleased as punch with his male prowess, he smirked.

"I can't be around you for a single second without acting shamelessly."

He helped her up, arranging her bodice and dropping her skirt. "You shouldn't feel bad. Or guilty. There's nothing wrong with you. Your reactions are perfectly normal."

"Maybe in your world, but they're certainly not in mine."

"Don't be too sure."

What was he implying? That her tiny village of Hailsham was a swirling hotbed of immorality? The insinuation was preposterous.

He appeared as if he was about to utter a profound remark, or explain an important fact, but couldn't. He stood before her, assessing her, pondering her, and out of the blue, he inquired, "Would you be my mistress?"

She gasped. "No. You insult me by mentioning it."

"Your talents are wasted in working as a governess."

"My *talents*?" How could he suppose that she had any aptitude for this kind of endeavor? He was the sole man who'd ever kissed her, and she was positive she wasn't very adept.

"I want us to be lovers."

"I'm not very experienced at this, but I believe we are."

"But there's so much more to it than this furtive groping. Wouldn't you like to find out how it could be between us?"

As she was convinced it would be wonderful, her reply was easy to render. "No."

"Let's go to your room."

Once they arrived, what naughty antics might he initiate? She was terrified to know.

"Absolutely not," she said.

"Emily?"

"Yes."

"Aren't you the least bit curious?"

She couldn't pretend no interest, for she was extremely
anxious to glean the particulars. It dawned on her that
there were probably ways in which she could please him,
too, and the notion was thrilling.

"Maybe a tad," she admitted.

"You can't tell me that you feel complete."

"What do you mean?"

"Concentrate on your body—on the inside." He stroked
her breast, his merest caress sending shivers down her
arms. "I want to lie down with you, in your bed. I'll take
off your clothes; then I'll touch you and kiss you all over."

She blushed, though not from embarrassment. The
image he painted was so stirring, and so vivid, that she
was eager to clasp his hand and lead him up the stairs.

"Michael . . ."

"Then *you* can take off my clothes and do the same."
He grinned. "We could order up a bath and wash each
other."

Men and women bathed each other? She thought of
having him nude, wet and slippery and at her mercy, and
even though she wasn't certain what she'd do with him
if he was naked, she suspected she'd quickly figure it out
and that it would be fabulous.

My, my! How swiftly she was becoming a strumpet!

"Just because I *can* doesn't indicate that I will." She hated how she sounded so prim and proper.

"After we are both naked, I'll arouse you again."

"To bring on the 'little death'?"

"Yes."

She gulped. "Then what?"

"Then, I'll make you mine in every way that counts."

"You're babbling in riddles."

"If I told you what it entails," he stated, "I doubt you'd believe me."

"Try it, and see if I will."

"Let's go to your room," he repeated. "It's simpler if I show you."

If she agreed, she couldn't begin to calculate the number of sins she'd likely commit. "Why not demonstrate right here?"

"Because I'm not about to debauch you on the desk in my library."

"Define *debauch*."

Apparently, she'd exasperated him, and he blew out a heavy breath. "It involves what you'd call mating or coupling."

"What is required?"

"We're built differently." He gestured between them. "In our private parts."

They were? She was so naive!

"Really?"

"Yes."

"Why?"

"So that we can fit together when we fornicate."

The word *fornicate* was new to her, and it seemed so

exotic and unusual that she mulled it, envisioning the places where she might use it in a sentence.

I fornicate all the time, she pictured herself gaily expounding at a party. Or, *Do you fornicate whenever you can?*

"How would we . . . would we . . . *fornicate?*"

"Well . . . you have a sort of sheath, while I have a sort of . . . a sort of . . ." He stopped, a muscle twitching in his cheek. "Emily?"

"Yes?"

"Quit asking so many questions."

He grabbed her and hoisted her over his shoulder. She was dangling upside down, her rear in the air, her head swaying across his waist. She struggled and kicked, but he tightened his grip and made for the door.

She shrieked and pummeled his back. "What are you doing?"

"We're finished talking." He swatted her on the bottom. "Now be silent, before someone hears you and sees what we're about."

"We are *not* going to my room!"

"You have no choice in the matter."

9

Michael walked into the master's suite, kicked the door shut with his heel, then marched to the bed and dropped Emily on the wide, plush mattress. She emitted a squeal of surprise, and tried to jump up, but he lay down and covered her with his body so that she couldn't escape.

He was so aroused that he was frightened. He'd reveled in decadent pursuits, had practiced seduction with a reckless abandon, but he couldn't recall ever having suffered such an unstoppable wave of lust.

He'd never desired a woman as he desired Emily Barnett, which, considering his position, was disgusting. How could he trifle with his wards' governess? It was so wrong, so unscrupulous, yet he couldn't desist.

"This isn't my room," she pointed out.

"No, it isn't," he replied.

"What are you thinking?"

"I haven't the foggiest."

"Have you any notion of the uproar that will ensue if we're caught?"

"Yes."

"The other staff members will crucify me," she said.

"I'm sure they will."

"Mr. Fitch will volunteer to act as executioner."

"Very likely."

"I could never show my face in public," she complained.

"Correct."

"The rumors would spread. I'd have to quit my job."

"I wouldn't go that far."

"I would. Do you care, even the slightest bit, about what might happen?"

"No."

He didn't care about anything. Not his servants. Not his neighbors. Not the possibility of scandal. The only relevant factor was that he remove her clothes as rapidly as he was able. What he planned from there on was anyone's guess.

Since the last occasion they'd philandered, naught had changed. She was still an innocent maiden, and he was still her employer. He wasn't about to marry her, so their dallying was inappropriate, but he was determined to forge ahead.

For reasons he couldn't comprehend, she goaded him beyond any sane limit, and he spent every waking moment avoiding her. In his concerted effort to behave, he'd absented himself from the house, invented false engagements, kept fictitious appointments, and drank himself silly at his club, but to no avail.

He was obsessed with her. She was like a dangerous drug, and he couldn't figure out how to break his addiction.

"If I don't have you naked in the next minute," he told her, "I can't predict what I might do."

"Naked!"

"Yes."

"Then what?"

"I'll show you what you've been dying to learn."

She was about to lambaste him with another lecture, but he couldn't bear it. He grasped the enormity of his reprehensible conduct, so what was to be gained by hashing out his misdeeds?

He kissed her, his tongue in her mouth, his fingers in her hair. Previously, if he'd been asked to state a preference, he'd have sworn he liked blondes, but after he met her, his tastes had altered. He'd never seen hair like hers before, and he delighted in how soft it was, in what a contrast it made when layered across the white of his pillows.

His hands were busy with her dress. It was a functional garment, with simple buttons and laces, so it loosened quickly. For once, she didn't fight him, and he was so glad. He was beyond discussion or debate.

He tugged off her gown, then her corset, and her chemise was all that stood between himself and paradise. Prolonging the excitement, he slowly drew the straps off her shoulders.

Finally—finally!—her breasts were bared, and he blazed a trail to her chest, sucking at a taut bud, and her reaction was instantaneous. She arched up, offering more of herself, and he feasted, traveling from one nipple to the other, as he caressed the pliant mounds.

Her passion swiftly escalated, and he couldn't get over what a licentious nature she had. She was a magnificently amorous creature, and he was so lucky to have stumbled upon her. He was anxious to spur the encounter to the next level, but when he glanced up, he was stunned to note that she had tears in her eyes.

His heart lurched. Had he been mistaken? Had she been resistant, with himself too enamored to realize it?

"What is it?" He couldn't abide her being unhappy, or imagining that he'd hurt her. A pretty tear dribbled down her cheek, and he swiped it away.

"I can't believe I'm doing this with you," she wailed miserably.

"But I thought . . . thought . . ." What precisely? She lived and worked in his mansion, which left her no choice but to obey his commands.

He was such a thick oaf! Of course she wouldn't wish to ruin herself. Especially for the likes of him. He was a fool to have presumed otherwise.

"I'm sorry," he muttered.

"What for?" she inquired. "I'm the one who can't behave."

"I assumed you were enjoying this. We'll stop."

He tried to cover her breasts, but she wouldn't let him.

"You think I want you to stop?"

He was so confused. "Don't you?"

"If you *stop,* I'll wring your neck."

"You want to keep going?"

"Yes!"

Women! He'd never understand them! "Then why are you crying?"

"Because I'm so weak!"

"You're not weak," he declared, and he grinned. "Easy to seduce, maybe. But definitely not weak."

"Shut up." She punched him on the shoulder, and she sighed. "I always pictured such a different life for myself."

"What had you envisioned?"

"I expect what all women do: my own home, a husband, and many children."

"But you don't see that happening?"

"No." She studied him, an unsettling quiet filling the room. "You'd never marry me, would you?" He must have flashed an expression of horror, because she hurried on. "Don't look so panicked. I haven't an angry father or brother hiding behind the drapes. I just need to hear your answer."

"Why?"

"I must be very clear that if we proceed, you'll never propose afterward."

He was amazed that she was brave enough to raise the issue. She was the sort who would give herself with marriage in mind, while he intended to evade the matrimonial noose till the last possible moment; then he'd pick someone from his class who was boring, plain, and unremarkable.

His bride would be in love with his title and fortune, rather than himself. She would comprehend the ways of his world, would never demand that he be a real husband, would anticipate deplorable treatment from him, and would constantly receive it.

Emily deserved a spouse she could trust and cherish. He was so far removed from the man she ought to have that he couldn't calculate how he'd fail her if he pondered such an idiotic path.

"No, I would never marry you," he bluntly announced. "Were you hoping that I might?"

She shook her head. "I'm not sure of what you're planning for us to do, but I'm positive it will mean much more to me than it ever could to you."

He hated that she had such a low opinion of his character, but she was correct, and he wasn't about to lie. Sex was only sex to him. Ages ago, he'd resolved never to have his philandering be anything more than a physical and pleasurable act.

Still, he asked, "Why would you say that?"

"I'm not stupid. This is a normal peccadillo for you, while for me, it's new and thrilling—very likely a once in a lifetime occurrence. But I'm not anyone special to you, and I never could be."

It was on the tip of his tongue to contradict her, to inform her of how unique she was, but he wasn't accustomed to expounding on his most private sentiments, and he couldn't decide what good it would do anyway. If he confided as to her exceptional qualities, she'd embrace his comments, would attach much more significance to them than she should.

"Why must we talk about it at all?" he inquired.

"Because I have this annoying habit of ascribing more importance to events than I should, and I need a hefty dose of reality before we start. That way, I won't have any illusions."

To his surprise, he felt terrible, crushed that he couldn't tell her what she was anxious to hear. With another female, he might have been tempted to allow his unreliable, deceitful male self to disgorge whatever falsehoods were necessary to have her compliant, but he liked her too much to mislead her.

"I won't ever marry you, Emily."

For a lengthy interval, she stared at him, and he was deluged by the notion that she'd actually assumed his reply would be the opposite. Evidently, she had an elevated view of his integrity that didn't match his situation. Hadn't she listened to the rumors?

One part of him was tickled by her high esteem, but the other—the sordid, corrupt part—was irked. He didn't want her admiration, for then, he'd be worrying incessantly about his behavior toward her. He was in deep enough, and he didn't require any more reasons to obsess over his conduct.

He was simply keen to dally, and he couldn't have her imagining their association to be more than it was.

"Thank you for being honest," she said. "I appreciate it." Calmly, and with no further discussion, she began unbuttoning his shirt.

He wasn't certain what he'd expected. Anger? Accusation? Hysterical weeping? As usual, he'd misjudged her and, with her bland acceptance of his rejection, his irritation increased.

What did she want from him? What was he supposed to say? How could she blithely carry on? Were they to pretend the awkward subject had never been raised?

He was desperate to explain, but apparently, she didn't need clarification. Wasn't that just like a woman! He was ready to hash it out, to beat it to death like a jockey on a losing horse, but she'd rather keep on as if the tedious topic hadn't been broached.

He'd insulted her, had denied her the respectability that marriage could bring, had relegated her to the ranks of the whores with whom he consorted. How could she be so indifferent?

He took her hand and kissed it.

"I'm sorry," he repeated.

"Don't be. I asked for the truth, and you gave it to me."

"But I shouldn't have been so harsh."

"You weren't." She shrugged, tossing off his disavowal. "I'm not a child, and I'm capable of making my own decisions. But as I appear to have arrived at a difficult junction, I merely wish to know the condition of the road I've chosen to travel."

He felt even worse. She sounded as if he was turning her into a harlot. What next? Would she be walking the streets at night, soliciting customers?

As if she'd dumped cold water on him, his desire fled, yet she commenced with removing his clothes. She couldn't presume they'd continue, could she? Not after he'd rebuffed her!

It occurred to him that he'd never entirely grasped the benefit of purchasing prurient services. When his paramours were paid, he wasn't required to read their minds. He could cavort without all the strife.

He was abysmal at having relationships with women. He had no female friends, no adoring fiancées, no doting aunties or younger sisters. His bond with Emily was the first time he could recall engaging in anything vaguely resembling a connection, and it was obvious that his thirty years of living hadn't gifted him with a greater understanding of feminine wants or needs. He hadn't a clue.

He rolled off her and shifted to the side, and he rebuttoned his shirt.

"What are you doing?" she snapped, and she grabbed the fabric.

"We should probably stop. Until we think this through."

"Are you mad?"

"We can't keep going," he said.

"Why not?"

"Well . . ."

They were grappling over his shirt, and the moment was so absurd that he flopped onto his back and howled with laughter. It was a full-on belly laugh, the likes of which he hadn't enjoyed in ages.

"What's so funny?" she demanded.

"For once in my miserable life, I'm trying to do the right thing, but you won't let me."

"I don't want you to do the *right* thing. I thought we were clear on that."

"We're not clear at all!" He laughed harder. "You're determined to be ravished, and I'm fighting to prevent it."

"Have I asked you to be my moral compass?"

"No, and I don't know what's come over me. I must be hallucinating, or maybe I'm asleep, and this is the strangest dream I've ever had."

"Don't go all honorable on me. I'm in a pitiful state, and you'll drive me to commit mayhem."

He smiled and rotated them so that she was trapped beneath him.

"You are so good for me," he admitted.

"Am I?"

"You make me happy."

"I do?"

"In the very best way."

"But why and how?"

"You're just . . . you . . . and I'm delighted to have you here."

"What a divine sentiment." She sighed with contentment, gazing at him with such affection that he rippled with unease.

He'd never been one for spewing flowery comments or ridiculous flatteries, so he wasn't positive what was transpiring, but he was changing, and he couldn't guess what his next move might be.

Would he be picking bouquets? Delivering boxes of candy? Writing bad poetry?

There was simply no telling.

For an eternity, he had merely existed, not letting anyone or anything matter, but gradually, he was awakening, his weary spirit thawing after a lengthy winter of loneliness and isolation.

She'd been in his house a few weeks. If she stayed six months, what would remain of his old self? He'd be so altered that no one would recognize him.

If there was a chance that his randy, depraved character might disappear, he ought to revel before he was an empty shell of the man he'd been.

He sat up, jerked his shirt over his head, and pitched it on the floor. "Miss Barnett, I'm all yours. Explore at your leisure."

"Are you serious?"

"Leave no stone unturned."

She chuckled and reached out, her palms on his chest. "Ooh . . . your skin is so warm."

She looked nervous, as if she wasn't certain how to proceed, so he gripped her wrists and guided her in slow circles. She worked over his shoulders, his arms, his back, but she never dipped lower, never caressed him where he urgently needed her.

He pulled off her chemise, so that she was naked. Down below, he saw the dusting of auburn hair between her legs, the sweet puss shielded within. He was in perilous shape, and he untied the drawstring on his pants, slackening it so that the front was loose. "Touch me," he ordered. "Touch me all over."

He directed her inside, and she was elated to follow wherever he led. At encountering his cock, she was incredibly surprised.

"We're built differently," he remarked. "Remember?"

"You told me so, but why?"

"So that we can mate."

"You keep saying that, but I don't understand you."

"I'll show you."

Would he? Could he steal her virginity? He didn't think so, but if he didn't find a release and soon, he was concerned for his well-being. It couldn't be healthy to be so hard, for so long.

He wrapped her hand around his erect rod, and he taught her how to stroke him. She quickly adapted to the task, and he felt like a lad of fourteen, ready to spill himself at the drop of a hat.

"What do you call this thing?" she inquired.

"It has many names. A phallus, a cock."

"What is it for?"

Her gestures were excruciating, and he didn't know how much more he could endure. "For pleasure. And for making babies."

"How is it accomplished?"

"You have an opening in your body. Here." He delved

his fingers into her sheath. "If we were to mate, I would push my cock into you."

"Really?"

"Yes, and then I would thrust it back and forth. The motion is very satisfying, and it creates a friction that causes a white cream to erupt from the tip. It is my seed, and it can plant a babe in your womb."

"This . . . this mating, would it hurt?"

"Only the first time. You have a thin piece of skin covering the entrance—it's your maidenhead—and when a man initially takes you, it tears and bleeds."

"Aah," she mused, "that clarifies the stories I've heard. Will you . . . will we . . ." She blushed, not possessing the terminology for salacious discussion.

"Will I penetrate you?"

"Yes."

"Not today."

"When?"

"Maybe never."

She scowled. "Why not?"

"Because we could make a babe."

The enormity of what they were about occurred to her. "So we must be very careful."

"Yes. And if I deflower you, you can never marry."

"Why?"

So many questions! He hadn't realized that bedding a virgin could be so tiresome. "Because your husband would know that you've lain with another. That you're not a chaste bride."

"I don't believe we have to worry about that situation ever arising."

"You can't predict what the future will hold."

"Trust me," she assured him, "it will never be a problem."

What was she claiming? That she had no wish to wed? Or was it a more personal comment? After him, would she forsake all others? He was foolish enough to hope that he meant that much to her, but such strident emotion was hazardous.

He couldn't deduce her rationale and wouldn't try. There was one thing that he wanted from her, and that was fabulous sex. He would come as close as he could to that grand event without stepping over the ultimate line.

"So if we're not about to . . . to . . . mate," she ventured, "what are we going to do?"

"I can experience the same pleasure as you," he explained. "I'll instruct you in how to give it to me with your hands or your mouth."

"My mouth? You'd put it in my mouth?"

"Yes, but no child would be conceived."

He couldn't imagine using her so badly, tutoring her to perform a whore's tricks, but the notion of impaling himself between those lush ruby lips was nearly his undoing. Throughout their conversation, she hadn't ceased her rhythmic stroking, and he was goaded beyond sanity, while striving to appear under control.

"May I look at you?" Not waiting for permission, she'd scooted down and hovered over his crotch.

"I suppose." If he shed his trousers, they were in trouble.

She must have noticed the agony in his voice, because she halted. "Are you in pain?"

"I want you so much it hurts."

"You're ailing physically?"

"Yes."

"Can I relieve your distress?"

"Very easily."

"Then perhaps I should."

She grabbed his trousers and tugged them down, baring his loins with a fast yank. He stared at the ceiling, ignoring her, pretending she wasn't inches away.

She inspected him, checking every detail as a scientist might a novel invention. She traced a path from root to tip, journeying over and over, trailing across the ropey veins, the velvet skin, the smooth end.

"It's so big," she finally murmured. "How can you walk around with it in the way?"

"It's only enlarged when I'm aroused."

"Then you must be very, very aroused."

"Oh, I am."

Without warning, she bent down and took him into her mouth, gliding over the crown as if she'd implemented the maneuver a thousand times. She was so wet, so tight, and the deed so unexpected, that he almost spilled himself, and he lurched away, dragged her to him, and rolled on top of her.

"What's the matter?" she frantically queried.

"I have to come." He crushed her to his chest. "Now!"

"What should I do?"

"Just hold me."

She hugged him, his phallus wedged to her belly. He thrust once, twice, and he exploded. Usually, he could last forever, but she'd pushed him over a spectacular edge. He couldn't recollect ever being so provoked.

How did she manage it? How did she keep him so inflamed?

He soared to the heavens, his orgasm going on and on until he wondered if his poor heart might quit beating. Eventually, he reached the peak, and he tumbled down, falling and falling, then landing in her embrace. He collapsed, his face buried in the pillow, his weight squashing her, and he was terrified to look her in the eye, terrified to learn her opinion of the endeavor.

He must have revolted her. How could she have found any satisfaction in what he'd done?

Slinking to the washstand, he dipped a cloth, retrieved a towel, and returned to her. He swabbed away all evidence of his sin, accomplishing it without meeting her gaze.

But as he finished, he had to glance up, and he was stunned to see her smiling. She stretched and arched up, which made him want to jump on her like the rapacious creature he was.

"I love your body," she asserted. "I didn't realize a man's torso could be so . . . inspiring."

"Is that what you'd call me? An inspiration?"

"I've definitely been moved." She assessed his flaccid cock, and she was annoyingly smug. "You're not hard anymore."

"The erection passes with the pleasure."

She fondled him, noting the change in size and texture. "Is this an indication that you enjoyed yourself?"

"Yes, you scamp."

"So I did everything correctly?"

"If you'd been any more *correct,* I couldn't have survived it."

"When can we try it again?"

She was caressing him, utilizing the slow, captivating

strokes he'd taught her, and the unruly rod leapt to life, pulsating with a rekindled energy.

How could he be titillated so swiftly? What was happening to him? He was thirty years old. Was he planning to kill himself with dalliance? What a way to leave the earth!

She was like a carnal disease for which there was no cure. He was crazy for her, impatient to proceed, and he couldn't refuse.

"How about right now?"

"I thought you'd never ask."

She opened her arms, and he snuggled into them, eager and ready to begin anew.

~ 10 ~

Pamela looked down the park's congested promenade and was certain she saw Amanda Lambert. Miss Barnett was busy at the pond, helping Margaret and Rose toss bread to the ducks, so it was simple to slip away. She took a hasty step, then another, and the crowd swallowed her up.

Since the day she'd discovered Miss Barnett's loathsome affair with Michael, Pamela had been dying to confer with Amanda, to ask her advice as to what she should do with the information.

Amanda had been a favorite of Pamela's father, had been regularly invited to his unending parties. She was independent and sophisticated in a fashion Pamela hoped to be, herself, when she was older. Though others whispered as to Amanda being a fallen woman, and snubbed her because of it, Pamela had never witnessed any questionable conduct.

Her father had cherished Amanda's company, so Pamela would, too.

She hurried along, and eventually, she espied Amanda

as she climbed into a fancy coach. The vehicle had Michael's family crest on the door. If Amanda was riding about in his carriage, they had to still be close, so it was even more imperative that Pamela impart her secret about Miss Barnett.

"Hallo! Amanda!" she called, waving and gesturing. "It's me, Pamela."

Amanda paused and grinned. "Pamela Martin, as I live and breathe."

"I've been searching for you everywhere!" Pamela exclaimed as she hastened up.

"Have you now?" Amanda glanced about. "Where's your chaperone?"

"Back by the lake. With Margaret." Pamela leaned in and whispered. "I had to speak with you, so I sneaked away."

"Fabulous. Why don't you join me in my carriage?" She clambered in and darted out of sight.

Without hesitation, Pamela followed, not fretting over whether she should parlay with Amanda. If there was anyone watching who might be upset or shocked, Pamela could not care less. She wasn't about to have the stuffy snobs of the *ton* choosing her acquaintances.

Pamela made herself comfortable, as Amanda pulled the curtains, hiding them from prying spectators. Amanda murmured directions to her footman, and momentarily, they began a slow trip down the tree-lined lane.

"How are you?" Amanda started. "I've been so worried. I've sent you a dozen letters, but they keep being returned, when I can't imagine why."

Pamela fumed. Who would have stopped her mail from being delivered? It had to have been Barnett, the witch.

"It's been awful," she confessed.

"Has it?" Amanda patted her hand. "You poor thing."

"I'm treated like a child. I can't go anywhere or do anything without permission. I feel as if I'm in prison."

Amanda clucked her tongue in dismay, her empathy a welcomed relief.

"Why . . . you're absolutely distraught, aren't you?" Amanda commiserated. "If I'd had any idea your situation was so vile, I'd have visited." There was a chest tucked under the seat, and she opened it to retrieve a glass and a decanter of brandy. She poured a hefty amount and offered it to Pamela. "Try this, darling. It will calm your nerves."

Pamela gulped at the liquor, delighted to have it so effortlessly dispensed. She emptied the contents and, without her having to plead for more, Amanda poured a second serving. Pamela swilled it, too, downing it so rapidly that her eyes watered and her throat burned.

Instantly, the brandy soothed her, and she felt smarter and more in control. "Amanda," she ventured, "Michael is so fond of you. Could you talk to him for me? Could you make him listen?"

"Of course, my sweet. What is it you need me to say?"

"I have to know about my finances, but he won't confide in me."

"Well, I don't have to consult with Michael to ascertain the facts. Your father was my dearest friend, so I'm fully cognizant of your dire straits."

"What do you mean?"

Amanda assessed her, then sighed. "Oh, I hate to burden you with such tedious issues."

"Tell me!" Pamela insisted.

Amanda oozed sympathy. "I suppose you must be apprised sooner or later."

"Concerning?"

"When your father died, he was beggared. He left you nothing, because there was nothing to leave."

Pamela gasped. "Why hasn't Michael notified me?"

"He realized that you'd be devastated, and he hasn't known how to break it to you."

"But what will become of me? What about my debut? What about my dowry?"

"All beyond you, I'm afraid."

Amanda refilled Pamela's glass and, anxious to ease her panic, Pamela guzzled the liquid. Her mind whirled with the prospects for disaster.

She'd met a girl once whose father had gambled away their fortune, and Pamela had publicly commiserated but had privately snickered, being flagrantly sure of her own stable circumstance. How humiliating to be in the same degrading state!

She had big dreams—of marrying a rich husband, who would furnish her with all the money she could ever spend. She would lead an exotic life like her father's, would be the most regaled hostess in London, but she needed cash to pay for her entertainments.

Oh, how could her father have placed her in such a predicament?

"We should discuss your options," Amanda was commenting.

"For what?" Pamela asked. The liquor had her confused.

"I've always been your friend," Amanda pointed out. "Haven't I, Pamela?"

"I guess so." Had Amanda been? With her reasoning growing muddled, Pamela couldn't recall.

"Haven't I helped you? Haven't I given you good advice?"

"That's why I had to find you," Pamela said. "I had to warn you about my governess, Miss Barnett."

"What about her?"

"Michael is in love with her."

Amanda scoffed. "Why would you presume something so ridiculous?"

"I saw them together."

"Really?"

At hearing the shocking news, Amanda appeared to be humored, rather than disturbed, and Pamela was angry at not being believed. "I saw them!" she repeated.

"I'm positive you misunderstood."

"He's completely smitten. I have no doubt."

"How droll, Pamela." Amanda chuckled. "You've had a little too much to drink for one afternoon."

The coach had halted, an indication that their chat was over. Amanda put the liquor case away, then took Pamela's glass from her. Pamela was enraged, but she was extremely lethargic and couldn't seem to react.

"Let me finish it," she complained.

"No." Amanda tugged on the curtain and dumped the remnants into the road. "Now, swear to me that you won't tell anyone about Michael and Miss Barnett."

"But why? It's horrid. She's a slattern, and the entire world should know it."

"I'll handle Miss Barnett, so she won't be around to plague you much longer. In the interim, I'm thinking we should select a husband for you. And we should hurry."

"A husband?"

"Yes, Pamela. Concentrate for me, will you? We'll convene tomorrow night. At the ball you're scheduled to attend. Watch for me. Can you do that?"

"Yes."

"We'll sneak off and talk about Michael."

"Michael?" Pamela echoed. "What about him?"

"It's time he wed. Wouldn't it be best if he married you?" The door was opened, and Amanda gripped Pamela's elbow and urged her out.

"Tomorrow night, Pamela," Amanda needled. "You must remember."

"I will," Pamela vowed, and at the notion of wedding Michael her heart pounded with excitement. It was the perfect solution, and Amanda would know how to achieve it.

The carriage rumbled off, and she tarried, befuddled and blinking in the bright sunlight. She peered around, trying to get her bearings, and she was still in the park, and very near to where she'd started her furtive coach ride.

Down the lane, she located the path to where Miss Barnett and the girls had been feeding the ducks, and Miss Barnett was coming through the trees. She was frantic, furious, gaping in every direction, and obviously in search of her lost charge.

Drunk and disoriented, Pamela giggled and stumbled toward her.

"You've been very naughty, Pam."

"I know, Michael."

Michael and Pamela were practically cooing at each

other, and Emily yearned to slap them both. Michael had no idea how to relate to a female, except in a sexual way, and in the secluded environment where she worked and lived, Emily had forgotten that fact.

Though Pamela was sixteen, she wasn't a child, and he was laughing and flirting as if Pamela's offense were a harmless prank.

As to Pamela, she was an expert at manipulating him. She batted her lashes, flaunted her cleavage, and acted like a seasoned coquette, while he reveled in her attention. On their tense trip home from the park, Pamela had insisted that Michael wouldn't care that she'd run off, that he wouldn't so much as scold her, and she'd been correct.

Emily was so incensed that she wanted to grab an antique vase off the mantle and smash it on the floor.

"Promise me you won't do this again," he pouted. "It upsets Miss Barnett."

"We wouldn't want that, would we?" Pamela mocked, though Michael was too full of himself to catch her sarcasm.

"No," he replied. "Everything is so much more pleasant when she's happy."

"She can be such a stick in the mud," Pamela whined.

"That's how governesses are," Michael agreed, the two of them conferring about Emily as if she weren't present. "They're born to be grumpy."

They chuckled, and Emily had had enough. She jumped to her feet. "Lord Winchester, I told Pamela that we would let you determine her punishment. What would you recommend?"

He flashed his most dazzling smile, the one she was sure had women swooning all over London. Usually, when he focused it on her, she grew weak in the knees, but in this instance, it was so aggravating that she felt like gagging.

"She doesn't need any reprimand," he claimed. "She's learned her lesson. Haven't you, Pam?"

"Certainly," Pamela purred.

"There. See?" As if he'd solved every crisis in the kingdom, he shrugged. "Why don't you head to your room and rest a bit before tea?"

All meekness and compliance, Pamela nodded. "Will you join us this time?"

"Probably not."

"We'll miss you terribly." She rose, and once she'd spun so that Michael couldn't witness her expression, she gloated with triumph, and she jostled Emily and roughly shoved her aside, though Michael was too intent on studying Pamela's curvaceous bottom to notice.

At the last second, she glanced over her shoulder. "By the by, Michael, I chatted with Amanda in the park. She sends her regards."

With that deftly tossed intimation, and Amanda's name hovering in the air, she strutted out, her footsteps fading down the hall.

Emily was so livid that she was shaking. She couldn't count the ways she wanted to murder Pamela, then Michael. It would be so sweet to be shed of them both, perhaps with a single, well-aimed pistol shot.

Michael grinned. "She's something, isn't she?"

"Is that the best you can do?"

"On the spur of the moment? Yes."

She couldn't figure out what she'd been hoping to accomplish by demanding a meeting with him, but when she'd stormed into the mansion, dragging an inebriated, obnoxious Pamela by the hand, she'd needed his assistance. She'd had him summoned from his club, but it had taken several hours for him to arrive, and by then, Pamela had sobered up. Emily had foolishly expected to receive some support, but he'd written off the incident as if Emily were a nosy busybody, and Pamela a misunderstood angel.

Emily had to quit imbuing him with traits he didn't possess! He'd hired her to watch over Pamela and Margaret, and he'd made it plain that he couldn't be bothered about them, yet she hadn't a clue how to be a governess or deal with their enormous problems.

"Do you care about this situation, at all?" she asked.

As if he'd cloaked himself in a blanket of nonchalance, detachment swept over him. He went to the sideboard, and insulted her by pouring himself a drink; then he returned to his desk and sat down, the expanse of polished oak stretching between them.

"Not really," he admitted, and her spirits plummeted. Could anything move him?

"Then what am I doing here?"

Looking bored, he sipped his whiskey. "You're very angry, Emily, so I suggest we have this conversation at a later date, lest we say things we don't mean."

"Have you any comprehension of the extent of her recklessness?"

"You're making too much of this," he insisted. "She's a child, and she's having fun pestering you."

"She's *not* a child."

"She wandered off while you were involved with Margaret and Rose. She didn't consider the consequences, and she—"

"She went for a ride in your ex-mistress's carriage!"

"A regrettable choice of companion."

He blushed, and she wondered why he would. Was he recollecting what Emily had seen him doing with Amanda? Was he embarrassed that he'd done the same with Emily? Was he afraid that Emily might wise up and realize he'd do the same with any woman?

She was so pathetic! She yearned to be special to him, but how could she be? He was a roué of the first water, while she was naught but a passing fancy with whom he'd trifle until he lost interest.

Reality was so discouraging, and suddenly, she was hankering for a fight. "Is that your only comment?"

He downed his whiskey, walked over, and poured another. "What factor would you like me to review that hasn't already been raised?"

"Stop drinking when I'm talking to you!" His indifference ignited her temper, and though she sounded like a shrewish fishwife, ranting at her beleaguered husband, she couldn't be silent.

He set down the glass, and whipped around, and she was delighted to note that she'd finally gotten a reaction. He was angry, too, and she was curious as to what he'd be like when he was infuriated. But for physical passion, she'd never witnessed much emotion from him, though with how he was assessing her, maybe it hadn't been such a good idea to provoke him. He was chafing like a lion whose tail had been pulled.

"Emily," he said very quietly, "you're presuming on our friendship. I've asked you to drop this subject, but you're too distraught to honor my request, so I'm ordering you to desist. Your appointment is concluded."

He'd goaded her beyond any boundary of propriety.

She felt too close to him, felt as if she should be able to broach any topic, and she was enraged that he would shut her out.

How dare he issue commands! She wasn't his slave, and she wouldn't be treated like one.

"She was with Amanda!" Emily shouted. "Have you any notion of what would become of Pamela if they'd been observed? It could have wrecked her entire life. And how about your repute? If you're not concerned as to what people think of you, I'm certainly concerned as to what they think of me. Can you conceive of the stories that would spread if word got out that I'd allowed her to do something so irresponsible?"

"So I'll speak with Amanda, and it won't happen again."

Her heart skipped a beat, a deadly pause stretching between them. "Are you in contact with her?"

The possibility hadn't occurred to Emily. When she'd agreed to work for him, he'd sworn that Amanda would never cross her path. Afterward, when Emily had begun to philander with him, she'd assumed that he'd split with the notorious consort.

She was so naïve! How many sexual partners did a man need? Apparently, more than one!

He blushed an even deeper shade of red. "Emily, leave it be."

"She's not your *ex*-mistress, is she?" At voicing the question, she felt so sick that she worried she might retch on the priceless rug. "When do you see her? Is that where you are when you're out all day? Is that what you've been doing when you come in so late at night? Lord, but I'm so stupid."

"I won't discuss her with you." He gestured to the door. "Now be off, before this gets any worse."

"Is she the only one? Or are there others? Are you still . . . still *interviewing* for a paramour?" He was obstinately, doggedly silent, and faced with his stubbornness, she bellowed, "Answer me!"

"You're acting daft. Please go."

He was calm, curt, and she stared him down, a thousand remarks perched on the tip of her tongue, and she bit them down to keep from spewing ultimatums he would never countenance.

She was prepared to resign her post, to stomp out in a huff, but how could she? Her life, as well as the security of Mary and Rose, was so intertwined with his that they were linked together like strands in a braided rope. She couldn't yank her family out of his mansion and onto the streets.

As to his liaison with Amanda—or with any other woman, for that matter—it was none of her business, and as he'd so aptly indicated, she'd imposed on their relationship by supposing she had any influence over him. Why had she believed otherwise?

The explanation, when it dawned on her, was terrifying. She loved him! She did! Perhaps she'd been in love with him from the moment they'd met.

She wanted to chastise herself, but she wouldn't. No ordinary female could share such intimacies with him and fail to develop a serious attachment. She'd been incapable of maintaining any distance, and with the blossoming of their affair, she'd jumped into an inferno from which she couldn't emerge unscathed.

She wrongly thought that he belonged to her, which had produced the deceptive impression that she had the right to complain, to demand better behavior, but she didn't. She was raving at him as if they were married, as if she'd uncovered an infidelity for which he needed to atone, but she had no claim on him. None whatsoever.

Oh, how had she fallen into such an untenable trap? She had to be the most imprudent person on earth. She lived in his house, she ate his food, and she joined him in his bed. She was no more than a prostitute, no different from Amanda, whom he paid, the distinction being that Emily had nowhere to go, and no other options, so she couldn't depart. He'd ensnared her as neatly as if she'd been his prisoner, and she had no one but herself to blame for her predicament.

She gazed at him, finding no hint of the affection she imagined lurking there, and she realized that it had been a ruse, a false perception she'd convinced herself was genuine. He looked at every woman the same way, even Pamela, even little Margaret. It was a trick, a flirtatious trait inherent to his male nature. It had nothing to do with her.

She'd stepped far across any line of what was appropriate between them, and she wouldn't be surprised if he fired her, when she absolutely could not lose her job.

"I beg your pardon, Lord Winchester," she stated, "and I most humbly apologize. I hope you can forgive me for my many lapses in judgment."

Dying on the inside, mortified beyond measure, she whirled away.

"Emily!"

He was commanding her to halt, but she raced out and down the hall, too frightened to hear whatever else he might say.

11

"You've been drinking."

"So I have."

Alex stumbled into Mary's room. He was making more noise than he ought, but he was too foxed to care. If he was discovered, so what? Who was to tell him to stop?

In another period of his life, he'd never have behaved so despicably. Notwithstanding his parents' lack of morals, he'd been raised to know the difference between right and wrong. It was dishonorable to lead Mary on, for he was sure she presumed that he'd turn out to be a better man than he appeared.

Hah! Wasn't she in for a surprise?

Every decent attribute had been extinguished, and he had no redeeming qualities remaining. Considering himself to be strong, brave, and wise, he'd joined the army, but he'd learned many bitter lessons.

He was a coward, so weak that a little scar had destroyed him. People stared on the street, children pointed, beautiful women—including his prior fiancée—blanched with disgust, and he couldn't bear it. He was neither courageous nor resilient, and he wanted his old existence back, wanted to be handsome, dashing Alex Farrow, who'd had the world at his feet. Like a spoiled child, he was raging at everyone.

He staggered to the bed and crawled under the blankets. When he was feeling lonely or blue, he would sneak to her, would fornicate until he was sated, until he'd shed some of the demons that plagued him; then he'd depart and ignore her until he was deluged, once again.

What was her opinion of his conduct?

She never said, and the fact that she didn't induced him to keep on.

In his more lucid moments, when he was vaguely sober, it occurred to him that he was coercing her, that due to his position as Michael's brother she couldn't refuse to dally. He couldn't abide that he'd plummeted to such a contemptible low.

By forcing himself on a dependent female, he'd become an emboldened cad. What if he impregnated her? What if she beseeched him to marry? He wouldn't compound his plunge down society's ladder by wedding the governess's sister.

He was a merciless, cruel snob, but he hated to picture himself in such an appalling light, so whenever the perception arose, he drowned it with brandy.

As usual, she had no comment as to his uncouth arrival. She pulled him near and kissed him, holding him in a fervent embrace that titillated despite his inebriated condition.

During the day, he never acknowledged her, strutting about as if she were beneath his notice. For hours at a time, he could pretend she wasn't in the house, that he wasn't thinking of her. He'd gambol at his favorite gambling halls, would fraternize with whores and other seedy characters, but when he came home, and the four walls of his room closed in around him, he stealthily climbed the rear stairs.

"Where have you been?" she scolded. "You smell as if you bathed in beer."

He'd never had a woman fret over him. His mother had had no maternal tendencies, and his nannies had been removed, stuffy employees who hadn't viewed their posts as requiring affection, so he hadn't realized that feminine hovering could be so soothing, so welcome.

"I've been playing cards."

"And overimbibing."

"That, too."

"I wish you wouldn't. I worry when you're off gallivanting. Anything could happen when you're so tipsy."

"I'm cautious," he contended, which wasn't true. Occasionally, he blacked out and awakened in strange locations with his pockets empty and his head throbbing.

He was fumbling with her nightgown, but he was clumsy, and he couldn't work it up her legs, which frustrated him. When he was with her, he was desperate to copulate, and he couldn't slow down.

His annoyance boiled over, and he gripped the garment and ripped it down the center, baring her body in a thrice.

"Alex! I don't have any money to replace my clothes. When you visit me, you can't act like a barbarian. I won't permit it."

"I'll buy you a dozen more," he lied. His allowance

was squandered, so he'd have no cash for several weeks, unless he debased himself by begging to Michael.

He'd made promises to her before but hadn't kept them, so she'd deduced how unreliable he was, and she murmured, "I can't wait to receive them."

"I want you," he tossed out as his justification. "Always. Every second."

"You're insatiable."

"Insatiable for you."

He struggled with his trousers, his inept fingers too awkward to loose the placard, and assuming the task for him, she chuckled and shoved him away. Shortly, she had him in her hand, her crafty thumb tracing over and over the inflamed crown.

She scooted down, licking him, sucking him into her mouth. She knew what he liked, how he liked it, having rapidly adapted to the sordid games he relished. The more intoxicated he was, the more revolting some of his preferences, but she didn't mind. If anything, she appeared *more* eager than he to revel in a debauched way.

Almost immediately, he was at the edge, and he couldn't figure out how she provoked him when he was so indisposed by liquor.

Anxious to be inside her, to be staring into her pretty face as he finished, he lurched away. He rolled them, so that she was beneath him, and with no finesse or wooing, he entered her and began to thrust. He treated her like a harlot for whom there was no need to show respect, and she endured it all without complaint. As he reached his climax, she did, too, joining him in ecstasy, finding her own release without any assistance.

He was a monster, a scoundrel, and he withdrew from her and flopped onto his back. His thoughts in turmoil, there were a thousand words he should utter, a thousand questions he could ask, but what emerged was, "Why do you put up with me?"

"I haven't the faintest idea," she calmly replied.

"You could refuse to let me in."

"Yes, I could."

"Or you could go to my brother and protest as to how I've been abusing you. He'd stop me."

"I'm sure he would"—she stretched and smiled—"but how could I convince him that I've been *abused*? I'm not a child; I've been an active accomplice in our folly."

"But why? There must be some explanation."

For a lengthy interval, she was silent; then she laid her palm on his chest. "Because, for some peculiar reason, I like you, and when you're with me, I'm not so lonely."

He hated hearing the comment. It hinted at an attachment and fondness he didn't share, and he was irked that he'd inquired. He loathed talking to her, didn't want any incentive to like her in return, or to fixate on her in more than a sexual fashion.

He yawned, the combination of orgasm and alcohol sweeping over him, and he closed his eyes as unconsciousness sunk in.

She elbowed him in the ribs. "Don't you dare fall asleep." When he didn't respond, she shook him. "What if you don't wake up till morning? What if a servant catches you in here?"

She shook him again, but he was beyond rousing. She sighed, grumbling about impossible men, and she nestled onto the pillow. Serene, content to be snuggled with her, he started to snore.

"She's your fiancée?"

"Yes."

Michael shifted in his chair and tried to fathom why he'd granted an audience to Reginald Barnett. The pompous buffoon had gained entrance by mentioning Emily's name to Fitch, and Michael hadn't been able to resist a meeting. He was dying to learn more about her.

While most women of his acquaintance liked to wax on about themselves, and he couldn't get them to shut up, Emily was entirely too reticent. It was like pulling teeth, gleaning details of her life before she'd moved to London.

In the hopes that he might garner a few pathetic tid-bits, he'd actually taken to commencing conversations with her sister, Mary Livingston, but Mrs. Livingston was as taciturn as Emily.

As he wasn't supposed to be familiar with Emily, he was relegated to inane queries: *How are your accommodations suiting you?* and, *How is your sister enjoying her employment?,* to which the answers were that everything was fine. Fine. Everything was so bloody fine that he'd like to strangle somebody.

Since their horrid argument over Amanda, he and Emily hadn't communicated, and since he wasn't at fault, he wasn't about to apologize. He was frantic to avoid her, so he was in hiding, a virtual prisoner in his own home.

Who would have imagined that a mansion with eighty rooms could be so small?

He had no clue how to deal with females and their troubles, no notion as to how he should handle Pamela. That's why he'd hired Emily! Why couldn't she understand how vexed he was?

He was in the process of severing his protracted association with Amanda, but such nasty affairs took time. During their quarrel, Emily had accused him of betraying her. She'd been hurt, had acted as if they were in a committed relationship, which he considered to be the height of gall.

They'd made no promises to each other and he, in fact, had been explicit in tendering none when she'd demanded to be apprised of his intentions. She'd insisted that he be clear, that he be honest, and he had been. Brutally so. Yet now, she was behaving as if he'd used her badly, as if he'd lied to her.

What did the blasted woman want? What did she expect?

He was not—and never would be—faithful, and she had him spinning in circles, so confused that he constantly felt dizzy.

"How long have you been engaged to her?" he probed.

"Since we were children," Barnett replied.

"Really?" The news was so disturbing that he couldn't listen to it. He'd wondered about the circumstances that had sent Emily rushing to the city but hadn't questioned her. Oh, to discover that she was betrothed! That her fiancé was this bloated oaf!

He went to the sideboard and poured himself a stiff whiskey, but he didn't offer one to Barnett. He'd welcomed the boor into his library, which was as much courtesy as he could extend.

"It became official after her father's death," Barnett clarified.

"I see."

"We've been planning the wedding for months."

"Have you?"

Michael studied Barnett, disliking everything about him. He was a pompous clown, and Michael tried to picture Emily married to him, but the vision wouldn't gel. Barnett was much older than she—by fifteen or twenty years—an obese, balding fellow, with a ruddy complexion, rotting teeth, and beady eyes. He wasn't particularly clean, either.

"Why are you here?" Michael asked. "What exactly is it that you want from me? Miss Barnett is a servant, but other than that quite tenuous connection, I haven't had much contact with her. I can't grasp why you're bothering me with your family's problems or history."

Barnett puffed himself up. "Will you grant me the liberty of speaking to you man-to-man?"

"By all means," Michael sarcastically retorted. "I wouldn't have it any other way."

"Emily is very independent."

Michael kept his expression blank, but on this topic they agreed: Emily was much too autonomous. Too bossy. Too obstinate. By being involved with her, he'd suffered an incessant headache, and he was perpetually reminded of why he preferred sane, male company.

"Is she?"

"She has many havey-cavey, modern ideas," Barnett stated, "ideas I don't countenance myself."

"Such as?"

"She thinks it's perfectly acceptable for a young lady to work, and she's always wanted to earn her own living.

Can you conceive of any woman of good breeding pining for such a thing?"

Michael couldn't, but he shrugged. "Perhaps she wasn't as *eager* for the union as you claim."

"She was eager, all right," Barnett maintained. "Especially after I taught her the private side of what marriage entails."

Barnett winked, and Michael's stomach churned. Was Barnett implying what he appeared to be? Was he insinuating that he and Emily had been lovers?

During Michael's trysts with her, she seemed so innocent, but how could he be sure? Presuming her to be a virgin, he'd never progressed to the ultimate conclusion.

Had he been wrong? Had she trifled with this foul, pretentious ass?

The possibility set a fire to his temper, though he couldn't figure out why he was upset. She was just a female, one of many who'd passed through his sorry life, but in view of how incensed he was, he had to ponder whether he cared for her more than he realized.

Could it be? Was he smitten?

At the absurd notion, he nearly guffawed aloud. As if he'd allow himself to be infatuated! How ludicrous! How droll!

Checking his emotions, he took a deep breath. "If she was so enthused, why did she come to London?"

"She begged me to permit her to have a little excitement, a big-city adventure. I'm a generous man. How could I refuse?"

"How, indeed?"

Michael seethed. Was Barnett aware of the dire straits Emily had been in during her attempts to garner employment? Had he understood the perils? Barnett was a fool.

"But I've humored her long enough," Barnett continued, "and it's time for her to return home."

"And you're telling me this because . . . ?"

"I doubt that she'd consent to quit her job." He chuckled in a manner that grated. "She's stubborn that way."

"You're asking me to fire her?"

"Well . . . yes."

"On what grounds?"

"Have you need of any?"

His knuckles white with rage, Michael gripped his desk, so that he wouldn't leap across and pummel Barnett. He was scheming behind the scenes so that Emily would lose her post. What a knave! What a despicable swine!

"I'm a fair individual," Michael pointed out. "She's performed excellently, and I see no reason to part with her."

"Then I suppose I could refer to my personal relationship with her, which might cause you to speculate as to whether she's fit to supervise children. But I *am* a gentleman and would hate to spread gossip."

Michael rose so quickly that his chair fell over, and he summoned Fitch, though he wasn't surprised to find that Fitch had been eavesdropping outside the door.

"Yes, Lord Winchester?"

"Is Miss Barnett in the house?"

"She's in the nursery, sir."

"Fetch her, would you? Inform her that I must meet with her at once." He leaned closer and whispered, "Don't take no for an answer. If she declines to attend me"—Fitch blanched at the prospect—"notify her that it is a command and not a request."

Michael trudged to his desk, praying that she'd arrive without a fuss, but he wasn't positive she'd obey his dictate. She was likely still as angry as he was, himself, but he wasn't about to brook any nonsense. Not with Reginald Barnett looking on.

Michael scrutinized Barnett, unable to prevent his disgust from seeping out. "I won't fire Miss Barnett."

"Then why have you sent for her?"

"If she wants to leave with you, so be it, but I won't force her."

Michael was anxious to witness her reaction to her cousin's presence, to evaluate the expression on her face. If she was glad, if she agreed to go with Barnett, Michael couldn't predict what he might do.

He couldn't let her make such a huge blunder, but what were his options? He had no hold over her, wasn't even certain she regarded him as a friend. If he tried to intervene, she'd probably tell him to bugger off.

But if she was inclined to depart with Barnett, what inducement would Michael utilize to convince her to stay? While Barnett seemed sincere in his plan to marry her, what was Michael's intent?

If she remained in London because of him, he would dabble with her until he grew bored, and he'd move on to another. Then what?

He had no future to offer her, save for the next few weeks or months of philandering. Wasn't she better off with Barnett? Shouldn't Michael sever their connection immediately? Shouldn't he cut her off like a rotting limb?

He sipped his whiskey and glared at Barnett, until finally, footsteps echoed in the hall. Fitch escorted her in and announced, "Miss Barnett, sir."

"Thank you, Fitch. Shut the door, would you?"

Fitch complied as Emily entered. Instantly, she espied her cousin, but she shielded any response.

"You have a visitor, Miss Barnett." Michael strove to sound cordial. "Won't you join us?"

He gestured to the chair next to Barnett's, and she walked to it without peeking at either of them, which was aggravating. Michael didn't care if she ignored Barnett, but Michael was on her side. He was determined to have her trust him, to comprehend that whatever she wanted, he would help her accomplish it, but apparently, she was smarting from their earlier fight.

Accursed female! He longed to march around the desk and shake her.

She seated herself but gave an illuminating sign of her attitude toward Barnett when she scooted her chair away to create more distance between them.

"Hello, Reginald," she said.

"Hello, Emily. How have you been?"

"Fine," she replied coolly.

She frowned at Barnett, and they appraised each other in a mutual and festering silence that had Michael conjecturing over the truth as to what had happened.

Was Emily off adventuring in the city as Barnett claimed? Had they had a lovers' spat? Had Emily spurned his proposal?

Michael couldn't believe she would have. What woman—even the most independent one—would abandon her heritage? What woman would rather fend for herself on the streets of London than be wed to her father's heir?

Her exploits made no sense, unless Barnett had

mistreated her. What was Emily's story? He was kicking himself for his prior lack of interest.

Michael interrupted their staring match. "Your cousin wishes to talk with you."

"Why?"

She shifted her gaze to Michael, and a thrill rushed through him at seeing her again. He felt as if it had been months—nay, years!—since they'd spoken, and his memories of their quarrel faded away.

"He advises me that felicitations are in order," Michael explained. "He says the two of you are about to wed."

She whipped around and scowled at Barnett. "My cousin is wrong, Lord Winchester. We had discussed marriage, but I declined."

"He would like you to return to Hailsham with him."

"Are you commanding me to go?" she inquired.

"No. It's entirely up to you as to what you desire, and I'll abide by your decision." He smiled, yearning to convey that all was forgiven and forgotten. "My preference is that you would stay on."

"Then I choose to remain." She peered at Barnett. "You shouldn't have come here. You shouldn't have bothered Lord Winchester."

Barnett was red with humiliation and temper. "Emily, you're being foolish, and I've had it with your games! This charade must end."

At his sharp tone, Emily flinched, and Michael calmly stated, "Mr. Barnett, you have the answer you sought. There's no reason to extend this appointment."

Embarrassed and chagrined, Emily mumbled, "May I be excused?"

"You may," Michael told her, and she hurried out. She was visibly distraught, which enraged him. What had Barnett done to her?

They both watched her exit; then Barnett stood as if he might chase after her.

"Sit down, Mr. Barnett," Michael instructed.

Barnett didn't obey but didn't follow her, either. Through clenched teeth, he insisted, "I must persuade her!"

"I'm afraid that won't be possible."

"But . . . but . . . I have to make her understand! She has to agree! We're to be wed. It's all arranged. The banns have been called."

"If your vicar called the banns, he was a tad hasty. It's obvious that she has no intention of marrying you."

"It's not up to her!"

"This isn't the Middle Ages. You can't force her."

"We'll see about that!" Barnett boasted.

"Why don't you go?" Michael urged as politely as he could. "I've had enough discord for one day."

Barnett didn't budge, and he assessed Michael with an enormous amount of contempt. "Oh, I get it," he mused.

"What is it you *get,* Mr. Barnett?"

"You want her for yourself." He was so angry that he was trembling. "You despicable libertine! Have you already corrupted her? Or are you merely planning on it? I'm sick. Just sick!"

At the slur to Emily, Michael couldn't ever remember being so livid. In a flash, he was out of his chair and around the desk. As he'd been dying to do, he grabbed Barnett by his jacket and lifted him off the floor, his feet dangling in the air.

"Leave my house," Michael growled, "before I toss you into the gutter like the rubbish you are."

He flung Barnett toward the hall, and Barnett stumbled but regained his balance.

"Bastard!" Barnett dared to hurl.

"Fitch!" Michael bellowed, and Fitch poked his nose round the door frame.

"Yes, milord?"

"Mr. Barnett is going," Michael declared. "Should he ever have the misfortune to show up on my stoop again, he should be denied entrance, and you should summon the law to cart him off as a public nuisance."

"Very good, sir." Fitch grinned, delighted at having the opportunity to physically escort someone out. He clasped Barnett by the sleeve, but Barnett shrugged him away and started out on his own.

"Have I made my position clear, Mr. Barnett?" Michael demanded.

"You haven't heard the last of me!" Barnett bragged.

"I think I have."

"Emily is mine."

"Only a person with your deranged mind would believe as much."

"I'll get even with you. If it takes the rest of my life, you'll pay."

"I'm quaking in my boots."

Barnett stomped away, Fitch dogging his steps, and Michael walked to his desk, sat down, and finished his drink.

~ 12 ~

Michael walked down the darkened hall and stopped at Emily's door. He wasn't exactly sober, so he'd lost whatever resolve might have kept him away.

After Barnett's eviction, he'd tarried in the library, presuming she'd reappear, that she might wish to discuss what had occurred or thank Michael for defending her.

He was such an idiot!

He'd assumed—wrongly!—that she would be appreciative of his efforts. But no! She couldn't be bothered to express any gratitude.

In fact, when he'd finally lowered himself to asking Fitch about her, he'd been informed that she was out! That she'd totted off on an afternoon jaunt to the park. While he was fretting and stewing, she'd been going about her business with his two wards.

The situation had to change. He couldn't continue on, hiding and avoiding her. She didn't want to marry her cousin. That much was clear. She wanted to stay on in

London. That much was clear, too. But why? Why had she chosen to remain?

The answer was eating at him.

Was she fond of him? As she looked down the road, what conclusion did she envision? Where was he located in her dreams of the future? Had he a part to play?

Why any of it mattered was a mystery he couldn't unravel, but from the first moment he'd met her, something had happened to him, something inexplicable and crazed. He was so disordered that he wondered if he wasn't about to pitch himself off some ledge of sanity from which he might never return.

He tried the door and was relieved when the knob spun. In case it had been locked, he'd brought a key and would have used it. He was that determined to be with her. It was his own damned house, and he wouldn't be denied.

He tiptoed in, and he could see her standing by the window, gazing out at the black sky. She was ready for bed, her shapely body perfectly outlined by a blue robe. The belt was cinched, accentuating her thin waist, her flared hips. She wore a nightgown underneath, the white fabric dotted with lavender flowers. Her feet were bare and pressed to the cool wood of the floor.

Her hair was down and brushed out, the wavy tresses falling across her back, and he studied her, thinking how delicate she was, how exquisite. As always when he was in her presence, his torso responded, his senses afire and eagerly anticipating what would come next.

She'd heard him, and she stiffened but didn't glance in his direction. "Go away."

"No."

"You can't be in here."

"I can *be* wherever I want," he pompously claimed. He was acting like a spoiled child, but he couldn't desist.

"You're impossible." She whipped around. "Do you ever listen? Do you ever pay attention to what anyone says? You are not welcome here!"

"Tell me about your cousin," he demanded.

"No."

"Tell me!"

"Why are you interested in my past? Have you suddenly decided you're human?"

She was incensed, her eyes flashing, her pulse pounding at the base of her neck, and he approached until they were toe to toe. She was spoiling for another fight, furious—in typical female fashion—over issues he couldn't fathom, and the realization set a spark to his own temper.

He was the injured party. In her misguided snit over Amanda, *he* had been maligned and insulted. *He* had suffered through her cousin's diatribe. Against his will, *he* had been immersed in her family's squabble, so that he worried about her constantly.

He refused to care about her! Refused to spend every second of the day fussing and fashing. He wanted peace and tranquility. He wanted his dissolute, scandalous life to be restored.

These sweltering, recurrent feelings of guilt and remorse were abhorrent to him. He couldn't be relentlessly vexed over whether he was doing the right thing.

What the hell was the *right* thing anyway?

"I'm sorry I didn't ask about it before," he said, reining in his irritation, and he reached out and pulled her to him.

She started to cry, tears dripping down and wetting his shirt. "My father wanted me to marry him, and I was prepared to go through with it. I was!" she added as if he'd argued the fact.

"But you couldn't?"

"I found some papers. He'd arranged to send Mary to an asylum after the wedding."

He frowned. "But she's not deranged. She's blind."

"So? He would have had the money to accomplish it."

"But he couldn't have had her committed for no reason. There are laws to prevent such atrocities." At least, he assumed there were.

"A mere woman has no power against a man like Reginald."

"I'm certain you misunderstood," he asserted, though he was placating her. Reginald was an ass and a bully, who might have perpetrated any depraved deed, and Michael wished he'd pummeled the swine when he'd had the chance.

"I can't bear much more of this," she told him. "I'm anxious to leave, but I have nowhere to go."

At the admission, he was reeling. Would she rather hazard the perils of London than stay in the safety of his home? "I won't let you depart," he advised. "I can't."

"This is killing me. I want to be alone."

"No, you don't."

"It hurts to be around you, to care about you and to have you so angry with me."

"I'm not angry." His wrath had faded like leaves on the wind. "You're everything to me. I adore you. I . . . I . . ."

He halted. He'd almost blurted out that he loved her,

and he was astounded. He didn't love her. He didn't love anyone, and his nearly proclaiming himself was a further indicator of his muddled condition.

Such an exclamation would be folly. She would embrace the words, when they weren't true. Heightened sentiment had no lasting value, and around her, he had to be cautious.

"If you're fond of me, as you contend," she rebuked, "you have a terrible way of showing it."

"I admit it. I'm an oaf, a boor. Forgive me."

He'd never been so at a loss with a woman, but then, she wasn't like the harlots with whom he consorted, and she had to be treated differently. He kept forgetting.

Needing to be closer, needing to communicate what he couldn't convey aloud, he dipped down and kissed her. They might quarrel, but they never failed to connect physically. When he was holding her, their problems seemed petty, their disparities minor.

She didn't resist his advance, and she joined in, clutching at his jacket as if it was a lifeline. Their bickering had drained the energy out of her. She felt lighter, rubbery, as if her bones had melted, and he had the distinct impression that if he released her, she would crumple to the ground.

He jerked at the belt of her robe and yanked off the garment; then he lifted her, propelling her back so that she was braced to the wall, her legs wrapped around his waist. The hem of her nightgown was bunched up, and she was open wide, her privates splayed, his crotch flattened to her own, with only the fabric of his pants separating them.

His tongue was in her mouth, his cock a hard rod at

her center, and he thrust against her, the motion relieving some of the ache but increasing the agony, too.

Her gown was summery, her shoulders bare, and he tugged at the straps, exposing her breasts, relishing their weight in his hands. He thumbed her nipples, making her squirm, making her writhe. Breathless and distraught, she broke off the kiss.

"Please don't," she begged. "I can't revel with you anymore."

"I can't stop. I have to have you." She emitted a soft groan that might have been joy or despair, but he ignored it.

"What do you want from me?" she wailed.

"I don't know," he honestly replied.

"Where are we headed?"

"I haven't the foggiest."

"Where will we end up?"

"I couldn't begin to guess."

"You're mad," she stated.

"Very likely."

At that moment, he was a bit crazed, capable of any nefarious conduct. He spun her, lugged her to the bed, and dropped her onto it.

Emily wasn't sure what had happened, but suddenly, they were wild for each other. He was pinning her down so that she couldn't wriggle away, but she wasn't about to escape. Amazingly, she was impatient to dally, and she couldn't wait for the spiral of ecstasy to commence.

She would try anything to forget Reginald and the gruesome day she'd endured.

Her knees were bent, her feet dangling over the edge of the mattress, and he knelt on the floor, positioning himself between her legs. He drew off her nightgown, revealing her thighs, her loins, her belly, and she let him look his fill.

"What are you doing?" she asked.

"I'm going to kiss you." He shoved two fingers inside her. "Here, where you need it most."

"No, it's too personal, too wrong."

"It's not wrong, Emily." He stared up at her. "When we're together like this, everything is allowed. Everything!"

"But I don't want you to know me like this."

"It's not up to you."

"Michael!"

"Be silent!"

He leaned down and licked his tongue across her, tasting her, delving into her tight, wet sheath. He found her sexual center, and he jabbed at it until her hips were flexing, until she was arching up in a desperate attempt to avoid the sensation he was inflicting.

"Desist!" she pleaded. "I can't bear this."

"Just about there," he coaxed.

"No . . . I don't . . . I can't . . ."

Her mind and body were at war. When ardor flared between them, her body welcomed it, but her mind couldn't abandon the moral restraints she'd been taught. She recognized that their actions were wicked, but in view of what he could give her, limitations seemed irrelevant.

She was rigid with desire, her feminine core weeping with its need for release.

"Let go, Emily," he urged.

"I can't."

"Do it for me."

He sucked at the taut nub, as his fingers kneaded her breasts. In an instant, she leapt into the inferno, and he held her down as she struggled and cried out.

The spiral went on and on, and as it waned, as she floated to earth, he was nuzzling up her torso. He blazed a slow trail to her cleavage, her nape, her chin, her mouth, as he kissed her, and she savored the tang of her sex on his lips. It was an aphrodisiac that inflamed and provoked, and she sighed with resignation. "I can't believe I allowed you to do that."

"I scarcely gave you a choice."

"I hate you," she claimed.

"No, you don't."

"Yes, I do. You bully and coerce me so that I can't ever say no."

"Why would you want to?"

"Because I'm hurting. I can't abide it that you mean so much to me, but I am so insignificant to you."

He scowled. "Is that what you think? That you don't matter to me?"

"How could I presume otherwise? You're like a sultan with a harem."

"I'm not, Emily."

She supposed they could have entered into a lengthy debate over whether he had any genuine feelings for her, over why he trifled with her and with others at the same time, but it was futile to argue over the kind of man he was, and the kind of woman she was. They were oil and water.

"I don't care," she insisted, waving away any declarations he might make, declarations she wouldn't credit. "I don't care about any of it."

And she truly didn't. Not at that moment anyway. Later on, she'd rue and regret, but when she was still quivering with pleasure it was difficult to concentrate on anything but her uncontrollable, baffling need for him.

He clambered onto the bed, dragging her with him so that she was draped across him, and he commanded, "Remove my clothes."

"What?"

"You heard me."

"But if I remove your clothes, we're likely to . . . to . . ."

"Precisely."

She understood what he planned. There was no need for conversation or extensive deliberation. "My common sense has flown out the window."

"Good."

"You tempt me to commit sins I never imagined."

"You're an absolute wanton. I'm convinced of it." He rotated them, so that he was on top and she was on the bottom.

"Are we going to mate? Right here? Right now?"

"Yes."

"I'm not ready."

"I am."

He tugged off his jacket, his cravat, his shirt, so that his upper body was bared, and he raised up, his breast at her lips. "Lick me," he instructed. "As I do to you."

Tentatively, her tongue flicked out, dabbing at the pebbled nub. "Like this?"

"Yes, and suck it into your mouth." She complied, and he added, "Harder."

She nipped and played till he couldn't stand any more, and he fumbled with his trousers, loosing them, easing them down around his flanks. Where previously she might have panicked and stepped back from the precipice, on this occasion she did nothing to stop their forward progress. Wherever he led, she was happy to follow.

Holding him, massaging him, she took his cock in hand, her thumb teasing the crown. He was shaking, beads of perspiration on his brow, and he clasped her thighs and lowered himself between them. His phallus brushed across her. "I have to finish this. I can't wait any longer."

She considered protesting, but what would be the point? She craved this, too. It seemed as if she'd always been searching for him, as if her entire life had been a chain of events delivering her to this place.

"Are you sure?" she queried.

Surprisingly, she was more worried about his subsequent reaction than her own. She wasn't positive he should proceed, was certain he hadn't reflected on the ramifications and that he'd feel awful afterward.

"I'm very sure." Stretching her, he nudged in the blunt end. "This will be painful. The first time."

He wedged it in farther, and she squirmed, suddenly unnerved by the swift escalation, by his steely determination. She'd thought she was prepared, but it was happening too rapidly. She was eager to discuss what was about to transpire, to pry out more of the details, or cuddle while she came to grips with what she was about to relinquish.

"Can we talk for a minute?"

"No."

She tried throwing him off, but she had no leverage. "I've changed my mind."

"You can't."

"It's too big. You'll never fit."

"Hush." He kissed her, every fiber of his being focused on completion.

"I'm frightened."

"Don't be."

"Michael!"

Briefly, he paused to assess her nude torso, and he smiled, a feral, possessive smile that thrilled her, that terrified her.

"You're mine, Emily," he said. "All mine from now on."

In a smooth, exact move, he broke through her maidenhead, impaling himself to the hilt. There was a tear, the rush of her woman's blood, and she cried out and arched up.

He was very still, letting her acclimate, and gradually, the ache faded. She exhaled a slow breath, and on her relaxing, he began to thrust, pushing in and pulling out, then pushing in again. With each penetration, her distress diminished, her anatomy accepting him. She joined in, flexing and adopting the rhythm he'd set.

He was resolute, his tension extreme, and he'd abandoned any pretense of gentleness or sympathy for her virginal state. His hips were methodical, disciplined, working like the pistons of a huge machine, and she clutched at him as if she were on a ship at sea and navigating stormy waves. The uproar increased, the tumult at a fevered pitch, when he moaned and went taut, every

muscle suspended; then he yanked away and spilled himself on her stomach.

Exhausted by the intense effort, he collapsed onto
her, and she cradled him, reveling in the quiet aftermath,
but assailed by the enormity of what they'd done. What
would they say to each other? How would they act?

Without a word, he slid to the side and walked to the
dresser to fetch a towel. He returned to her and wiped
away the stain of his seed. There was blood on her thighs,
on his phallus, and he swabbed it away.

He couldn't—or wouldn't—look at her, and she was
left with the distinct impression that he was embarrassed.
She shifted with unease. Was he lamenting his behavior
so soon?

"Are you all right?" she inquired, unable to bear the
awkward silence.

"Me?" He was startled by her question. "Of course.
How about you?"

"I'm fine."

As if afraid to touch her, he dawdled on the edge of
the mattress, so she opened her arms in invitation, and
he snuggled into them.

"Did I hurt you?" he asked.

"I'll live."

"I didn't mean to be so rough."

"You weren't."

"You arouse me beyond my limits."

"What joy to my ears." She smiled. There was something immensely satisfying about driving him to distraction.

He kissed her and smiled, too. "Any regrets?"

"Nary a one. How about you?"

He shook his head and chuckled. Down below, his cock was partially erect and prodding at her abdomen. "I want you again. Already."

"I can tell."

"I can't get enough of you. So . . . can we put to rest this silly notion that you don't matter to me?"

"Yes, we can definitely put it to rest."

The moment was wonderfully intimate. He was staring at her, his blue eyes searing her with his affection and esteem, and she was delighted to read the fondness written there.

Though she might occasionally have her doubts, his regard was more strident than he could ever admit. He was a male, after all, so perhaps verbal professions were beyond him. He had to show her physically what he couldn't articulate aloud, and for now, she'd let it be enough.

She'd be patient, and she'd hope for the best. She was convinced that, deep down, an honest and reputable fellow was lurking, and if she could bring him to the surface, they could have a future together.

"I'll spend the night with you," he said. "We'll make love till dawn."

"Amorous activity seems to be rather draining for you. Are you certain you should dare it more than once?"

"Hah! I can do it till morning," he boasted, "if you can keep up with me."

"Rascal."

"Always."

She hugged him, content and excited to begin anew.

~ 13 ~

Michael tiptoed out of Emily's room and quietly closed the door. He'd finally driven them both to the point of exhaustion, and she was sleeping.

Dawn was breaking, and he'd stayed much later than was wise, but he hadn't been able to force himself away. The encounter had been too glorious, the bliss too welcome.

Like the cur he was, he turned to slink up the rear stairs when, to his horror, a door opened down the hall. He froze, curious as to who else could be sneaking around at such an ungodly hour. In view of his disheveled condition, there was no way to pretend he hadn't just crept out of Emily's bed, so what excuse could he make?

To his utter amazement, his brother emerged, skulking out in the same despicable fashion as Michael. Across the lengthy expanse of carpet, they studied each other. They were both in the same pathetic shape—rumpled and scarcely dressed—and it was apparent that Alex had spent the evening fornicating, too.

Michael struggled to recollect whose room Alex had been in, and he was sickened to surmise that it was occupied by Emily's sister.

If Michael cared about anyone, it was Alex, but his brother wasn't the same as he'd been before the war. In his current state, Alex was the last man Michael would want cavorting with Mary Livingston. Only trouble could result.

Mrs. Livingston was sheltered under Michael's roof, living under his protection, and he couldn't let her be illused. Alex could have no honorable intentions. When he married, he would wed for money, which had been the plan until his fiancée had tossed him over. In a thousand years Mrs. Livingston couldn't provide Alex with what he needed.

Michael waved toward the stairs, indicating that he was going down, and that Alex should follow, and Michael scowled so that Alex knew it wasn't a request, but a command. Michael was still the elder sibling and strong enough to pound Alex into submission if he was too recalcitrant.

Michael departed and headed to the family dining parlor, where he surprised a maid who was up and preparing the kitchen. He ordered the American-style coffee Alex preferred, then sat down to wait.

It took Alex an eternity to appear, and when he entered, he was insolent and taunting. In the lamplight, he looked like death warmed over, his skin pasty, his clothes soiled, his hands shaking.

Without a greeting, he proceeded to the sideboard, poured himself a brandy, and raised it toward Michael as if toasting him.

"Hair of the dog," Alex grumbled. "Would you like one?"

"No."

In a single motion, Alex swigged the contents; then he refilled his glass and did the same. By the third serving, he was enjoying a beneficial effect. His pallor had receded; his quaking had lessened.

When had Alex fallen to such a dreadful level? Why hadn't Michael noticed? His beloved brother was wasting away, right before his very eyes!

Michael gestured to the chair opposite, and Alex seated himself. The maid delivered their coffee, and as soon as she left, Alex fetched the brandy and mixed his half-and-half. Michael was aghast and grappling with what he should say, but he couldn't figure out how to comment without sparking an argument.

He decided to ignore Alex's problem and focus on his conduct.

"Why were you in Mrs. Livingston's bedchamber?"

"Why were you in with the governess?" Alex shot back.

"Don't be flip." Michael wouldn't discuss his own depraved circumstance. "I want an answer."

Alex assessed Michael, making it clear that Michael had no secrets, no lock on decadency, and Alex shrugged. "I expect I was doing the same thing you were doing." Defiantly, he grinned. "Now you know. Are you feeling better?"

"How long have you been carrying on with her?"

"We started up just after she arrived."

"How could you?"

Alex scoffed. "You're screwing her sister, and you have to ask?"

Michael bristled with fury. "I won't dignify your remark with a response."

"Why not? If you're about to tell me that it's permissi-
ble for you to fuck the hired help but not me, you can shut
the hell up, because I won't listen to any moralizing."

"You've really become a horse's ass."

"As if I give a shit what you think."

Michael wondered when they'd strayed so far from
being friends. "What are your plans toward her?"

"My plans?" Alex jeered.

"What if she winds up pregnant?"

"What if she does?"

"What will you do?"

"I ask you the same," Alex carped. "If your darling
governess develops a little bulge in the tummy, what
then?"

"She's not *my* anything," Michael lied, declining to
have the quarrel switch to his own misbehavior. He
didn't understand his passion for Emily, couldn't explain
it, and he most definitely couldn't defend it.

"Well, Mrs. Livingston isn't *my* anything, either." Alex
gulped more of his spiked coffee. "Here's to the two of us.
Aren't we a pair?"

Michael wanted to rail and shout, to clarify why
Alex's situation with Mrs. Livingston was different from
his own with Emily, but how could he spew such a frivolous claim?

Was he ready to assert that it was acceptable for himself to act badly, but not Alex? By what standard? Because he was an earl and Alex wasn't?

He couldn't maintain that it was appropriate to debauch Emily, while it was wrong for Alex to dabble with

her sister. So what point—precisely—was he trying to make?

There was no rejoinder that seemed fitting or that adequately conveyed his concern. Any chastisement was hypocritical.

"Could you please be more circumspect?" he lamely inquired. "At least consider her reputation. She's our guest. What if you were caught? The servants would crucify her."

"You have the gall to lecture me?"

Michael wasn't surprised by the question. He was on a slippery slope, his own choices hardly above reproach. "You're being crazy these days," he declared as gently as he was able. "Be a bit more prudent. That's all I'm saying."

"Why don't you keep your own trousers buttoned, before you expend so much energy worrying about mine?"

Alex swilled the last of his brandy and strolled out.

Mary dawdled, as Emily puttered around, dishing up their breakfast. Winchester had insisted they take their meals in the family dining parlor, that they shouldn't eat with the staff, and Mary constantly speculated as to why he was so generous.

Emily contended that he'd been desperate for a governess, that he was simply grateful for her assistance, but his offering of the private room was beyond the pale, and Mary didn't comprehend it.

Briefly, she pondered whether she should use the moment to admit her affair with Alex Farrow. She had few secrets from Emily, and all the sneaking about was killing her.

After the winter she'd been struck blind, her life had been one tedious ordeal after the next. Her furtive liaison with Alex was the only outrageous, exotic deed she'd ever attempted, and she couldn't fathom what had driven her to acquiesce, or what insane force goaded her into persisting.

Since moving into Lord Winchester's house, she'd metamorphosed into another person. Stuffy, boring Mary Barnett Livingston had ceased to exist, and another, more outlandish woman had seized her place. She was frantic over her conduct and frightened that she might have put them in a predicament where Emily could lose her job.

If Lord Winchester found out that Emily had a wanton for a sister, if he determined Mary was unfit to be around his wards, she would be back on the streets in a thrice. Or what if Alex tired of her and had Winchester toss them out? Then what?

Oh, what a fine state she was in! Fretting and stewing and not a soul to tell! How could she confess? How could she justify her recklessness?

Emily came to the table and centered Mary's plate. "I've brought you some eggs, a slice of ham, and a piece of bread with jam. There's tea by your right hand."

By the aromas wafting from the food, Mary knew what had been provided, but she murmured, "Thank you."

Emily passed behind Mary's chair and seated herself. Discreetly, Mary sniffed at Emily, and she was distressed to perceive that Emily smelled different again. When Mary had initially noted the change, she'd written it off as being triggered by their new surroundings. However, with the two of them sequestered in the small salon, there was no mistaking the alteration, and Mary was confused.

If pushed to describe the modification, she would have said Emily smelled as if Lord Winchester had rubbed himself all over her.

Winchester had an unusual scent—most people did—that was unique to him, and long before Mary ever ran into him in the halls she always deduced when he was approaching.

The odor was so strong on Emily that Mary could almost swear he was present and emitting it, himself.

She queried, "Have you been with the earl?"

Emily paused, her fork missing a swipe across her plate. "No, I rarely see him, and when he is here, he's much too busy to spend time with paltry old me." As if she'd shared a funny joke, she laughed.

"You're sure?"

"Yes. Why?"

Mary kept her focus on the table, but she scowled. She was wrong about many things—where furniture was located, or which dress was which in her wardrobe—but she was never wrong about what her nose detected. It was too keen, too accurate.

"I heard him in the foyer," she fibbed. "I thought you might have talked."

"No. We haven't spoken in days."

"Wasn't he eager to receive regular reports about the girls?"

"That was before Pamela's shenanigans in the park. Since then, he's decided that raising children is a tad more difficult than he'd imagined, and he doesn't wish to be bothered."

Typical male, Mary mused, but she didn't dare utter the derogatory sentiment aloud. Lest others eavesdrop,

she had to be careful. Emily, on the other hand, was perfectly at ease with denigrating the earl, but then, Emily
had an uncommon relationship with him, and Mary
wouldn't try to unravel it.

"Tell me about Reginald," she urged, glad that they
had a minute to discuss the disturbing development.

Emily leaned closer so their voices wouldn't carry.
"He visited Lord Winchester."

"What did he want?"

"He claimed that we were to be married, and he demanded that Winchester fire me and send us home so
that the wedding could proceed."

Terrified by the prospect, Mary blanched. She was
aware of Reginald's penchant for cruelty. Before she'd
been married, herself, he'd accosted her and attempted to
ravage her, though Mary had escaped. After she'd wed,
he'd left her alone, but she still despised him, and she
was positive that his scheme to lock her away was a re-
venge over her earlier refusal to submit.

She'd never told anyone about the incident, but the
notion of returning to Hailsham, of being under his control without a male family member to act as a barrier,
was more than she could abide.

"What did the earl say?" Mary probed.

"He declared that it was my choice, and when I informed him that I wanted to remain here, he had Fitch
escort Reginald to the door, with instructions not to let
him in if he comes back."

"He didn't!"

"He did!"

"I'll bet Fitch enjoyed that."

"I'll bet he did, too."

They chuckled, but Mary was unnerved. It was dangerous to cross Reginald. He never forgot an insult, and he would find a way to retaliate against Emily for Winchester having championed her cause.

"Was Reginald very angry?" Mary ventured.

"Yes, but he went without causing a scene, and he hasn't shown his face again."

"Let's hope he has the good sense to stay away."

"I doubt he'll risk offending Lord Winchester," Emily asserted. "Reginald isn't that brave, and the earl was incensed by his audacity."

"Was he?"

Mary was quiet, letting the strange comment sink in. Though Emily downplayed her connection with Winchester, and pretended she scarcely knew him, Mary was dubious. Why would Winchester have any interest in their petty troubles? Why would he even deign to meet with Reginald?

Was there more to Emily's association with him than she could admit?

Mary was in a quandary. She yearned to talk about Michael Farrow, to learn if Emily might have done what she oughtn't, but Mary wasn't sure how to broach the delicate issue. Emily was a very private person, and if Mary's suspicions were incorrect, they'd both be mortified.

But what if a worse event had occurred? What if Winchester had pressured Emily? Mary was the elder sister. Shouldn't she intervene? Shouldn't she counsel or caution?

Considering her current peccadillo, she was hardly in a position to chastise or condemn, but she'd hate for Emily to be hurt.

Should Mary inquire? And to whom should she speak? To Emily? To the earl?

While Winchester seemed polite and friendly, Mary couldn't envision approaching him over such an indiscreet topic. Particularly if her reservations were unfounded. She'd look like a fool.

"Emily," she guardedly started, "may I ask you a question?"

"Certainly."

"Is there anything special you'd like to confide about Lord Winchester?"

Emily had popped a bite of egg into her mouth, and she sounded as if she choked, but she quickly recovered. "Lord Winchester? No, why?"

"I was just curious."

Emily was silent, and Mary reached out mentally, assessing the situation. Emily's mind was racing with so many denials and equivocations that Mary was left with the only possible impression: Emily was in an awkward fix with Winchester, but she would never acknowledge it.

At having guessed Emily's secret, Mary sighed. How pathetic they were!

Neither had been immune to the charms of the Farrow brothers, and there was no predicting what disasters might befall them.

Mary was tired of being a burden, of worrying about Rose and Emily, but, because of her disability, never being able to alleviate their problems.

Well, she'd given much to Alex Farrow, more than the bounder deserved, more than he should have been allowed. Maybe it was time to demand a bit more for herself, time to stabilize her circumstance. Occasionally, he hinted that he cared about her, and she needed to find out if he was serious.

"I barely know Lord Winchester," Emily was claiming again. "Other than a few chats about Pamela and Margaret, we've rarely conferred."

"My mistake," Mary replied, keeping her tone detached and neutral.

The response provided no opening for a frank conversation, so Mary wouldn't instigate one. Besides, she was no more eager to discuss Alex than Emily was to discuss the earl.

Mary would handle the crisis on her end, would consult with Alex and exact a better conclusion for herself. She was weary of relying on others, of sitting idle while they scraped and scrounged to support her. For once, Mary would be the rock upon which her family rested, would supply the umbrella to shelter them if Emily lost her post due to her fraternizing with Winchester.

At the notion that she was about to assume control of her life, a surge of excitement swept through her. If she had to wrestle Alex to the floor and drag a proposal out of him, she intended to have him for her husband.

She wouldn't let him refuse.

"I have it all planned."

"Have you?"

"Yes."

Amanda glanced down the deserted hall, ensuring that no one had seen them; then she led Pamela off the verandah and into the garden. It was a cool, wet evening, with the revelers dancing inside, so the chance of bumping into any guests was small.

Michael had sent a curt note, advising her to stay away from Pamela, so she had to be vigilant, lest she be discovered and incur his wrath. Matters were coming to a head, his solicitors proceeding with the details of wrapping up their relationship.

She was barred from his house, barred from his side, about to be evicted from her residence, about to lose her income and status in the demimonde, and she blamed it all on Emily Barnett.

Amanda wouldn't relinquish her place without a fight. Not when she'd worked so diligently to earn it. She would do whatever it took, would employ any ruse, would devise any scheme, would plot and finagle until she righted her affairs.

Desperate measures had to be implemented. The governess had to go, and Amanda had to reestablish herself with Michael. Pamela was the perfect avenue by which Amanda could achieve her objectives.

The girl was greedy, stupid, and prone to addiction, thereby an ideal candidate to be used for nefarious purposes, and Amanda had no qualms about her gambit. This was war, and she would muster her best defenses. When Amanda was finished, Emily Barnett wouldn't know what had hit her.

There were many ways for the calamity to resolve in Amanda's favor. Michael needed to wed, and why not Pamela? Being his bride, Pamela would manage the Farrow household, would hire and fire the domestic staff, and, as Amanda had already gleaned, her first order of business would be to dismiss Barnett.

As to Michael and Pamela, Pamela was too weak to dominate him, so Amanda's influence wouldn't be threatened. If, however, Michael declined to marry Pamela, if she was merely ruined by the scandal Amanda was about to initiate, Amanda couldn't care less.

She owed loyalty to no one but herself.

Amanda ushered them into the bushes, and she retrieved a flask from her bag and offered it to Pamela. The younger woman ravenously sipped at the potent brew.

"As I mentioned before," Amanda began, "your father left you beggared."

"Don't remind me," Pamela seethed. "I can't bear to hear it."

"So your position is extremely precarious. If you want to have any security you must wed and soon. You can't depend on Michael's charity. What if he cut you off?"

"He wouldn't," Pamela mutinously contended. "He's charmed by us. I've ingratiated myself."

Amanda chuckled, pretending great knowledge she didn't possess. "If that's what you think, you're a fool."

"You've spoken to him about me?"

"Of course," Amanda lied.

"What has he said?"

"He's weary of the fuss that's arisen since your arrival. He'd like to be shed of you." She shrugged. "Since he's determined that you have no funds, he doesn't wish to continue supporting you."

"But he was my father's friend!"

"Not really." The two men had been as close as any

drinking chums could be, but there'd been no genuine fondness.

"He was!" Pamela insisted, but Amanda scoffed.

"Have your illusions, if you must."

Up on the verandah, Miss Barnett rushed outside. She was at the balustrade, staring out into the shadows and trying to locate Pamela. Amanda had but a few moments to bait her hook.

"There's a viable solution," Amanda maintained.

"What is it?"

"*You* must marry Michael."

"If he detests me so much, why would he?"

"We're not about to give him any choice."

"What do you mean?"

"There are methods of bringing about a proposal," Amanda clarified, "even if the man is dead-set against tendering one."

"How?"

"You'll have to be compromised, and I know just how we'll accomplish it. In fact, I believe Miss Barnett will play an important role."

"I don't understand what that involves," Pamela said. "Would it entail something horrid? Would I have to humiliate myself?"

Amanda wasn't about to explain the details of what would be required. Later on, there would be plenty of opportunity to steer Pamela in the wrong direction. She seized the empty flask and tucked it into her reticule. "Your nanny is searching for you. You'd better go."

"But I need to know what you've arranged."

"Hush!" Amanda sharply admonished. "Miss Barnett is on the patio"—Pamela whipped around and glared— "and if she learns that we've been talking, it will complicate everything. Be off, before she sees us."

She shoved Pamela, pushing her onto the walk so that she was visible to Barnett. Then, as if she'd never been there, Amanda vanished into the trees.

~ 14 ~

"I must ask you a question."

"What?" Alex snapped.

He glared at Mary and halted his rhythmic thrusting. He was in a foul mood, annoyed at having gambled away several hundred pounds. When Michael learned how much he'd frittered away, he'd be driven to commit murder.

Alex needed the peace and oblivion he found with Mary. When he was with her, he managed to banish his demons, so he wasn't about to stop and chat. He tried to start in again, but she wouldn't participate.

"Is your brother having an affair with my sister?"

He scowled. "What an absurd topic to raise at a moment like this."

"Is he?"

Briefly, he considered whether he should be truthful or not. What was best?

"Yes," he ultimately said, "they've been carrying on." He flexed, but his response had cooled her ardor, and he cursed and pulled out of her.

"What does his attention signify?"

"Nothing. How could it?"

"But he's been so kind to her—when there was no reason for him to be. Surely, that must indicate a heightened affection."

Was she really so obtuse that she supposed Michael required a logical incentive to philander? "For God's sake, Mary, you're a widow. You know how these matters go."

"No, I don't. Why don't you tell me?"

She was peeved, frowning in a maddening feminine fashion that apprised him the sex had ended, and there'd be no recommencing, unless he engaged in the spat she was determined to have. They'd have to hash it out to its bitter, futile conclusion; then he'd have to seduce her all over again.

"Michael is a lusty man. He'll tumble anything in a skirt."

"But Emily isn't a strumpet. How could he trifle with her?"

"She's an adult woman, who can make her own choices."

"She was a maiden!"

"So? I doubt he forced her."

"What if she winds up pregnant?"

"He'll . . . he'll . . ."

Alex stumbled for an answer. Michael had never fathered any children, so Alex couldn't begin to guess what he would do. His brother's sense of right and wrong was a tad skewed, and Alex couldn't picture him shackled in holy wedlock over such a bothersome problem.

"He'll what?" she pestered.

"He'll buy her a cottage in the country. The tot will have a trust fund, she will have an allowance, and she'll be set for life." He blew out a heavy breath. "There! Are you satisfied?"

"Hardly."

"Hasn't she been wrangling for just such an arrangement?"

She gasped and sat up in a huff. "Are you suggesting she's involved with him for the . . . the *money* she could pry out of him?"

"That's precisely what I'm saying."

"You actually believe that my sister is an opportunist? That she's naught but a leech, out to blackmail him into parting with some of his fortune?"

"Don't act so surprised. It happens all the time."

"Maybe in your world, but not in mine."

"I'm sure you lived around saints," he facetiously retorted, which ignited her temper.

She jumped to the floor, fumbled for her robe, and hastily covered herself.

"Why don't you go?" When he didn't move, she pointed to the door. "Now."

He was perplexed by her sudden fury, and he needed her to be perfectly clear as to what was transpiring, for he hadn't the vaguest clue.

"Why are we fighting?"

"We're *fighting* because you are a rude, unfeeling oaf, and I'm sick of you. Get out!"

He'd never understand women. She'd wanted his opinion; he'd given it. Why was she in such a snit?

"I'm not leaving. Come back to bed."

"I'd rather eat a toad."

He sighed with exasperation. "You've started an argument, when I can't fathom why you would, but you should end it immediately. I'm not in the mood to squabble."

"Why are you doing this with me?" she countered.

"Doing what? Quarreling?"

"No." She gaped as if he was the thickest dolt in London. "Why are you sleeping with me?"

"Because it's enjoyable."

"Do you care about me?"

"What?"

"You heard me. Don't pretend you didn't."

A second earlier, they'd been discussing Michael and her sister. How had the subject been switched to himself? He'd had too much brandy to be thinking straight, or making rational statements, and he wanted her to shut the hell up, to return to where they'd been before she'd decided on talking.

They were at their best when they were copulating. There were no words to trip them up, no tricky issues to review, no feelings to hurt.

Desire he could handle. Emotional outbursts were beyond him.

"Of course I care about you." How else was a fellow to reply? And, in an indistinct sort of way, he was sincere.

"Fine," she concurred, nodding. "You *care* about me. What does that mean to you?"

She'd dragged them to a hazardous spot, and he hovered between telling her to sod off and telling her he loved her. He took the coward's route. "I'm not certain."

"You must have some idea."

"I like having sex with you."

"Our fornication is a physical exploit we perform together. I'm inquiring about your sentiments toward me personally."

He couldn't announce he had none, for that wasn't true. Nor could he claim that he adored her, that he wanted to spend the rest of his life with her, for that wasn't true, either. His attitude was somewhere in between nothing and everything, but candor wouldn't suffice. She had to be angling for a marriage proposal, but he couldn't give her one.

Didn't she comprehend who and what he was? Even if he was inclined to matrimony—which he adamantly was not—what kind of husband would he be? What sane woman would bind herself to a drunken, lecherous gambler? She was being crazy.

"Don't do this, Mary," he pleaded.

"I asked you about Emily," she continued, as if he hadn't spoken, "but what if it was me? What if I was pregnant?"

The question sucked the air out of the room. "Are you?"

"No."

"Then why rattle that cage?"

"I'm in a precarious situation. What if your brother learns of our affair and fires Emily because of it?"

"He wouldn't."

"You can't be positive. In case you haven't noticed, I have a daughter. Where would we go? What would we do?"

It was on the tip of his tongue to declare that he'd look after them, but he swallowed down any imprudent offers he wasn't prepared to render. "Nothing bad will happen."

"When you tire of me, will you have your brother cast us out?"

"Mary!" he scolded. "I could never behave so despicably to you."

"Why should I believe you?"

"You have to trust me."

The request that she *trust* him was insulting and preposterous. What had he ever done to merit higher esteem? He'd used and abused her in the worst fashion, and now, with her practically begging for recompense, he was too spineless to supply it.

"If I become pregnant"—she was like a feral bird, swooping in for the kill—"I have to know your intentions. What are they?"

"I'll marry you," he insisted, quickly and without deliberation.

"Swear it."

"I swear."

She chuckled wearily. "I hate it when you lie to me."

"I'm not lying."

She raised a hand, the motion stopping further protestation, and he was silenced. She was quiet, too, blankly staring at the fireplace. Finally, she murmured, "Sometimes, I'm so afraid."

The comment did something funny to his insides. His dormant conscience woke up and wiggled around, reminding him that he'd once been a compassionate man.

Where had that individual gone? Why was it so difficult to bring him back?

"Of what are you afraid?"

"I'm *afraid* of our being tossed onto the streets without a penny in our pockets." She gestured around her room. "You've always resided in this grand mansion, and you've had your brother to watch over you, the family coffers to provide an allowance, so you have no clue what it's like to struggle. Can you imagine how any of this might frighten me?"

"Yes, I can," which was another fib. He was so selfish, so bent on his own pleasure, that he'd rarely pondered what her plight would be after they were through.

He was living in a bubble, where naught was real. Not his liaison with her, not her unstable position, or the fact that she had a daughter who needed a father. He'd never so much as said hello to the girl, had never inquired as to her name.

He was an ass. A certifiable, unrepentant, unreliable ass. Why did Mary put up with him?

"So," she persisted, "I'm sorry if I've disturbed you with some uncomfortable questions, but I've earned the right to ask them."

She was talking as if she had no value to him, as if he considered her no more than a whore, and he had to admit that he'd done little to leave her with any other impression. Suddenly, he was eager to pose a few questions of his own. If she could dig and poke, so could he.

"You're badgering as to whether I care about you, so let's turn the tables. Do *you* care about me?"

"Yes," she answered without hesitation.

"And what does that mean to you?" he prodded.

"I love you."

He blanched. "You couldn't possibly."

"Why not?"

"You can't have any genuine regard for me. Not after how I've acted. You're being foolish."

"No, I'm not. I know there's a better man lurking inside you. I'm hoping you'll set him free."

He gazed up at the ceiling, and an idiotic rush of tears surged to his eyes, and he was so glad she wasn't able to witness them. He couldn't stand to hear that she'd placed him on some absurd pedestal.

If he dared to pledge himself, ultimately he'd fail her, and when she discovered that there was no white knight beneath the gruff exterior, she'd be crushed.

The notion that he might hurt her, that he might break her heart, was too distressing. It knocked at the door to his emotions that he kept tightly locked. By dallying with her, he was wallowing in oblivion, pretending that the world outside her bedchamber didn't exist. There was just him and her and the licentious things they did together. Peripheral issues, such as integrity and honor, had ceased to signify. As he was immersed in a void, Society's tenets no longer controlled him. Due to his obsessive and insane need for her, they'd been nullified.

Hadn't they?

The sex he had with her was his entire universe, and he was anxious for the shallow, superficial experience to continue on forever. He felt like a jester at a fair, as if he were juggling balls in the air and he couldn't drop one, lest his whole life crash to the ground in pieces.

"Come here." He held out his hand, but she didn't take it.

"No. I don't want this from you anymore. I never should have started. It's been folly from the beginning."

"You're wrong, Mary. It's been grand. Every second has been more than I deserved."

"I'm sure it's been magnificent for you, but for me, it's been a tad less fulfilling."

He was desperate for his illusions to remain intact, and he climbed off the mattress and went to her.

"I love you, Mary." The declaration slipped out before he'd realized he would utter it. Apparently, he was ready to express any crazed sentiment in order to have her compliant and willing.

"No, you don't," she interjected. "You insult me by saying so."

"I do love you. Let me show you how much."

He kissed her, his lips tentatively falling on hers, as he worried about how she'd accept the embrace. She didn't push him away, so he deepened the kiss, his tongue in her mouth, his fingers in her hair.

She'd donned her robe, and he abhorred that she'd hidden herself from him, and he untied the belt, the lapels flopping open, so that he could massage her breasts. He petted his thumbs over her nipples, reveling as they hardened.

While she might fuss and stew, might fret and agonize, she was as captivated by their carnal antics as he was, himself. She couldn't deny the pleasures in which they engaged.

Moving to the bed, he drew her down on top of him. He rooted to her nipple, sucking and biting at it, until her hips responded.

He gripped her thighs and spread them so that she was perched over his loins. She was wet, relaxed, and with the barest thrust, he glided inside.

This was what he wanted, the only thing that mattered.

Their quiet, comforting ability to join, to bond without words, was a treasure unlike any other.

He reached between them, stroking her, driving her to the edge, and tossing her over, and he followed, spilling himself as recklessly as ever, and he was amazed by his negligence.

Why would he proceed down such a dangerous path? Fleetingly, he wondered if he didn't hope that she *did* become pregnant. How else could he justify his actions?

Holding her, cherishing her, he rocked them to the end, but as their passion waned, she glanced away. Naught had changed. They could fornicate till Armageddon and not arrive at a mutually satisfying resolution.

He pulled out of her, and the instant he did, she rolled away, and he hated that she was so forlorn. He hadn't the flowery language necessary to smooth over their disagreement. He spooned himself to her, nibbled at her nape, and kissed at her shoulder.

"Will you marry me?" It was what she was frantic to hear, the sole remark that would repair their rift.

"I've humiliated myself by begging for a proposal, but that doesn't mean you have to offer one."

"You've been a veritable nag," he teased.

She elbowed him in the ribs. "Shut up. You needn't remind me of how pathetic I am."

"Marry me," he repeated. He waited for a reply, but when he didn't receive it, he asked, "How could I convince you that I'm serious?"

"I suppose if you marched down to inform your brother. I *might* believe you then."

His heart pounded. How had he ascended to this perilous precipice?

"All right, I will." As if he was prepared to stride out, naked as a jaybird, he shifted away.

Would he? Could he?

To his vast relief, she stopped him. "Don't you dare."

"Why not?"

"Lord Winchester would talk you out of it."

"I'm a grown man, Mary. I make my own decisions."

"Yes, but you respect him, and he's dear to you. If he advised against it, how could you refuse him?"

A valid point. "What about your sister? If you went to her, what would she say?"

"She thinks you're a lunatic."

"Why, thank you."

"You're welcome." She grinned, relishing the opportunity to bring him down a peg.

"So . . . she'd be against it, too?"

"She'd tell me I was mad to consider it."

She sighed, as did he, and he spun her toward him so that he could look at her.

"Let's elope," he said, and his suggestion stunned them both.

"You're joking."

"No, I'm not. Let's do it."

"Emily is correct: You are deranged."

"I'm not. Listen: Our biggest obstacle is the people we know, that they'd disapprove, and if we were to wed here in London, we'd have to have my vicar call the banns. That gives our relatives an entire month to dissuade us."

"Or for you to back out."

Precisely, he mused, though he wasn't about to admit as much aloud. He was swept up in the rashness of the moment, ready to spew any contemptible promise that he might—or might not—keep.

"An elopement is for the best," he contended.

"But how would we accomplish it?"

"We'd travel to Scotland. To Gretna Green. That's where everyone goes. It's a town across the border."

"*Everyone* goes there? You make it sound as if lovers are popping up there by the thousands."

"Only those who are in a hurry."

"Hmm. . . ." She was silent again, wanting to trust him, but she couldn't.

"We can race up in Michael's curricle. We'll return in a few days, with the event concluded, and no one will be able to complain." He paused and chuckled. "At least, not to our faces."

"When would we leave?"

"When can we most easily avoid your sister?"

"On Saturday. She's escorting the girls to a country house party. They'll be visiting for a week."

He bit down the urge to moan. He was hesitant to set a specific date, for that would bind him and it would be impossible to renege.

"Saturday morning it is then." He nodded and smiled. She was buying every word. "We'll head out after they depart."

"What about your brother?"

"He's so busy, he won't realize I'm gone."

She studied him, her shrewd perception reaching out, and he kept his expression blank, his mind still, not wanting her to discern how disordered he was.

"Are you sure?" she queried.

"Very sure."

"You'll never regret asking?"

"No, I never will."

How he yearned for it to be true!

Before she had a chance to question him further, he pulled her into his arms, determined to immerse them in carnality.

She joined in, as eager as he to seal their pact, to pretend that they would go forward. With all the vows he'd uttered, with all the persuading he'd done, how could he fail to follow through?

15

Emily wandered into the solarium, pausing to admire how the afternoon sun shone through the windows. It was her favorite room in the large mansion, and she frequently stopped by to sit and think.

Her world was spinning too fast, and the routines of daily life were beyond her. The person she'd once been had ceased to be, and a new, wild woman had taken her place. She wanted things she couldn't have and dreamed about things that could never be.

She felt so wonderful!

She was so miserable!

She was hopelessly, desperately, in love. With a man who would never love her in return, who would never marry her or make a commitment to her. Oh, what folly had led her to this forlorn, gloomy precipice?

She didn't have the courage to end their destructive affair, yet she couldn't keep on. Every time they were together, she grew more smitten, but no good could be generated from the disaster she'd wrought.

"Emily Barnett Farrow," she whispered, trying out the name to hear how it sounded, and, at her whimsy, she blushed bright red.

How could she presume such a preposterous outcome? Yet she couldn't help yearning for a conclusion that was more satisfying than each of them ending up lonely and alone.

Why couldn't she be his wife? The prospect was absurd, but she couldn't set it aside. He wasn't the sort to dwell on titles and bloodlines, and they could be so happy. If she was clever enough, she ought to be able to wrangle the result she craved, and Michael could be hers forever.

She walked through the last wall of ferns, expecting to encounter a secluded bench and that it would be empty, so she was startled, and she jumped.

"Hello, Emily," Amanda said, cool as a snake. "You don't mind if I call you Emily, do you?"

Emily frowned, a thousand questions careening through her head: Why was Amanda in the house? How had she known when Emily would be in the solarium? Obviously, she'd been lying in wait. What did she want?

"Actually, I mind very much," Emily replied. "It's *Miss* Barnett to you."

She spun on her heel, and Amanda spoke to her back. "Don't go just yet. We have a few topics to discuss."

Emily whipped around.

"We have naught to *discuss*," Emily declared. "Be off. This instant!"

It was the height of arrogance to order Amanda's departure. Emily held no position of significance that gave her any authority over who came in and who didn't. Still, she couldn't bear to see Amanda so comfortable, so at ease, and acting as if *she* were the hostess and Emily the interloper.

"Won't you join me in a glass of wine?"

Amanda gestured to a table where there was a tray of wine and goblets, and Emily was furious. A servant had to have assisted Amanda, had to have parlayed with her over Emily's schedule. Who would have?

How could Amanda have free access to the mansion? How often had she been on the premises without Emily's being aware? Was she a regular visitor?

Trepidation swept over her. Amanda wouldn't have entered without Michael's consent. He had to know, and Emily's heart pounded. There were too many secrets swirling about. What should she say? What should she do?

"No," she responded, "I won't *join* you. I am a respectable gentlewoman, and I'm not about to consort with a strumpet."

Amanda raised a brow. "Isn't that the pot calling the kettle black?"

At the insinuation, Emily tamped down any reaction. No one had detected her liaison with Michael, and she intended to keep it that way. "What are you implying?"

"Sit down, Emily." Amanda indicated a chair that had been situated directly across from her, and Emily was faced with further evidence of how much effort Amanda had expended in preparing for Emily's arrival.

"I won't. I have no desire to speak with you."

"Don't be tedious. You're trying my patience."

"As if I care."

She started to turn again when Amanda barked, "If you don't hear me out, we'll have to have this conversation in front of Michael. Would you rather? I can summon him from his club, though I imagine he'd be annoyed." Like a lazy, dangerous cat, she shifted and leveled her lethal stare. "At the moment, he's gambling—which he always does on Friday afternoons—and he loathes being interrupted."

Emily had no notion of where Michael went on Friday afternoons or any other day. When he left the house, he never explained his absences, nor did she feel she should pry.

She was out of her league. Amanda possessed the type of information gleaned through years of association, through familiarity and longevity. She'd been acquainted with Michael for ages, and she was intimate with him in a manner Emily couldn't fathom.

Emily took a slow step, then another, and she sat as Amanda had commanded. Was she to be terminated? By the mistress? How humiliating! How galling!

"Has Lord Winchester asked you to talk with me?" Emily queried.

"What do you suppose?"

"I have no idea."

Amanda poured herself some wine, and she studied Emily over the rim of the glass. "You are very pretty," she stated, "in a fresh, innocent fashion. I guess I can appreciate Michael's interest. He never could resist a virgin."

Emily bristled with outrage. "Is there a point you wish to make?"

"It's time for you to leave."

"Am I being fired?"

"I hate to label it a *firing*," Amanda mused. "The word is so callous, and you have been so . . . helpful. How about if we refer to it as a parting of the ways?"

"Is this at Lord Winchester's request?"

"No, but he wants me to be happy"—she flashed a treacherous, ruthless smile—"and I have decided that you are not welcome here. You see, when I'm not happy, neither is he."

"Have I done something to offend him? Or you?"

"Don't be impertinent." Amanda downed her wine and refilled the glass. "Let's be frank, shall we?"

"Of course. Let's be *frank.*"

"I know all about your affair with him."

Emily kept her expression blank. "I have no clue as to what you allude."

"Don't bother denying it."

"Really, I—"

Amanda held up her hand, halting any protestation. "I gave him permission to proceed with you."

"What?"

"You can't think his peccadilloes are any secret to me."

"You and Lord Winchester confer over such dastardly details?"

Could it be true? Would Michael have sought Amanda's acquiescence? Would he have garnered Amanda's blessing? Had he consulted with her afterward? Did they snuggle in bed and laugh over what Michael had done with Emily?

She felt sick.

"Yes, we confer," Amanda asserted. "I insist on it. I even find him some of his partners. He could never be satisfied with one woman. He likes variety, so I allow him to stray, but when he wanders too far, I rein him in."

"That's disgusting."

"Why? He matters to me in a way you couldn't begin to grasp, and I would do anything to ensure that he's contented."

"But if he's important to you, as you claim, how could you share him?"

"Sex is just sex for a man, and Michael is no different than any other. He'd fornicate with a goat if he thought it would bring him pleasure. I've come to terms with the kind of individual he is, with his perverted tastes and preferences. How about you? Can you accept him as he is?"

"I'm merely his governess," Emily fibbed, though she was dying inside. Hadn't she wondered about his philandering, about his ability to be faithful? He'd offered no promises, not even when she'd degraded herself by begging for them. "It's none of my business how he chooses to conduct himself."

At the disavowal, Amanda chuckled and raked Emily with a contemptuous sneer. "I can understand why you fell victim to his charms. He is a handsome devil, and you're so provincial. You wouldn't have had any experience in fending off such a libertine. His attention must have been very flattering."

Emily was desperate to flee, to stomp out in an angry huff, but she was confused as to how she should act. She didn't believe Amanda, but at the same juncture, she couldn't be positive that the stories were false.

Mesmerized, she dawdled like a stump, and she couldn't muster the courage to defend Michael, to shout that he was a good man, a loyal man. As she wasn't supposed to know him very well, how could she have an opinion?

"I've heard enough," Emily forced herself to say, and

she stood. "It's not proper for the two of us to discuss Lord Winchester. He is my employer, and I admire him very much."

"You're not listening, Emily. Your interlude in the Farrow household is ended. I've let him have his fun, but it's over."

"I'll go when Lord Winchester notifies me, and not a second sooner."

Amanda sighed. "Michael had so hoped I could persuade you without creating a huge fuss."

"You? Why would he send you to speak with me?"

"I was to obtain your agreement without hurting you, but Michael is a bit thick about females. He's not aware of how smitten you are." The weight of the world on her shoulders, she sighed again. "I can see that it won't be possible to spare your feelings."

"On what topic?"

"Another girl has tickled Michael's fancy. He's about to take her as his next lover. In fact, he and I may initiate her together. Two women and one man. It's called a *ménage à trois*. Are you familiar with the phrase? Michael absolutely adores a threesome."

"You're lying." The words slipped out before she could stop them, and all pretense of distance was abandoned. "Michael would never behave so terribly to me."

"Wouldn't he?" Unruffled, Amanda sipped her wine. "I can still summon him from his club. Shall we have him rush home, so that you can ask him face-to-face? Have you that much temerity?"

"No . . . no. . . ." Emily's head was reeling, her stomach churning. In her immoral fling with Michael Farrow, she'd endured much, had relinquished much and given much, but such a confrontation would be beyond the pale.

"We simply deemed it was best for all concerned if you left before he started in. He's prepared to pay you a severance, but you must go immediately." Amanda reached to a bag on the floor and retrieved an envelope, and she placed it on the table between them.

"What's in it?" Emily probed.

"It's the money Michael owes you for watching over his wards, plus a little extra. He's penned a letter of reference, too, so that you can find a new job. The cash and the letter are yours, so long as you and your family vacate the premises in twenty-four hours."

Emily's mind was awhirl. She didn't trust Amanda, yet why would Amanda concoct such a ruse? Amanda had to realize that Emily would inform Michael.

Or would she?

She tried to envision herself cornering Michael and demanding an explanation, but she never would. They didn't have the type of relationship where she could pose such appalling questions or where he would answer them.

And what if Amanda was telling the truth? Could Emily bear to have Michael reiterate Amanda's comments?

Emily had painted herself a fantasy, where reality didn't exist. Her liaison with Michael was finite, a temporary lark for him. She'd built an elaborate illusion, where she'd convinced herself that he loved her, that he would throw aside his wild tendencies and marry her.

Bit by bit, she'd erected sturdy walls to shield herself from the hazards of her situation, but with each of Amanda's remarks, the bricks were falling, pummeling her with the folly of her choices, the danger of her precarious position.

Nervous and unsure, she licked her lip. "If I don't take the money and go . . . then what?"

"You'll be tossed out, without your compensation, without a character recommendation." Amanda shrugged. "Mr. Fitch is awaiting orders from me to have the maids pack your bags. It is up to you as to the conditions under which you elect to leave."

Despairing and afraid, Emily gazed at the rug.

What to do? What to do? Finally, she murmured, "I must talk with Michael."

"But he doesn't wish to meet with you. That's why I am here."

"I don't care. I have to hear what he says."

"Daft ninny!" Amanda chided. "You were a plaything to him, a pretty vessel where he spilled his lust. Are you presuming that you're the first virgin he's ever ruined?" She scoffed cruelly. "I procure young girls for him all the time."

It couldn't be! It just couldn't be! Yet Emily thought of her initial encounter with him, of the spiked punch and late-night appointment. Perhaps, he regularly lured women off the streets, women such as herself who were unsuspecting as to his motives.

How many had there been before her? How many would come after?

No! No! a voice shouted. She wouldn't believe it. She couldn't. Still, she found herself inquiring, "Who is this girl you claim has caught his eye?"

"Can't you guess?"

"I haven't a clue."

"It's Pamela."

The response was so shocking that it took several seconds for the impact to register. "Pamela . . . Pamela Martin?"

"Don't look so surprised. He's been considering it for years. She hasn't exactly been a model of propriety, and she's tempted him enormously. So far, he's held back, but she's sixteen, and without her father in the way to protest, there are no obstacles. He's ready to sample her fruits—so to speak."

Emily remembered the occasions she'd observed Pamela and Michael together. They were always flirtatious. Emily had ignored their teasing and repartee, writing off Michael's interest as being due to his male nature, but what if she'd been wrong as to his intentions?

Pamela was capable of any treachery, but what about Michael?

Could he debauch his ward? Was he that low?

She had to flee before she learned anything worse, but she couldn't force herself toward the door. "He would never seduce Pamela. As soon as I can arrange it, I plan to advise him of what you've said."

"Be my guest," Amanda replied. "I'm positive he'll be more than happy to discuss his peculiar sexual habits with you."

Amanda didn't flinch, didn't blink, and her calm certitude rattled Emily even more. "He's not the roué you allege him to be. You'll never persuade me that he is."

"Aren't you the little champion?" Amanda laughed, then sobered. "You're in for heartbreak. You know that, don't you?"

"He'd never deliberately hurt me."

"There are many kinds of *hurt*. Could you stay in this house when he was slipping into Pamela's bed one moment, then into yours the next?" Amanda's lips pursed into an unbecoming pout. "Think, you pitiable fool. Why put yourself through such agony?"

Emily couldn't survive such a horrid circumstance, but insecurity had muddled her reasoning, fear trouncing her better sense.

Amanda noted her confusion and she prodded, "Why don't you save everyone a colossal amount of grief by simply returning to the village from whence you came?"

Amanda was too confident, too certain. Emily was anxious to confront Michael, but what if Emily approached him, only to discover that Amanda had been doing her a favor? What if Amanda was giving her a chance to slither away before she was humiliated?

"I don't know what's best." She lurched to her feet and stumbled away, barely seeing the path through the potted plants as she rushed out.

"You have till tomorrow morning, Emily," Amanda called from behind her. "Don't wait too long to make a decision, or it will be made for you."

~ 16 ~

Michael crept in the door at the rear of the house. It was very late, everyone asleep, and he stood in the dark, listening to the creaks and groans of the old mansion. He was soothed by the familiar aromas of beeswax and polishing, of banked fires and baked bread.

"Oh, Alex," he murmured to the quiet halls, "where are you?"

His brother had been missing for days, but Michael hadn't noticed his absence. Fitch had been the one to whisper that Alex's bed hadn't been slept in, that he hadn't been home to change his clothes. Considering Alex's current disposition, he could be anywhere, doing anything.

Michael had searched every hovel, every brothel, every gambling hall. He'd even lowered himself to asking Mrs. Livingston if she was aware of Alex's location, but she'd been shocked by what the inquiry implied and claimed to have no idea. No one had seen Alex. No one had heard from him. How could a man vanish into thin air?

Alex was his only brother, his only family. They'd
survived their upbringing as a unit, had suffered the
same shames and humiliations. In a childhood fraught
with trauma and strife, Alex had been Michael's rock,
his sole companion. Without Alex to lean upon, Michael
couldn't gain his balance.

He glanced up the stairs, thinking of Emily. It was so
wonderful to know that she was waiting for him, and just
pondering her, he felt better. He needed her as he needed
air to breathe or water to drink, and before he could talk
himself out of it, before superior judgment could prevail,
he was hurrying to her room.

He tiptoed in, and he walked to the bed. As he stared
down at her, he was inundated by a surge of unusual
emotion. She looked so young and innocent, and he
yearned to pull her close, to vow that he'd always watch
over and cherish her.

Near to love, he mused as the peculiar sentiment
swirled away. It explained his level of infatuation and
obsession. She simply affected him as no one else could.

He shrugged out of his clothes. As he mulled what
was pending, and how marvelous it would be, his
anatomy stirred to life. She roused him to recklessness,
and there had to be a point where he'd grow weary of
her, where his fascination would peak and wane, but he
couldn't imagine when it would arrive.

The more he was with her, the more he wanted her.

His cock was hard, aching with his desire for her, and
he wrapped his fist around it, squeezed and flexed to relieve the tension, then crawled onto the mattress and slid
under the blankets.

She was slumbering soundly, and he stretched out, his

body making contact with hers. He kissed her, using the pressure to roll her onto her back, and he came over her, covering her, wallowing in sensation.

For the briefest instant, she smiled and kissed him in return; then consciousness dawned. She stiffened and wrenched away, glaring at him as if a stranger had crept in, as if she didn't know who he was.

"What are you doing?" she snapped.

"I missed you."

"So? You're not welcome here." She studied his torso, irked by the fact that he was naked, that he'd disrobed and lain down. "I don't understand you. I never have."

"What's to understand?" He put his hand on her bottom, urging them together, so that his phallus was wedged to her belly. "I want you."

"You're like a dog in heat," she muttered.

"Excuse me?"

For some odd reason she demanded, "Pay me my salary."

"Your salary?"

"When I agreed to work for you, you promised that you'd pay me hundreds of pounds, yet I haven't received a penny. I want it."

"No."

"You promised me!"

Yes, he had, and sometime in the future he would remunerate her, but he'd offered her a small fortune. If he gave it to her, he wouldn't have any hold over her. She'd be at liberty to leave him, would have the resources to reside elsewhere.

"What need have you for money?" he asked. "I've provided you with everything you require."

"You owe it to me!"

"Have I said I wouldn't compensate you?"

"You don't have to. I can read your mind without any problem."

Had he wandered into the wrong room by mistake? "I have no idea why you're talking this way."

"Please go. I have to decide what I'll do, and I can't think clearly when you're here."

"What is it you have to *do*?"

"Stop it!" she begged. "I can't bear it when you act like this."

"Like what?" The word *what* seemed to be the only one he could articulate. He was confounded by her wrath, by her enormous hurt. It was careening off her in waves.

"Are you denying that you had Amanda meet with me?"

Amanda? This was about Amanda? "Yes, I am. I haven't seen her in days."

"In days? Really?"

Realizing his slip, he squirmed, which no doubt made him appear guilty as hell. He was no longer fraternizing with Amanda—as least not for any carnal purpose—but Emily couldn't know how difficult it was to avoid Amanda, how intertwined their lives and associates were. It was tricky business, getting their affairs settled, particularly when Amanda was opposed to the split. She was like a second skin he was trying to molt, but he couldn't slither out from under her cloying grasp.

"So I suppose"—Emily was almost sneering—"you're not tossing me over so you can move on to another?"

"Of course not. Where did you come by such an absurd notion?" Although he didn't need an answer. If she had spoken to Amanda, Amanda would have tormented her with horror stories.

"It's too dark," she complained. "I can't see your eyes." She wriggled out from under him, lit a candle, and lifted it toward him. "Tell me the truth, and don't lie. I'll know if you are."

He rippled with frustration. Why should he have to defend himself? Why couldn't she trust him?

"Emily"—he started slowly, as if clarifying something for an imbecile—"I haven't conferred with Amanda, I haven't discussed any plans with her, nor would I."

"Swear it."

"I swear."

"I don't believe you."

He flopped onto the pillow and blew out a heavy breath. "Then why interrogate me?"

"I have to hear you say it."

"Say *what*?" He nearly shouted the query.

"Do you want me to leave?"

"No."

"How can I be sure you mean it?"

"Listen: If Amanda claimed as much, she must have learned about us, and she's hoping to rattle you, hoping you'll flee. She's jealous of you."

"Are you attracted to Pamela?"

"Pamela who?"

"Pamela Martin."

"My . . . my ward?"

"Yes."

How could she assume that he would have sex with his ward? Pamela was a confused, annoying girl, scant more than a child, and his temper flared. "Have you gone completely mad?"

"How many virgins have you ruined before me? Or have you lost count?"

There was no more despicable remark she could have hurled. In the corrupt circles where he was wont to roam, he flaunted his dissolution, letting his colleagues have whatever foul opinions they chose. Some of the gossip was accurate, but most of it was false, especially the rumors involving his infatuation with innocent maidens.

He'd been certain that Emily understood him, that she'd delved to the man lurking below the surface. Her disdain wounded him, and he was livid over the denigration. She was more blind than her sister!

He yanked the candle away from her, hot wax splashing his wrist as he set it on the nightstand. He ignored the burning pain and rolled them so that she was trapped under him. She fought and clawed to escape, but he wouldn't release her.

"How dare you lay such sins at my feet! Apologize at once!"

His fury registered, and her wrestling halted, but her own rage hadn't dissipated. "Answer my question," she retorted. "Was I just another virgin in a long line of them?"

As he assessed her, he was stunned to find that she was genuinely worried as to his motives. After all they'd shared, how could she be so wary?

"My God," he murmured, "you don't know me, at all."

It was a crushing deduction. He'd presumed they were friends, that she liked him and maybe even loved him, but obviously, his perception was wrong. In his pathetic need for acceptance and approval, he'd deluded himself.

She was no different from any of the other people who flowed through his life, people who'd always anticipated the worst from him, and had always received it. He was perverse in his ability to live down to their expectations.

"I absolutely adore chaste females," he crudely declared, "and you were the best of the lot. By far."

He sat up, his feet dangling over the edge of the mattress. His clothes were scattered across the floor, and he knew he should tug them on and stomp out, but he couldn't compel himself to go.

She was the only grand thing that had ever happened to him. She made him smile, made him happy in ways he couldn't explain. She gave him something to look forward to, a reason to come home, and it occurred to him that this was why a man might marry, why he might bite the bullet and propose.

What would it be like to have her with him forever, to have her constantly by his side? It was such a pretty picture that he yearned for it to be real, but the possibility was ridiculous. If he was foolish enough to bind her to him, she would ultimately grow to hate him, and he refused to have them both so wretched.

He had to depart, had to make a clean break and put them both out of their misery, yet if he left, he wouldn't return. He wouldn't lower himself to begging. If she didn't have faith in him, so be it, but an obstinate, forlorn piece of him was desperate to remain.

Drained and despairing, he closed his eyes, praying that she would move to him, that she would display some indication that affection still flickered, but it never arrived.

He began to rise when she startled him by leaping up and draping herself across his back, her arms around his neck, her hands on his chest.

"Don't send me away," she pleaded.

"I won't," he assured her. "I can't."

"Can you forgive me for what I said?"

"I already have."

"I'm sorry."

"It's all right."

"I was so afraid."

"You shouldn't have been, you silly girl." He reached over his shoulder and linked their fingers.

"I love you," she proclaimed, and his jaded spirit soared.

I love you, too! The affirmation was on the tip of his tongue, but he was too much of a coward to admit it. He'd never uttered the words to anyone, wasn't positive what they meant, or what such a confession would do to the shaky ground upon which their relationship rested.

He couldn't acknowledge how much he cared, but he could show her.

He spun around and seized her lips in a searing kiss, and he pressed her down. This was what he wanted, this tempestuous, heedless rush to ecstasy. Nothing else signified. Not his brother or Amanda. Not the future or the past. There was only now, and the flagrant, inexplicable desire he felt for her.

He had to be joined with her, and he struggled with

her nightgown, drawing it off; then he dipped down and took her nipple in his mouth. He was too rough, biting too hard, but he coveted her with a resolve he'd never previously experienced, and his lust spiraled to a frightening height.

What if she'd let him march out of the room? What would have become of him?

If she'd decided she'd had enough, he couldn't envision what his life would be like. For the first time in ages, he had a purpose to drive his existence, and the fact that he could have lost her was too agonizing to contemplate.

He centered himself and entered her in a smooth, brutal thrust. He hadn't relaxed her, or prepared her for such an invasion, and she arched up and cried out, caught off guard by the strength and depth of his need.

With no concern for her comfort or welfare, he reveled, pushing in all the way and pulling out to the tip, then pushing in again. Harshly, viciously, he used her, not worried if she would be torn or bruised. Like a crazed animal, he had to mate or die, and his pulse was pounding so wildly that he wondered if his heart might quit beating, if he might finally fornicate till he perished.

"Tell me that you'll always love me," he demanded.

"Yes, I always will."

"No matter what!" he growled. "No matter where you go, or what happens between us, promise me that you'll never stop."

"Never," she vowed.

"I have to know that you're mine."

"I'm yours forever, Michael. I swear it."

He spilled himself inside her, his hot seed spewing into her womb. In all the prior occasions they'd dallied, he'd never hazarded so much. He'd been cautious, prudent, but in his current condition, rational reflection was beyond him.

He ached for her in a fashion that transcended explanations or justifications, that surpassed logic or sanity. There was no excuse for his rash behavior, no defense he could provide.

As his mind whirled with the recipes for disaster, his body celebrated, a primal urge sweeping over him. He was elated to have made her his in the sole manner that truly counted.

Was he deranged? Was he hoping to impregnate her? Was he bent on fatherhood?

No! The fervent denial rang in his head, yet he smiled, satisfied with what he'd wrought. She'd stirred an ancient, potent compulsion that he couldn't resist, and he was pleased to have risked all.

In the morning, he would curse and lament, but not now. Not while he was still throbbing deep in her sheath. Not while she was trapped beneath him, subjugated, and under his control. He was preening, cocky as any rooster.

He reached his peak, and he floated down, but instantly, he wanted her again. If he had his way, he'd copulate all night, would rut until he was too sore to walk, until she was too sore to move.

He collapsed onto his side, but he couldn't look at her, for he didn't know what to say. He wasn't sorry. Not a whit. He gazed at the ceiling, while she studied the wall.

For a lengthy interval, she was silent; then she contended, "You shouldn't have done that."

"Probably not."

"If I wind up pregnant, will you marry me?"

The question had his heart racing. He never planned on matrimony, couldn't imagine himself as a husband, which was the reason his deed had been so absurd. If she was increasing, he'd have to wed her, but he had no idea how to be faithful, how to be loyal. Why would she want him?

"Don't let's fret about it."

"Would you?" she prodded, jabbing an elbow in his ribs.

"What if I said *yes?* What would you do with me if you had me?"

"I might surprise you."

"You might at that."

"I think you're worth having, Michael Farrow. I think you're worth keeping. Am I crazy?"

"Very likely."

"I'm such a fool," she murmured.

She sighed, the sound so forlorn and resigned, and he couldn't abide her woe. He spooned himself to her, and he nestled in the quiet, holding her, relishing her essence, when the worst, most depressing sensation of conclusion washed over him.

Was this the end for them? Was it the last time he'd ever be with her? What could possibly transpire to separate them?

Yet there was such an aura of doom and tragedy that when he inhaled, it seemed as if he could smell them in the air. He couldn't fathom why he felt calamity approaching, but he shoved away the impression, writing it off to his elevated emotional state.

"Let's rest a bit," he suggested. "Then I want to love you again."

"You can't stay in here," she insisted. "You can't fall asleep."

"I won't," he claimed, but his rowdy fornication was taking its toll, and he was terribly drowsy.

She sighed once more, and he suffered the strangest surge of unease, as if he should make special note of the moment.

Would these innocuous words be the final ones they ever spoke? Would this be her final memory of their relationship?

The horrid prospect couldn't keep him awake. His eyes drifted shut, and he slumbered.

$\sim 17 \sim$

"What's happening?"

"Hush!" Amanda scolded. "He'll hear you!"

"But I can't see," Pamela whined.

"You don't need to *see*. Just do as I tell you, when I tell you, and everything will work out as planned."

Amanda peeked through the door to Michael's bed-chamber, spying on him as he sat in a chair by the fire-place. Deep in thought, he stared at the empty hearth.

She and Pamela were huddled in the adjacent room, which would be his wife's boudoir, although whether that woman would turn out to be Pamela was anyone's guess. Pamela was merely a means to an end, and Amanda couldn't care less whether any union was brought to fruition.

So far, he hadn't approached the cupboard in the cor-ner, where he had various decanters of liquor. It was early Saturday, the start of the weekend, and he ought to be drinking himself into a stupor, but when would the blasted man take a shot? If he didn't imbibe, how was she to pull off her scheme?

Over the years, there'd been many occasions where he'd reveled till he didn't recollect his exploits, till he'd had lapses of memory, and she was positive she could goad him into like condition, then persuade him that he'd committed numerous horrid deeds.

Timing was critical, but he wasn't participating as she'd intended.

She sighed. She'd have to show herself, would have to enter and spur him to his doom. She hadn't wanted to be personally involved, but there was no other choice.

Her window of opportunity was closing. Very soon, Miss Barnett would be calling for the girls to attend her, would be prepared to leave for their party. It was the perfect moment for affairs to resolve.

In light of what was about to occur, the servants would blab. Despite how devoted they were to Michael, and how much they valued their jobs, the tale would be too juicy to keep secret. Whether or not Michael would succumb to pressure and marry Pamela was a gamble, but by evening, he might be engaged. Depending on how fast the scandal exploded, he might be wed by the following morning.

Miss Barnett would be crushed and flee the house forever.

Amanda would be shed of Barnett, would have weak, stupid Pamela ensconced at Michael's side, after which she'd have no trouble regaining his affection and resuming her role as his mistress.

The sole wrench in the machination was Margaret Martin. Margaret was too astute, too clever. Amanda didn't like the child, so she wouldn't be allowed to remain in the mansion. Permanent boarding school was the most likely option.

Amanda had given Emily Barnett sufficient warning, which she'd ignored, so it was Barnett's own fault that matters had come to this dire conclusion. Amanda felt no remorse.

She glared at Pamela. "I have to hurry him along. Hide until I summon you."

"But I still don't know what I'm supposed to do."

"As the event proceeds, I'll instruct you."

"I'm afraid," Pamela complained.

Amanda reached in her reticule, retrieved a flask of liquor, and handed it over. "This should calm your nerves."

Pamela took a greedy gulp, and Amanda shook her head in disgust. The girl had no concept of restraint, and she was destined for a bad end, but Amanda couldn't worry about her. There were bigger fish to fry.

She opened the door and slipped through. Michael was so distracted that he didn't notice her until she was a few feet away.

He scowled. "Why are you here, Amanda?"

"I must speak with you. I've asked you to visit me, and you refuse. What would you have me do?"

"Have you considered that there might be a reason I don't wish to talk with you?"

"You're being stubborn."

"Absolutely."

"Which is nothing new, but I'm weary of these games."

"Bully for you."

She went to the cupboard, poured him a brandy, then

offered him the glass. For a second, he hesitated, and she was so frustrated by his moderation that she wanted to rail at the heavens. If he didn't partake—at once!—she'd wrestle him to the ground and dump the vile brew down his throat.

"How did you get in?" he inquired.

"I have a key."

"Why would you presume you're welcome to use it?"

"I'm still your mistress. And your hostess. Though you seem to have forgotten, I occupy a position of importance in your life." She struggled to be flirtatious. "I haven't earned my keep in ages."

"We're through, Amanda. Why are you being so obstinate?"

"Oh, posh. You've told me we were through on a hundred different occasions. You never mean it." She grinned. "Remember all the times we frolicked in that chair? Shall we give it another go?"

"I don't think so."

She rested her foot on the cushion, and tugged her skirt to her knee, having him view an expanse of shapely leg. She had a maid who shaved her, even her privates, so that she was smooth, silky, just for him. She leaned over, her cleavage flaunted, her breasts barely contained by the neckline of her red gown. It was his favorite dress and a reminder of a better period between them.

"Drink up, darling," she urged, and she was pleased when he swallowed down the contents. She grabbed the decanter and dispensed more.

"How were you able to convince the servants to admit you? I can't understand why Fitch didn't sound an alarm."

"Why would they deny me?"

"Because I ordered them not to let you in."

"They're terrified of me. After we kiss and make up, as they are certain we will"—she winked—"they need to be on my good side, so they don't dare cross me."

"You are the most exasperating woman I've ever met."

"Aren't I though?"

He swigged his brandy again, and she could scarcely keep from bellowing in triumph. One or two more servings would do the trick.

"My governess advises me that you've been harassing her."

"Your governess?" As if she couldn't place the aggravating strumpet, she acted baffled. "Is that the ninny who saw us fucking in the library?"

"Yes."

"Why would I bother with the likes of her?"

"That's what I would like to know."

"I haven't done anything to her." *Not yet, anyway!* "Besides, what is she to me? What is she to you?"

She almost hoped that he'd remark and indicate the depth of his feelings, although she couldn't believe he had any. He simply wasn't a man who grew attached. He loved a new conquest, reveled in the chase, but once he caught his prey, his interest waned.

He didn't comment on his relationship with Barnett, but he frowned. "Leave her be, would you? She's not corrupt, as you and I are, and she shouldn't be exposed to you. When you pester her, I have to hear about it. She hasn't learned how to ignore you—as I do."

He swilled a third glass, and Amanda was extremely happy to pour a fourth. The change was gradual, but his movements were slowing. Perspiration popped out on his brow, his speech slurred.

"Is it hot in here?" he asked.

"Very hot," she replied, and she reached out and stroked his phallus. Though he pretended to be angry with her, his body responded, his cock hardening under her adept fingers. "Would you like me to suck you off? It's been an eternity since I have. You must be about to burst."

"No . . . I . . ."

He gaped around, as if he was lost or couldn't find his balance. His cravat was already off, and she opened his shirt. His arms were like lead, so he didn't resist.

"Let's cool you down," she suggested.

She dropped to her knees and snuggled herself between his thighs. He was unsteady, woozy.

"I don't feel well. Have you put opiates in the brandy?"

"Of course not," she murmured. "I recall how much you detest them. You merely drank too much too fast. You shouldn't overindulge so often." Later on, he'd be confused and disoriented, and she wanted to plant seeds of memory, wanted him to think that he really had been foxed. "Pamela is eager to fornicate with you, darling. She's anxious for you to be her first. Wouldn't you like to be?"

"No . . . no. . . ." He tried to decline but couldn't raise much of a protest.

Not long now, she mused. "You've always lusted after Pamela. You've always wanted the three of us to do it together. You can't have forgotten. You begged me to bring her to you."

"That's crazy," he managed to mumble. "I would never . . ."

"Relax, Michael." She unbuttoned his pants. "Let me take care of you. I know what you like best."

She pulled his cock from his trousers and sucked it into her mouth, but luckily, she didn't have to perform to the end. After a brief interlude, his erection vanished and he dozed off. His head tipped to the side, and he snored.

Easing away, she paused to ensure he was unconscious; then she rushed to the door and dragged Pamela into the room.

"Help me get him onto the bed," she commanded.

"What have you done?" Pamela inquired. "He isn't . . . isn't dead, is he?"

"No, he isn't dead. I drugged him."

"Why would you?"

"You can't presume he'd do this willingly."

"Are you serious? My father told me I was very pretty, that men would be fighting over me when I grew up."

Amanda rolled her eyes in disgust. For a female with no funds and no prospects, Pamela was so set on herself. "Be silent, and let's finish this."

They lugged and heaved him to the mattress; then Amanda arranged him, mussing his hair, discarding his shirt and shoes, loosing his pants and lowering them to his hips. Once she had him looking as dissolute as possible, she focused her attention on Pamela.

"It's your turn," she explained.

"For what?" Pamela queried.

"Your hair needs fixing."

"My hair? What's wrong with it?"

"It can't be braided."

"But I always braid it when I'm in my nightclothes."

"Stupid girl," Amanda scolded, "it's a child's habit." Amanda untied the ribbon and riffled through the golden tresses.

"I hate this," Pamela griped.

"Shut up!" Amanda admonished. "You must trust me, and do as I say. You're overdressed. It must appear as if something naughty happened, as if Michael behaved very badly."

Pamela's nightgown was a pristine, maidenly white, and Amanda grabbed it by the front and ripped it from top to bottom. Pamela shrieked and clutched at the fabric, as Amanda wrestled it away.

"Let go!" Amanda ordered.

"You didn't tell me I had to be naked!"

"Well, I'm telling you now."

Amanda gave a hard jerk, and Pamela stood, nude and shivering, an arm across her bosom, the other over her crotch. Amanda walked around, assessing her, evaluating the competition.

Pamela's body was different from Amanda's more mature one, but Michael would probably enjoy it. Her breasts were pert, her waist tucked, her hips flared. Her pussy, with its dusting of blond hair, was inviting, tempting, her chastity ripe for the plucking.

When Michael awoke, Amanda couldn't imagine him declining to feast. What sane man would forego an amenable, compliant virgin who'd crawled into his bed?

She grinned. Maybe the three of them would engage in some trysts, after all. It might be amusing to watch and assist while he sawed away between Pamela's immaculate thighs. Amanda would garner no small amount of satisfaction from holding Pamela down if she resisted.

Pamela was whimpering and quaking, her knees knocking, and Amanda fetched her bag, carrying in a jar of red cosmetic coloring. She daubed some of it on her finger, and clasped Pamela to her side, rubbing the crimson gel round and round Pamela's nipples. The tiny buds swelled and tightened, and the motion revolted Pamela, so Amanda kept on much longer than necessary.

"Why are you doing this to me?" Pamela sniveled.

"We're emphasizing your titties, which will heighten Michael's interest. He might even kiss you here."

"I'd die if he did!"

"You'll get used to it."

"Never!" Pamela claimed. "I never will."

Amanda's hand slithered down, and she caressed Pamela between her legs, even going so far as to push a finger into her wet, unsullied sheath. The deed was actually quite exciting, more erotic than Amanda could have envisioned, and it occurred to her that she might someday seduce Pamela, herself.

Why not? It could be very entertaining, and who was to prevent her?

"He might kiss you here, too," Amanda noted, stroking back and forth, as Pamela struggled to break free. "If he does, you're to lie peacefully quiet and allow him to proceed. In fact, you must permit him to attempt whatever he wishes."

"I won't let him!" Pamela mutinously stated.

Amanda shoved her away. "Do you want to be his wife or not? Or would you rather have him throw you out without a penny? I thought you were adult enough to go through with this, but if you're not . . ." Her sentence trailed off, and she shrugged as if the end result didn't matter to her either way. "I guess this was a mistake. You really are still a child, so we'd better call it off."

Pamela was torn, and she stared at Amanda, then Michael, then Amanda again. Ultimately, she shook her head. "No."

"Then stop arguing with me and climb up on the bed."

"All right."

Thoroughly cowed, Pamela complied, but she scooted around Michael, being careful not to connect with any anatomical parts, and Amanda observed in frustration. Pamela was stiff as a board, as unflirtatious as a rock. How would she ever pull this off?

"Snuggle yourself to him," Amanda directed.

"I don't want to touch him!"

"Oh, for bloody sake! Am I to do everything?"

Amanda crawled to her and rolled Pamela, posing her so that she looked as if she belonged next to him, instead of having been dropped in against her will.

"Your hand should be here." Amanda placed it on the center of his chest. "The instant someone comes in, you should be massaging in circles. You have to appear as if you're enjoying yourself, as if you've both done something you oughtn't. Can you figure out how to seem ecstatic and guilty at the same time?"

"I . . . I think so."

Amanda gripped Pamela's leg and draped it over Michael, and as she pressed Pamela's loins to his thigh, she took another moment to toy with Pamela's privates.

"Keep yourself spread wide," Amanda instructed. "This spot must be flattened to him."

"Quit mauling me!"

"I'm showing you what Michael will be doing on a

regular basis, but he'll be much more rough. All men are—as you're about to learn."

"I'll never succumb!" Pamela vowed.

"As if you'd have a choice!"

If Pamela wound up as his bride, poor Michael was in for a life of miserable connubial fornication, which would improve Amanda's predicament enormously. Michael liked his women to be wild and willing, and if Pamela was a whining, frigid nag, he would need the solace that only Amanda knew how to provide.

Amanda slid to the floor, more than ready to be finished with the entire sordid business.

"Where are you going?" Pamela demanded. "You can't mean to leave me alone with him."

"He's out cold. Haven't you noticed?"

"He might wake up."

"I'm planning on it."

"What if he does? What should I do?"

Her hysterics were beginning to grate, and Amanda prayed for patience. "I told you: You are to smile and do whatever he says."

"I don't have any clothes on!"

"Precisely."

As if the drug was wearing off, Michael stirred and groaned. Pamela yelped and leapt away, but Amanda dragged her over and repositioned her so that she was wrapped around him.

"He's coming to!" Pamela whispered. "What if he's angry?"

Amanda assessed Pamela, her shapely breasts, her sweet, lush puss. "Trust me: He might be a lot of things, but he won't be angry."

"But . . . but—"

"I can't wait with you," Amanda said, cutting her off. "I have some last-minute details to clear up. You absolutely can't depart until Miss Barnett sees you. If he rouses before I return, you have to remain with him, even if he attempts to be rid of you. Do you understand?"

Pamela gulped. "I understand."

"He'll be a tad groggy at first, and you need to convince him that you've been here for quite a while. We've rehearsed what you're to tell him."

"Yes."

"The same for Miss Barnett. Do you remember the words you're to utter when she enters?"

"Yes," she repeated.

"Good." Amanda nodded. "I'll be back with her as soon as I can. Try to look surprised. Try to look happy."

"I will."

Barnett should have heeded Amanda's warnings, but she'd refused to walk the wisest path, and for that, she would be so sorry. Amanda always got her way, and this situation would be no different.

~ 18 ~

"Are you going to place a bet or not?"

"I'm thinking; I'm thinking," Alex muttered as he glanced around the table. The other players weren't the sort who'd take his markers. If he mentioned Michael's name, and swore Michael would square any debt, they'd laugh, then proceed to mayhem.

Though he was out of money, he was positive he could win. He felt it deep in his bones. He had to recoup what he'd lost, but he was befuddled by drink, by lack of sleep and food, and couldn't make lucid judgments.

How had he come to be in the seedy establishment? Why was he wagering with such a rough crowd? Was it night? Or was it morning? The building had no windows, so he couldn't see outside.

"Well, mate," one of the gamblers asked, "what's it to be? In or out?"

"Out." Alex threw down his cards.

"You can use your pocket watch," the fellow cajoled. "Can't he, gents? Same as cash."

The others nodded in agreement, and there was an air about them that Alex didn't like. It dawned on him that they might have been cheating. At a time when his fingers were clumsy and his mind scrambled, they'd quickly stripped him of every cent.

"No." Michael had given him the watch on his eighteenth birthday. It was his prized possession. He could never part with it. "Thank you for the game."

He stood, when he noticed that he was blocked in. When had they shifted their chairs?

"I really like that watch," the dealer mentioned.

"Sorry, but you can't have it."

The man snickered, and an ominous frisson of fear trickled down Alex's spine. He'd soldiered with many despicable villains, had done things that would turn any sane man's stomach, so he wasn't afraid of much, but he was by himself, with no one to protect his flank.

His situation was precarious, his enemies having formed an impenetrable wall, so he took the only possible action. He grabbed the table, piled high with money, and tipped it over. Precious coins rolled everywhere, and tavern patrons hooted with glee and scooped them up.

"I'll kill you for that," the biggest man vowed, and together, they lunged.

Alex fought like a madman, but they kept attacking. He was hit and hit and hit. Eventually, one of them pulled a knife, which Alex dodged successfully through many wild swings, but not all of them.

The blade sunk into his chest. Blood squirted into the air, and he couldn't breathe. The room faded to black, and he crumpled to his knees, then fell to the floor. He tried to rise, but he couldn't move. Somebody rummaged through his pockets, while somebody else slipped his watch off its chain.

No one in the bar came to his aid, no one intervened, though from far away, he heard a male voice say, "Leave the poor sod alone. He's had enough trouble."

Alex was on his back and staring up at the ceiling. He was detached, serene, as if he were hovering over his torso and looking down on it from above. Vaguely, he wondered if he was dying, and he thought that he probably was. The ruffian's knife was firmly wedged, though strangely, he couldn't feel it. The wound was bleeding profusely, but there was no pain.

If Mary could see me, what would she think?

The gloomy reflection slithered by, but he couldn't focus on who Mary was or why she was important.

A tavern maid strolled by, the hem of her skirt brushing his battered face. She leaned down. "You still alive, love? Can't believe that ya are."

He concentrated hard so that he could inquire, "What day is it?"

"It's Saturday." She patted his hand and walked away, and he attempted to cry out to her. He was very cold, and very scared, and he didn't want her to go, but he couldn't form the necessary words. Not that she would have helped him. To her, he was just another drunk.

Resigned to his fate, he chuckled morosely. For such a long while, he'd been praying to die, had chased mortality with a reckless abandon, and now that his demise was imminent, he wished he'd pursued a different course. There was so much left unaccomplished, so many pleasures he hadn't enjoyed.

"Farewell," he murmured to no one in particular.

There was something he was supposed to do on Saturday, but he couldn't remember what it was. The room grew darker, the sounds fainter, and he shut his eyes.

Quiet and forlorn, Mary sat on the edge of the bed, her hips barely perched on the mattress. She was anxious to leap up and be on her way. Her traveling cloak was on and tied, her valise packed and resting by her feet. Her pulse hammered with equal amounts of dread and excitement.

Footsteps echoed in the hall, but she didn't react. In the past few hours, many people had been by. In the beginning, she'd jumped at the slightest noise, certain it would be Alex and that they would actually go to Scotland.

Since the night she'd pressed him for a marriage proposal, she hadn't seen him. At his initial absence, she'd been panicked, had agonized that she might have pushed him away, but as time had worn on, she'd convinced herself that he was having a last fling before tying the knot, or that he was finalizing plans for the journey north.

She'd been so sure of him. How could she have been so wrong?

Dejected and crestfallen, she rubbed her stomach, terrified that he might have planted a babe. While she'd advised him she wasn't increasing, she was starting to fret. Ordinarily, she was regular as the moon, but her monthlies were late, and the sole occasion it had occurred previously was when she'd been pregnant with Rose.

What if she was with child? How would she explain her condition?

If Alex didn't fetch her, as he'd promised, she'd never tell a soul who the father was, would never admit in a thousand years what a foolish, foolish sin she'd committed. She would take her secret to the grave.

A more fleet stride rushed down the hall, and momentarily, her daughter knocked. Mary kicked her valise under the bed.

"Come in," she said, and Rose entered.

"Hello, Mother." As usual, Rose was pleasant and merry. Though the lives of the adults in the residence swirled with misery, Rose had never been more contented. She loved the large mansion, the nursery, the servants, and especially her friend, Margaret.

"Are you ready for your trip?" Mary queried, though she could discern from the scent of Rose's clothes that she had on her coat and bonnet. Emily was escorting the girls to a fancy house party, with Rose invited as Margaret's companion.

"Yes," Rose answered, "and I can't wait to be off. We're to ride in the earl's coach-and-four!" She crossed over and sat next to Mary. "Are you ill, Mother?" Rose was very astute, and having a blind mother had made her too attentive, too sensitive to Mary's moods.

"No. Why would you ask?"

"You seem very sad."

"I'm fine."

"Are you going out?"

Rose was assessing Mary's cloak, her gloves. "I was about to walk in the garden," Mary fibbed, "but I guess I've changed my mind. I won't be going anywhere, after all."

"Are you lonely? Would you like me to stay home with you? I could, you know. It's no bother."

"No, no," Mary hastily replied. She couldn't have Rose hovering. Mary would need the next few days to

regroup, to make decisions and hide her enormous broken heart so that no one would ever discover how desperately she'd been wounded. "You go with your aunt
Emily and have fun."

"Are you positive?"

"Absolutely."

Mary kissed her on the cheek, and Rose hesitated,
torn between assisting her mother and enjoying her adventure, but ultimately, she stood.

"I'll miss you every second," Rose proclaimed.

"As will I you." Mary smiled, though it was tremulous
and difficult to hold. "You're a good girl, Rose. You always were."

"Thank you." Rose knelt and hugged Mary tightly as
she whispered, "Whatever it is, Mother, it will be all
right. I'm sure of it. Nothing bad can happen to us here.
Lord Winchester has been so kind, and Aunt Emily is so
happy. Don't worry."

"I won't. Now, when Emily summons you, you must
be prepared."

"I've been packed for hours!"

Mary chuckled. "Farewell, darling. Have a grand
holiday."

"I will."

Rose hesitated again, then left, apparently recognizing
that she couldn't fix what was wrong. Mary listened to her
go, and she murmured a short prayer for Rose's safety.

When Rose returned, how perilous would their situation be?

Mary was a smart, experienced widow, a middle-aged
parent. How could she have been so imprudent?

Abhorring the silence, the ambiguity, she went to the

window and gazed outside. She could smell the flowers in the yard, could hear the bees buzzing.

He wasn't coming.

With a lethal certainty, she knew it, and she had to face the facts. He'd never intended to marry her. He was the son of an earl, the brother of an earl, an army veteran, a war hero. He was a man of means and wealth, of status and station, but what was she?

She was a disabled invalid, who was indebted to others for the food she ate, the clothes she wore, the roof over her head. She was naught but a burden. Why would he assume such an obligation?

She'd been pathetic in her need to believe that he cared about her, but he hadn't. She'd merely been a method by which he could slake his lust. No matter how she tried to shine a better light on his conduct, no matter how she rationalized or justified, his interest had been no more simple or complex than that.

She yearned to hate him, to blame him, but she was an adult, and she'd raced to ruin of her own accord.

Oh, how she wanted to go home, to her modest, humble life in Hailsham. She would give anything—anything at all—to flee London and the despicable people she'd met, but how could she arrange it?

She hadn't a penny in her purse. She was powerless, dependent, alone.

Devastated, she sank into a chair. She closed her eyes and wept for all that was lost.

Emily rushed toward the dining parlor. She and Michael had loved till dawn, and she was exhausted and had overslept. Much too soon, it would be time to depart.

She wasn't anywhere near ready, and she hurried into the room, expecting it to be empty, expecting to grab a scone to nibble while she finished her preparations, but she skidded to a halt.

To her shock, horror, and fury, Amanda was at the table, attired in a revealing negligee and matching robe. Her blond hair was down, brushed out, and it fell around her shoulders in casual disarray.

She looked sexy, wanton, and desirable, in a fashion Emily never could have managed. She glanced up, and they studied each other, their mutual loathing blatant, and Emily was so stunned that she couldn't think of what to say.

If Amanda had owned the accursed mansion, she couldn't have been more at ease, and it was obvious that this was not her first meal in the spot. She was too comfortable, too relaxed.

Amanda frowned and inquired, "Are you still here? I thought you'd gone."

Emily sputtered for a reply and finally countered with, "What are you doing in this house? Go at once."

Amanda ignored her edict and continued eating. "I'd have you join me, but I don't dine with the hired help. I suggest you retire to the kitchen where you belong."

Emily couldn't decide what to do. What was her authority?

She stomped to the hall and shouted, "Mr. Fitch, I need you."

Fitch eventually appeared. "Yes, Miss Barnett? What is it?"

Emily pointed to Amanda. "Amanda is on the premises."

"I see that." He was calm, unperturbed by the tidings. "Good morning, Miss Amanda."

"Good morning, Fitch." Amanda shrugged as if she couldn't comprehend why Emily was creating an uproar, and Fitch glared at Emily as if she were mad.

"I hate to be blunt, Miss Barnett," he counseled, "but you're relatively new to your position, so it seems you're confused. Amanda often *visits*. She has her own room upstairs. It's connected to the earl's. I must remind you that we're servants, and it's not my place—or yours—to worry about how they carry on."

Emily was appalled to learn that Amanda utilized the chamber next to Michael's. She hadn't realized how ensconced Amanda was in Michael's life, hadn't grasped the full ramifications of their relationship.

He'd left Emily's bed a few hours earlier. Since then, what had he been doing? She'd considered their romantic interlude to have quelled her doubts as to his affection, but suddenly, she was more perplexed than ever.

She ventured to Fitch, "Has Lord Winchester advised you that it's all right?"

"Why would any instruction from him be necessary?"

"Would you ask him for me?"

"I wouldn't presume to wake him with such a frivolous question."

"Frivolous? But his . . . his mistress is here, and so am I." Without further clarification, the statement sounded idiotic. She couldn't blurt out that she and Michael were involved in a torrid affair, that she loved him and was crushed over this horrid turn of events.

Fitch was untroubled by Amanda's abrupt arrival, and a niggling suspicion occurred to Emily: Perhaps this wasn't *abrupt*. Perhaps Amanda had been sneaking in all along.

Unless Michael had given Amanda permission to enter, she would never have risked so much, would she? Oh, what was the truth? There were so many ways Emily felt betrayed, but she couldn't announce that Michael was hers.

"As I explained, Miss Barnett," Fitch was saying, "Amanda's presence is none of our concern."

"But . . . but—"

Amanda interrupted. "Fitch, I awoke so late. Would you see if Cook has a minute to whip up some of those special eggs I enjoy?"

"She'll be more than happy to fix them for you. I'll talk to her immediately."

He exited, leaving them alone, and a dangerous silence festered. Emily knew that Amanda was trying to rattle her, but she stood her ground.

"Begone," Emily demanded, "or I swear to God, I will march upstairs and notify Michael, myself."

"I dare you."

"You can't be parading around so scantily dressed! The girls are about to come down. We're off to a party, and they'll be in any second."

"I wouldn't count on it," Amanda retorted. "Not Pamela anyway."

Emily's ears began to ring, her pulse to pound. "What do you mean?"

"I warned you. It was for your own good. You should have listened."

"You *warned* me about what?"

"About Michael and his budding interest in Pamela. Have you spoken with her this morning?"

Emily had been to Pamela's room, but Pamela hadn't been there, and her bed was neat and tidy as if it hadn't been used, but Emily lied. "Yes, and I expect she'll be down at any moment."

"There's no hope for it." Amanda sighed. "I guess I'll have to show you." She threw her napkin on her plate and rose. "Shall we go up together?"

Without waiting for Emily's response, Amanda swept by and proceeded into the hall, her perfume wafting behind like a poisonous cloud. As if mesmerized, Emily followed. For some reason, she couldn't stand up to Amanda, couldn't protest or wrest control of the situation from her. She could only tag after her like a puppet on a string.

What were they about to find? With every fiber of her being, Emily recognized that she didn't want to be apprised of the answer. They swiftly climbed the stairs to Michael's door.

"Shall we knock?" Amanda queried. "Or shall we walk in and surprise them?"

Emily started to tremble, and she backed away, too distraught to witness whatever was transpiring.

"No . . . no . . . I don't wish to . . . I can't bear it. . . ."

"You won't be convinced until you see for yourself."

Amanda seized Emily's wrist and dragged her inside and over to the bed.

Michael was blissfully asleep. His clothes were off, except for his trousers, which were around his flanks, as if he'd been in too much of a hurry to remove them.

Emily recollected the numerous occasions Michael had done the same with her, when he'd been too impatient to bother with disrobing.

A wanton, rumpled—naked!—Pamela was snuggled to him, her blond hair down, her young, lithe body draped across his. She rubbed his chest, as if she was intimately familiar with it, as if she'd touched him thus many times previous.

"Look, Emily," Amanda commanded, clutching Emily's arm so she couldn't wrestle free. "Look at your dear Lord Winchester."

"Oh my God! Oh my God!" Emily murmured over and over. It was the sole remark she could utter.

"Miss Barnett!" Pamela barked. "We're *involved* here. Do you mind?"

There were a thousand replies Emily could have made, but what was the point? Mr. Fitch had elucidated what Emily had forgotten: She was a servant in the house. It was a truth she hadn't been able to face, a reality she'd declined to accept.

Michael Farrow was the lord of the manor, a sort of powerful, autonomous god, who could do whatever he wanted to whomever he wanted. Emily had intrigued him, had fascinated him, and he'd trifled with her, but it had never been more than that.

Had she amused him? Had he been entertained?

How could she have been so blind? So stupid?

"I brought Pamela to him," Amanda was whispering. "I helped him arouse her. I held her down while he took her virginity."

"Be silent!" Emily pleaded.

"After we finished, he complimented me on how erotic

it had been, and he promised me a bonus for pleasing him." She paused to heighten the impact of her words. "It was the three of us, Emily. Together. Can you picture it?"

Emily lurched away, so off balance that she nearly fell, and she gripped the mattress to right herself. He'd been her world, her sun, her moon, and she was aghast, wounded to her very core. If he'd pulled out a pistol and shot her, the damage couldn't have been any more painful.

"Michael, oh, Michael," she keened, but he didn't stir. "How could you? I loved you," she shamed herself by admitting. "I would have done anything for you."

"Would you have?" Amanda prodded. "What if, for his next romp, he decides on a threesome with you and Pamela? Could you oblige him? Or what if he insists you do it with me? Could you refuse? He is *Earl* of Winchester, after all, and he's not terribly gracious when rebuffed."

Emily heard an odd cracking noise, and it had to be her heart breaking. "No, I never could. I'm not one of you. I don't belong here."

"No, you don't," Amanda concurred. "Go home, Emily. There must be someone who misses you, someone who will take you in."

Pamela stretched like a lazy cat. "He's mine, Miss Barnett. He wanted *me*. Not you. How could you not have known?"

Pamela began to cackle, then laugh, until she was quaking with mirth. Amanda joined in, the timbre of their voices jarring, how a gaggle of demons might sound.

Emily spun away and raced for the door. A crowd of servants had gathered in the corridor, and they were craning their necks and muttering in disgust. Even though

Cheryl Holt

they'd observed many ignominies under Winchester's roof, the sight was beyond deplorable. No doubt, the scandal would spread across London, from kitchen to kitchen, before the hour was through.

The Earl of Winchester was about to wed, but his countess wouldn't be Emily Barnett. She'd been such a fool, such a dreamer.

She shoved through the surly group, ignoring their snide comments, their condemning glances. She didn't care about any of them, and she was desperate to be away. Away from them and London and Michael Farrow.

She was from a small village and didn't understand the ways of people in the city, hadn't the strength to endure what was required. She didn't comprehend the members of the Quality, shouldn't have immersed herself in their society, shouldn't have reached so far above her station. She wanted her quiet life back, wanted to return to her simple existence, where she'd grasped the rules by which to conduct herself.

She'd been a good person once, had been virtuous and respectable, decent and principled. She hoped to be that woman again.

Eager to pack her bags, she ran to the stairs and dashed to her room.

~ 19 ~

Michael opened his eyes and groaned. His head throbbed, his ears rang, and though he didn't recall drinking much the night before, he was suffering from the worst hangover he'd ever experienced. He could feel the blankets on his bare skin. When had he undressed? When had he crawled into bed?

He lay very still, staring up at the ceiling and struggling to recollect the prior evening. He'd spent many divine hours with Emily, then he'd returned to his room, and . . . and . . .

Amanda had been waiting for him. They'd chatted, and he'd had some brandy. What else? He shuddered. A vision flashed of her going down on him, of her sucking him off.

Had it actually transpired? Would he have let her? He didn't know.

Suddenly, it dawned on him that he wasn't alone. He peeked to the side and was stunned to see a very naked, very rumpled Amanda curled next to him. Her presence was unexpected, but hardly a surprise. He'd passed out next to her on many occasions, though he couldn't fathom why he'd have perpetrated such a betrayal on Emily.

He . . . he loved Emily. Yes, he did. The splendid notion blossomed in his chest, and he was disgusted with himself. Had he any morals? Any integrity? Was there a shred of decency remaining? Or had it fled during his years of debauchery and vice?

"Hello, darling," Amanda purred. "I didn't think you would ever wake up."

"What time is it?" he asked, terrified by the probable answer, because it had to be very late. From the shadows out the window, clearly it was no longer morning. The maids would have been gossiping, and he couldn't risk that the rumors might make their way to Emily.

"I suppose it's the middle of the afternoon," she stated, not sure herself. "You wore us out."

At almost the same moment, he sensed that someone else was on the other side of him. Someone who was also naked. The individual was definitely a female. Praise be! Her breasts were flattened to his back, an arm across his waist, a thigh across his leg.

He had to roll over, had to discover who was with them, but he was too horrified to look. "What happened?"

"Don't you remember?" Amanda chuckled, raised up, and peered over him to the third person in the bed. "How could he forget, hmm?"

"It was fabulous, Michael," a very young and very familiar voice gushed. "I never dreamed it could be like this between a man and a woman."

Not able to avoid the inevitable, he glanced at Pamela. His friend's daughter. His ward. Emily's charge.

Oh, God! What have I done?

He shifted so that he was straight as a board, and he tried not to touch any bodily parts, but he was wedged tight. There wasn't sufficient space to evade either one.

He closed his eyes, took a deep breath, then opened them again. He'd hoped Pamela would have vanished, but she was really there. She gave him a tremulous smile.

"I've wanted this for an eternity," she claimed.

"Pamela?" he croaked. "How . . . when . . ."

Amanda butted in. "You demanded that I bring her to you so that the three of us could revel. You insisted."

He had an elusive memory of Pamela's name being mentioned, of Amanda talking about the girl, but he couldn't have agreed to such a ghastly indiscretion. He had many faults, extreme misbehavior being common, but he'd never previously attempted anything quite so foul.

"I said that *I* was anxious for the three of us to dally?"

"Yes. Pamela was interested. You were interested. Why not?"

He couldn't believe what he was hearing, but his brain was so muddled that he couldn't sort it out. They had to be lying, but why would they? Why would Pamela involve herself in such an absurd deception? Why would Amanda help her?

He studied Amanda, then Pamela, then Amanda, searching for a hint of treachery, an indication that mischief was afoot, but they both gazed back with innocent expressions.

He was bewildered as to what had occurred, and he had to get Pamela out of his room, and into her own, before she was spotted. His employees had witnessed him committing many sins, but he didn't imagine they'd ignore this one, or that they'd keep silent.

If stories were spread, he would have to marry Pamela, and he couldn't conceive of a more distasteful fate. Offering up a quick prayer, he questioned, "Have any of the servants been in?"

"Several of them, but I wouldn't let them rouse you." Amanda smirked. "It was hilarious to have them so shocked. The governess nearly fainted."

His heart raced. "Miss Barnett saw us?"

"Oh, yes." Amanda giggled. "The look on her face was priceless."

Pamela cooed, "I'm so glad I won't have to spend the week with her, that I can spend it with you instead."

What must Emily have thought? Where was she? What was she doing?

Oh, Emily, he wailed inwardly, *I'm so sorry. So very, very sorry.*

He had to find her, had to explain, but even as the frantic notion flitted by, he knew that she would never speak to him again. And why should she?

He was an unprincipled villain. There was no way he could convince her otherwise, no way he could make this right.

She was lost to him. Lost forever.

"Would the two of you excuse me?" He was desperate to be alone and truly wondering if he might retch. He felt ill, poisoned, as if his brandy had been tainted.

"But we need to begin planning," Pamela whined. "What about the wedding?"

"The wedding?" He must have seemed stricken, because she hurried on.

"You promised we would!" She peered at Amanda. "Didn't he promise, Amanda?"

Amanda appeared humored, and she shrugged. "You swore to it."

"The servants watched us and everything," Pamela complained. "You can't refuse. What would people say?"

He moaned, and his head hammered so ferociously that he worried the top of his skull might blow off. He glared at Amanda and mouthed, *Get her out of here. Now!*

For once, Amanda didn't argue. "Pamela"—she sat up—"let's retire to my boudoir and ring for a bath."

"I don't wish to leave," the recalcitrant girl declared. "I want to stay with Michael."

"He's not well," Amanda pointed out. "You know how unpleasant a man can be when he's been in his cups. When your father was hungover, he was a veritable beast. Michael desires privacy so he can freshen up."

Pamela bristled. "I won't have you bossing me about, Amanda. I'll go only if Michael asks it of me."

They stared, eager for his response, and Michael yearned to shake them both. In his miserable condition, he couldn't abide any bickering.

"Why don't you go with Amanda?" he requested. "We'll talk later."

"When?" Pamela pressed.

"Give me an hour. I'll meet you in the library."

"Will we pick the wedding date?"

"Yes, Pamela, we'll pick the date."

"We can't delay," she needled. "We should obtain a Special License so that we can hold the ceremony tomorrow."

His stomach knotted and heaved, and it was all he could do to keep from vomiting. "We'll discuss it downstairs."

Shimmering with triumph, Pamela rolled off the mattress. As she tugged on her robe, he caught sight of her appealing figure, and he tried to remember fornicating with her.

Even a very drunken man would recollect such a tempting treat. Wouldn't he? Yet no flicker of memory leapt to the fore. Had he deflowered her? Or was she still a virgin?

There was no maiden's blood on her thighs, none on his phallus, and he had no idea how to probe for the squalid details.

He sighed. He wasn't a saint, and when he was urged on by an abundance of liquor, he'd frequently demonstrated himself to be capable of any abomination. Over the years, he'd established, time and again, that he had no self-control. Pamela was living proof of how reckless he could be.

She leaned over and gave him an awkward kiss on the mouth. He suffered through it, not reacting or reaching out to her, but she didn't seem to notice or mind that he failed to participate.

"I'll see you in a few minutes," she chirped.

"Yes, you will."

Proud as a peacock, she strutted out, and after she exited, Amanda murmured, "Well . . . that was interesting."

"Did I have sex with her?" he queried. "For that matter, did I have sex with you?"

"What do you think?"

"Did I?"

"Are you telling me you genuinely can't recall? Honestly! It was rather sordid."

"Go away," he snarled, on the verge of strangling her.

"Will you really marry her?"

"Just go away!"

"Aren't we in a foul mood?" she snapped. "Don't blame me because you can't keep your trousers buttoned. This predicament is hardly my fault."

"Amanda! Have mercy on me! Please!"

Pamela poked her nose through the door. "Amanda, are you coming or not?"

At Pamela's audacity, Amanda was furious, and she huffed, "I'll join you shortly."

"I'm not about to leave you in here with my fiancé!" Pamela nagged. "Cease your prattling—immediately!—and attend me at my bath."

Amanda growled and stomped off to lock horns, and Michael was left in a blessed, welcomed silence. He gazed at the ceiling again, wishing he could vanish, wishing he could magically turn back the clocks so that he could redo the entire episode.

How had he landed himself in such a quagmire?

He couldn't wed Pamela! She was too young, too immature, while he was . . . was . . . He couldn't describe what he was. How could he, in good conscience, bind her to him? Yet what other choice did he have?

He fought down an urge to howl at the top of his lungs.

"What do you have to say for yourself?"

Reginald tipped his chair onto the two hind legs and studied Emily with cool disdain. She, along with her sister and niece, had shown up on his stoop in the middle of the night, the trio having homed in on his residence like a gaggle of geese on its homeward migration. He hadn't been able to refuse them refuge, though a less desperate man certainly would have.

He smirked. His patience had won out. She would be his. The inheritance would be his. He yearned to shake his fist in the air, to revel in his victory. She'd never understood her place, but she would soon learn it. He would be her lord and master, and she would submit to him as his dutiful and obedient wife.

Visibly nervous, she wrung her hands. "I'm sorry I went to London."

"Is that the best you can do?" he scoffed and assessed her. Her respirations were elevated, her breasts working against her corset, their pert shape clearly outlined.

He'd waited forever to see them, to touch them, to suckle them as he often observed in the indecent pictures he bought from his traveling peddler. Merely from pondering the images his phallus swelled to a painful length, and he was glad he was sitting behind the desk so that his bodily response was hidden.

How sweet his wedding night would be! He would tie her to the bedposts, would beat her for the humiliation she'd inflicted. The vision of her, shackled and forced to do his bidding, had his phallus enlarging even further.

"What else would you like me to say?" She was acting as if she had no atonement to make, when Reginald planned for her to spend the remainder of her life doing penance.

"I would like a sincere apology."

"All right," she said. "I apologize."

"And . . . ?"

"I hope you'll let us stay."

"Only if we marry."

At hearing his comment, she looked as if she'd bitten into a rotten egg. "Of course."

His temper flared. She'd had her adventure in London, had foolishly cavorted with her betters, but she still assumed herself superior to him. He rose and rounded his desk, and he towered over her. She glared at him, not cowed in the least by his position or authority, and he grew even more angry.

"You have nowhere else to go," he stated.

"No," she admitted, "I don't."

"If I toss you out, you'll be lucky to find shelter at the poorhouse."

"I'm sure you're correct."

"Yet you have the temerity to face me as if *I* am the wrongdoer."

"What is it you want from me, Reginald?"

"I want you to beg," he seethed. "Get down on your knees."

"No. I'll do whatever you ask, but you must promise you won't send Mary away. Give me your word."

She had the gall to make demands? To issue ultimatums?

"You betrayed me. You deceived me."

"No, Reginald," she claimed. "I've done nothing to
you."

She was so haughty, so proud, and he walked around
her in a slow circle. Like a brave soldier about to be disciplined, she stared straight ahead, resigned that the ax
was about to fall.

Vividly, he remembered every second of the degrading encounter in Winchester's parlor. Reginald would
never forgive her for the shame he'd endured on being
evicted from the earl's mansion. If she lived to be a
thousand, Emily would pay for the disgrace each and
every day.

"Answer one question for me," he commanded.

"If I am able."

"Are you still a virgin?"

"Reginald!"

"Are you?" he shouted.

She blushed bright red, and he couldn't decide if she
was embarrassed by the intimate query or if she was a
whore. He was paralyzed by the possibility of her being
seduced by Winchester. It was like a fetid wound, and he
couldn't let it go, but he wasn't positive how to verbally
probe for the facts.

He knew about the physical aspects, about the blood
and the tearing, so there were ways to become apprised
later on, but if, after he'd married her, he discovered that
he'd been duped, he would kill her, and there wasn't a
man in England who would blame him.

In the interim, he had to have a denial from her own

lips. Her perfidious, devious tongue would have to soothe his torment.

"I would have the truth," he insisted.

"There's naught to tell."

"Liar," he hissed, and he slapped her as hard as he could. Stunned by the ferocity of the moment, she lurched to the side and tumbled to her knees.

As far as he was aware, Emily had never been hit before. She'd been pampered and coddled, and in an instant, he discerned a fascinating component to his character: He relished the violence, relished how he felt powerful and omnipotent, how she cowered and cringed.

He hovered over her, where she was crouched on the rug, and he grabbed her by the neck and shook her as if she were a misbehaving dog.

"Where is your fancy *lord* now, Emily? There's no one to help you, no one to rise to your defense."

"No, there's no one," she concurred.

"You thought you were so high-and-mighty, snubbing me to impress *him*. How dare you!"

"I didn't mean to hurt you!"

"Beg me," he raged. "Beg me to permit you to stay."

"Please!" She was gasping, clawing at his fingers as he squeezed her throat. Her arrogance had finally fled. "Let me stay."

"Swear to me that it's for Mary and Rose, that you want nothing for yourself."

"Absolutely," she agreed. "I don't need anything for myself."

"You will be a respectful and acquiescent wife, and you will submit to me in all matters."

"I will," she agreed again.

He shoved her away, hating to be in her presence, to be fretting over how she might have been disloyal. She scrambled out of reach, weeping and adjusting her dress, and he reveled in her dishabille, in her terror and confusion.

This was how he wanted her—under his control, groveling, isolated, scared.

"Yes, Emily," he hurled, "we shall marry. I will speak with the vicar this afternoon about calling the banns, once more. But," he threatened, "you've made a devil's bargain. If you ever refuse to do as you are told, Mary will be locked away in an asylum. I guarantee it."

With a wail of despair, she clambered to her feet and ran out. He watched her go, and he chuckled, elated with how he'd bested her. In the future, she couldn't defy him, and she knew it. She was out of options.

He was aroused, his phallus rigid and aching, and he pushed at the placard of his pants, wishing he'd taken their relationship to the next level. When she'd been huddled on the floor, he could have raped her. Why hadn't he?

When dealing with her, he couldn't be timid. She had to constantly be shown who was boss. But then, the longer he delayed, the more satisfying her capitulation, the greater his reward.

The altercation had him eager to look at his naughty books, to touch himself and relieve the tension she'd induced. He especially liked the drawings of the auburn-haired harlots. He liked to gaze at them and pretend they were Emily, that he was witnessing the things he would eventually do to her.

He proceeded to his room, where he closed and barred the door. He opened the trunk at the end of his bed, and he pulled out his favorite envelope of pictures, of women being flogged, of women being ravished and tortured.

Emily's room was down the hall. She was alone, unprotected, with nowhere to hide.

He smiled and unbuttoned his trousers, his hand on his cock, and—slowly, rhythmically—he began to stroke. Soon, very soon, Emily would be performing the task for him, and he couldn't wait for her lessons to commence.

∾ 20 ∾

Margaret Martin huddled in the shadows and peeked through the door into her sister's room. Pamela had just stormed in, and Amanda Lambert had followed. Though it was the middle of the afternoon, they were in their nightclothes, and Margaret wanted to find out why.

Many peculiar events had occurred throughout the day, and though she kept asking for answers, no one would tell her what had happened. The trip to the country had been abruptly cancelled. The servants were aflutter with gossip. Miss Barnett had fled, taking Rose with her, and Margaret couldn't bear that her friend had left without so much as a farewell.

It was obvious that Pamela was up to no good. She thrived on causing trouble, and from the beginning, she'd resolved to be shed of Miss Barnett, but what had Pamela done? She had to be in league with Miss Lambert, and if she was, then turmoil was brewing, and Margaret was determined to unravel their scheme.

"I can't believe how well your plan worked," Pamela

said, and she grinned. "The stupid oaf bought every word, hook, line, and sinker."

"Of course, he did," Amanda boasted. "How could you have doubted me? I've been Michael's lover for years. I know how to handle him."

Margaret bristled. If Pamela had hurt Lord Winchester, Margaret would wring her neck.

"There at the end," Pamela mentioned, "he didn't look as if he was feeling very spry. He was white as a ghost."

"The drug I administered has that effect."

A drug? They'd given Lord Winchester a drug?

Margaret was so angry, she nearly burst in to demand an explanation, but she held herself still, anxious to hear more.

"Or maybe," Pamela interjected, "the concept of tying the knot was so distressing that he was ill. He brags about being the consummate bachelor."

"I wouldn't count on his marrying you," Amanda replied.

Lord Winchester was to wed Pamela? How could that be? Margaret was astonished. They must have tricked him.

"And why shouldn't I?" Pamela queried. "The servants saw what transpired. The sordid story is probably all over London by now."

"Yes, but he didn't actually do anything to you."

"*He* assumes he did." Pamela chuckled.

"Well, don't be too confident," Amanda chided. "He'll wiggle out of the trap we set."

"What do you mean?"

Amanda scoffed. "He'll never marry you."

"That's what you think."

"That's what I know."

A fit of temper swept over Pamela. She had violent mood swings, and though Miss Lambert was older and taller, she had no idea how furious Pamela could become. Should Pamela fly into a rage, Miss Lambert would be no match for her.

"Don't presume to lecture me," Pamela warned. "I am about to be the Countess of Winchester, and you cross me at your peril."

"Foolish girl," Amanda needled. "If not for me, you wouldn't have had the faintest notion of how to crawl into his bed, and if you suppose that you're on some fast road to matrimony, you're out of your mind."

"Listen, you aging hussy." Pamela grabbed Miss Lambert by the hair, yanking so hard that Amanda shrieked. "Your opinions have ceased to matter in this house. I've landed the best possible position for myself, so I no longer have to tolerate your presence." She shoved Miss Lambert away. "Get out of my sight."

"Michael is mine." Miss Lambert pushed Pamela back. "He will always be mine."

"As I'm about to have a ring on my finger, I'd say you're suffering from insane delusions."

Miss Lambert growled like a rabid dog and charged at Pamela. Pamela leapt to the side and seized a heavy candleholder, and she brought it down on Miss Lambert's temple. It was a glancing blow, so it didn't draw blood, but Margaret was frightened by the attack, and she gasped aloud.

Both women halted.

"Who's there?" Pamela whipped around to peer through the crack in the door. "Margaret! Is that you?"

Pamela lunged toward the spot where Margaret was hiding, so Margaret spun away and ran.

"How many left my employ?"

Michael sat at his desk and glared at Fitch. A bath, a clean suit of clothes, and numerous shots of whiskey hadn't helped in the slightest. His head was pounding, his stomach queasy, and he was dizzy and grouchy.

"Ten," Fitch responded. "The men didn't care, but the women were quite shocked. So we're short of maids, and I'll need to begin interviewing."

Michael's disgusting romp had been too much for his female workers. Several of them had donned their coats and walked out. "Could you convince them to reconsider?"

"I could try, but I doubt I'd succeed. They were extremely offended."

Michael sighed. Could the vile day get any worse? "Why are you still here? Aren't you ready to stomp out in a huff?"

"With all due respect, milord," Fitch bravely proclaimed, "there's very little you could do that would surprise me."

"A low blow, Fitch."

"Yes, it was, sir. My apologies."

"I imagine I'll survive."

"If I may point out, sir, Miss Pamela is a tad young."

"Isn't she, though?"

"I believe that's what upset most of the ladies. The others, who've agreed to stay, were wondering if there's to be a wedding."

Pamela had no one to speak for her, no father or brother to demand reparation. Michael wanted to shout *no*, but he'd stepped so far over the line of what was allowed that he had to pay the price for his reprehensible conduct.

"Yes, Fitch, you may assure them that wedding bells are about to chime."

"Very good, sir. They will be relieved to hear it."

Fitch started to go, but Michael stopped him. "May I ask you a question, Fitch?"

"Certainly."

"I was informed that many members of the staff saw me when I was . . . when we were . . ." He was too ashamed to complete the sentence. "Were you one of them?"

"No, but Housekeeper was. It took all my persuasive abilities to keep her with us."

"How about Miss Barnett?"

"She was gravely disturbed. She, and her sister and niece, packed their bags and fled about thirty minutes after the incident."

So . . . she'd gone. He'd been curious. He'd sensed her absence, but it was awkward to inquire without his interest seeming heightened and inappropriate. "Could we prevail upon her to return?"

"May I be blunt?"

"Please."

"Not a chance in hell."

"I owe her some salary. Do you have any idea of where they went?"

"I'm told that they proceeded to the village from whence they'd come."

"Hailsham?"

"I don't know the name of it, sir."

He thought of her scurrying home, of her having to beg her cousin to take her in, and couldn't bear that he'd driven her to such a dire fate. Would she marry her cousin? If Barnett refused her shelter, what would become of her?

She was devoted to her family's safety, and he couldn't have her living on the streets, nor could he stand by and have her forced into matrimony. In light of his abundant transgressions, he owed her the opportunity to build her own life, to be free of her cousin so she could make her own way.

"I need you to ascertain her whereabouts," Michael said. "I'll write her a note and enclose a bank draft. Have it sent as soon as you locate her."

"I will. Will there be anything else?"

"Is there any news from my brother?"

"Not a word."

Michael bit off an epithet. With disaster falling around him, he couldn't be worrying about Alex. Where was the blasted man? What could he be doing that would occupy him for so long?

"Miss Pamela will be down shortly," Michael explained. "I'll chat with her; then I'm to be left alone for the rest of the evening."

"As you wish."

"And, Fitch?"

"Yes?"

"If you ever catch Amanda in the house again, I don't care what she tells you, I don't want her here. Escort her out. If need be, you may fetch me, and I'll assist you in tossing her into the yard."

"It will be my pleasure."

Fitch exited, and Michael stared at the wall, trying to deduce how he'd tumbled into such a dreadful predicament. He had no one to blame but himself, yet oh, how it grated! He'd been snared like a rabbit in a trap.

His only hope was that Emily was so far away from London that she would never be apprised of any town gossip, that she would never learn of his marriage. After how he'd abused her, he was determined to save her that heartbreak.

He pulled out a sheet of paper, dipped his pen, and composed the letter. It took numerous attempts to figure out the correct tone. He'd never advised her as to how he truly felt about her, and at this terrible juncture, it was too late. She wouldn't believe him anyhow, but he was anxious that she have the money.

With her being so proud and independent, she might decline just on general principles, so he had to convince her to use it for her family but to ignore the source.

He was dabbing wax to seal the envelope as Fitch ushered in Pamela. She was smug and gleefully strutting around. Had she set her sights on him from the beginning? Had Amanda put her up to it?

He couldn't abandon the impression that they'd duped him, yet he couldn't imagine Amanda befriending Pamela, couldn't fathom why Amanda would do Pamela any favors.

She dropped into a chair and barked, "Fix me a brandy, will you, Fitch?"

At the request, Fitch was shocked, and he glanced at Michael, wondering if he should. Michael nodded. Pamela was about to be a married woman. They had to stop treating her as if she was a child.

Fitch poured her two fingers, and when he offered her the glass, she scoffed at the small amount. "Don't be cheap with Michael's liquor, Fitch," she scolded. "He has plenty more."

Fitch filled the glass to the rim, and Pamela was satisfied. She sipped the strong brew as if she was in the habit of imbibing hard spirits.

Michael sighed again. Was he about to bind himself to an adolescent sot?

Without preamble, she asked, "Have you obtained the Special License?"

"I'll start on it tomorrow. My solicitor will seek an appointment with the Archbishop. It may take several days." How he prayed that it would! Perhaps an immediate and generous contribution to his local parish would guarantee a lengthy delay.

"Pity," she purred. "I wanted to have it accomplished as quickly as possible."

"I'll bet you did."

The encounter was so strange, the concept of wedding her so absurd. Shouldn't they be discussing important aspects like how many children they would have or how they would carry on? Shouldn't he propose? Shouldn't she accept? Shouldn't there be a ring? An announcement?

As if it was a *fait accompli,* the formalities seemed unnecessary, but when it was such a monumental jump for him it was too casual, too slapdash.

"What about an allowance?" she prodded. "How much can I spend?"

Hadn't he provided her with everything she'd expected from the moment she'd moved in? "What do you need to buy?"

"A bride must have all sorts of clothes. A wedding dress. A trousseau. Now that I'm about to be a countess, I can't look like a pauper."

What a mercenary! They'd been engaged for a few hours, and she already had her hand in his wallet. "We wouldn't want that, would we?"

"No," she agreed, not realizing that he'd been sarcastic. "What would people say?"

"What, indeed?"

He studied her, curious as to what was going on in her sixteen-year-old head. Staring intently, he tried to rattle her, but she was a cool customer and couldn't be cowed.

"Are you positive you wish to go through with this?" he couldn't help inquiring.

"Of course. Why wouldn't I?"

"Have you considered what it will be like being married to me?"

"Actually, I've been thinking about it for ages."

"You have?"

"Yes. I'm about to receive all that I desire."

"Which is?"

"Money, position, notoriety. What would you suppose?"

She was smarter than he'd given her credit for being, more shrewd than he'd assumed. Emily had insisted that Pamela was a vixen and a schemer, but Michael had rebuffed her assessment of Pamela's character.

Emily had been correct. Too bad that he'd had to arrive at such a horrid place before he'd heeded her warnings.

"I'll have my secretary arrange accounts for you."

"Thank you."

"You may charge whatever tickles your fancy."

"Fabulous." She stood to go. "Let me know when the special license is prepared. I've hired an artist to design the invitations."

"Isn't that a bit fast?"

"Is there any reason to dawdle?"

As this was a disaster waiting to happen, he could conjure up a thousand reasons to defer the nuptials, but she was too bent on matrimony, and after what he'd done, he had no right to refuse.

"None at all," he concurred.

"There is another matter I'd like you to handle."

"What's that?"

"As this is my home, and I'll soon be your wife, I shouldn't have to suffer Amanda's presence. I demand that you bar her from the premises."

She swept out, her remark destroying any suspicion he'd harbored that Amanda and Pamela were conspirators. He listened to her footsteps as she whisked down the hall, and he tried to envision himself joined to her, tried to envision himself introducing her as his bride.

It was such a ludicrous notion that he couldn't get it to gel, and it occurred to him that he couldn't continue to reside in the mansion. He couldn't share a house with her. She was a stranger, one he didn't like and didn't care to know any better.

He had to escape, and he decided to dump the entire debacle into the laps of his attorneys. He'd party up the town, would drink till he couldn't see straight, and when the details were finalized, he'd appear for the ceremony.

You'll have to consummate the union, a niggling voice scolded. The very thought made him ill.

He rose to leave, when Fitch hurried in, his expression frantic.

"It's your brother, sir."

"What's wrong?"

"He's dying. You must go to him at once."

"Dying?"

"He was in a fight. There's a messenger. He brought you this note. . . ." Unable to explain further, he waved a piece of paper. Michael was already racing by and shouting directions as he went.

"My horse, Fitch," he commanded. "Have it saddled. And summon the doctor so that he's here when I return."

He ran toward the door, not pausing to don his coat, when Margaret popped out of nowhere and slipped her small hand into his.

In the chaos, he'd forgotten about her, hadn't spoken with her to clarify what was transpiring.

"Lord Winchester, I need to ask you a question."

He yanked away. "I haven't time, Margaret."

"But it's dreadfully important. When may I have a moment?"

As usual, she was incredibly polite, but he was too distraught for civility.

"Not now, Margaret!" he snapped, and the hurt look on her face was so colossal that he halted and dropped to his knee. "I apologize, darling, but my brother, Alex, is in trouble. I must rush to his aid. Immediately."

"I understand," she said. "Don't let me detain you."

She gazed at him, her big blue eyes pleading, and he felt like the lowest sort of vermin. In dealing with her, he was so out of his element, had never known what to say or how to act, and he was reminded of why it was for the best that he'd never fathered any children. She presumed he was someone he wasn't, much as Emily had before she'd learned the truth.

Would he disappoint Margaret as he had Emily? Margaret was about to be his sister. How long would it take to shatter her illusions?

"The minute I'm back, we'll talk," he promised. "We'll talk all night if you wish."

"All right."

He dashed out, and it seemed that she murmured, "I hope it's not too late by then," but he kept going.

Pamela strolled down the hall, pretending to have no destination, when in reality, she was on a mission. Michael had fled and hadn't had the courtesy to inform her. The corridors were quiet, the servants at supper.

She peeked into every room, eager to stumble upon Margaret. She hadn't found the girl yet, but when she did, she'd make her so sorry.

How dare she eavesdrop! There was no telling how much she'd overheard, and Pamela couldn't risk that Margaret would tattle to Michael. Pamela was determined to wed him, and nothing would stop her. Particularly not her irksome, annoying little sister.

She arrived at the library and glanced about. Espying no one, she tiptoed in, and within seconds, she was riffling through Michael's mail. When they'd chatted earlier, she'd observed the envelope he'd been addressing, and the thick oaf hadn't realized she had two eyes in her head, that she could read what was in plain sight.

She seized it and stuffed it down the bodice of her

gown, then hastened to her bedchamber, where she could examine the contents in private. After breaking the seal, she scanned the words, which reinforced her opinion that she'd been wise to follow up.

My dearest Emily . . . the letter began, and Pamela seethed. She dug further, discovering a bank draft, and the enormous sum had her livid. His money was about to be *her* money, too, and she had no intention of sharing a single farthing with Emily Barnett.

He'd written to the despicable tyrant! He'd offered to assist her! Why . . . he'd contacted her on the very day he'd become engaged to Pamela!

His gall was amazing, and he would pay for the insult; Pamela would see to it. He would pay in more ways than he would ever be able to count.

She tore the note—and the bank draft—to shreds and threw the pieces into the fire.

"Where's my brother, Mr. Drake?" Michael demanded.

"Your brother?"

The villain behind the desk was cool, calm, but his composure was a façade. The man was too alert, poised for action, and as his hand was hidden under the wood, he was very likely aiming a pistol.

"Show me to him."

"And you are?"

"You bloody well know who I am," Michael fumed, "or you wouldn't have sent for me. How much do you want?"

"For what?"

"Don't play dumb. I'm extremely wealthy. Name your price, and I'll forfeit whatever you require."

"You're not much of a negotiator."

"I have no time for games."

"A hundred pounds, and he's all yours."

Michael groaned. "I haven't such a large amount in my purse!"

Drake shrugged. "I don't extend credit."

Michael ripped his signet ring off his finger and tossed it on the desk. It was ornate, studded with rubies and diamonds, and he'd always loathed the gaudy bauble, detesting the rank and station it represented. "Here, you can have the blasted thing."

Drake assessed it. "What the hell would I do with it?"

"Do what you will. Just so long as you take me to Alex."

"You must care about him."

"For the sake of a few pounds, am I to tarry while my brother perishes?" Drake gaped as if Michael were speaking in a foreign language. "Have you a brother, Mr. Drake?"

"No, but I have a sister."

"Wouldn't you do anything for her?"

Drake was silent; then he surprised Michael by giving back the ring. "Keep your trinket, but you owe me a hundred."

Michael nodded as Drake led him out of the dark office where they'd been meeting. They were down on the docks, in an old warehouse. It was icy, and it smelled of rotten fish and moldy air. Michael shuddered, stunned that Alex had landed himself in such a dastardly place.

They walked down a lengthy corridor, and Drake pushed open a door. Another criminal was huddled inside a small room. A candle burned.

"Is he alive?" Drake asked his sentry.

"Last I checked," the fellow replied.

"Help the earl carry him outside."

Michael stepped into the cramped space, and his heart plummeted to his shoes. Alex was resting on a pallet on the floor, his shirt and boots gone. His skin was pasty, and he was deathly still. Someone had nursed him. A poultice had been applied to his chest, and it was secured by bandages wrapped around his arm and shoulder. He was battered from a fight, his face and clothes bloodstained, his knuckles raw, an indication that he'd held his own in the altercation.

"Oh, my Lord," Michael breathed as he slumped to his knees and clasped Alex's hand.

"One of my men was an army sawbones," Drake stated, "and we doctored him as best we could."

"Dare I move him?"

"Better you than me."

"How did you find him?"

"A tavern owner notified me. If your brother manages to survive," Drake counseled, "you should explain that this isn't the neighborhood to be flashing around cash and jewelry, especially when he's too foxed to defend himself."

Michael wondered if there was enough life force remaining for his brother to regain consciousness. "Alex," he whispered, "it's me, Michael."

He was glad the pair of ruffians was behind him, so

that they wouldn't notice his distress. The day had been sufficiently awful, and this was the very worst conclusion he could have imagined. He'd lost Emily. Would he lose Alex, too? How could the Fates steal them both?

"Michael . . . ?" Alex's eyes fluttered open. "What are you doing here?"

"I've come to take you home."

"I'm so cold."

Michael peered over at Drake. "Have you a blanket?"

A heavy woolen one magically appeared, and Michael tucked it around Alex's body, being careful not to touch the wound. It would need further tending, but Michael would leave it to the physician awaiting them at the mansion—if Alex lived till then.

"Tell Mary I'm sorry," Alex murmured.

At first, Michael didn't know to whom Alex referred, and it dawned on him that Alex meant Emily's sister, Mrs. Livingston. Perhaps their relationship had entailed a deeper significance than Michael had suspected.

"You can tell her yourself," Michael responded, "when you're feeling better."

He stood and lifted his brother, and when he staggered with his burden, Drake's man leapt forward to assist.

They lugged Alex out, trying not to jostle him, which was impossible.

As they passed, Drake commented, "Don't forget my hundred pounds. I'd hate to have to stop by to collect it."

"Don't worry, Mr. Drake. You'll get your money."

"You owe me a blanket, too."

"I'll send a dozen."

They went out into the cool evening. The sun had set and night had fallen, ending the terrible day. After much maneuvering and shifting, Michael mounted his horse, and Alex was hoisted onto his lap. Cradling his precious cargo, he raced for home, praying he would arrive before it was too late to matter.

～ 21 ～

"Tell me again. What happened?"

Michael sat at his desk and glared at Pamela, but she was unperturbed by his examination.

"What do you mean?" she inquired.

"It's an easy question. Did I remove your clothes? Or my own?"

"Well . . ."

"It can't be that difficult to remember. What was the order?"

"Amanda helped me with my clothes."

"What was I doing?"

"Ah . . . watching?" With each query, she grew less sure of herself, and he tamped down his fury.

Poor Margaret had finally caught him alone, had relayed the argument she'd heard between Pamela and Amanda. Having no background in sexual matters, she hadn't understood their comments, but they'd been more than clear to Michael.

Pamela knew that Margaret had eavesdropped, and

Margaret had been hiding for days, slipping in and out of rooms, sleeping in closets and sneaking food, so as to avoid her older sister's wrath. Margaret was now secreted in Michael's suite and carefully concealed from Pamela, but whenever Michael thought of the youngster's terror, he saw red.

Who was safe around him? Who was secure?

"When and how did we lie down?"

She hesitated, then claimed, "You went first, then me."

"I asked you to join me? Or I pulled you down?"

"I . . . I . . . simply crawled next to you."

"What about Amanda?"

"What about her?"

"Where was she?"

"She was . . . she was on the other side of you."

"Doing what?"

"Snuggling."

He said nothing. Amanda performed many deeds in bed, but *snuggling* wasn't generally one of them. "Then what?"

"Then . . . then . . . I expect we did the usual things couples do."

"Such as?" She was silent for so long that he probed, "Were we kissing?"

"Oh, yes, there was a great deal of kissing."

"And . . . ?"

"Touching. You touched me all over." As if the memory was delightful, she gave a fake little shiver.

"Where precisely?"

She gulped with dismay. "Where?"

"Which bodily parts?"

"You want me to speak of them aloud?"

"If you would, please." She was flummoxed, her juvenile age blatantly apparent, so he prodded, "Your breasts?"

"Yes." Unable to look at him, she stared at the rug.

"Was I caressing them, or was I sucking on them, too?"

"You . . . you . . ." She leapt to her feet, stomped to the sideboard, and poured herself a hefty glass of brandy. "Stop interrogating me as if I'm a criminal! I've done nothing wrong. *You* seduced me!"

"Did I?"

"Yes, everyone saw you, but you're acting as if I am to blame."

His skepticism obvious, he studied her. "I'm merely curious. You're parading around as if it was the most magnificent night of your life, yet I have no recollection of what occurred. Why would you suppose that is?"

"You drank too much."

"You're positive?"

"Amanda says it's typical behavior for you."

"You and Amanda certainly have become a pair of chums."

"She was close to my father," she declared.

"As close as Amanda ever is to anyone, I guess."

"She was his friend!"

"Your wishing it doesn't make it so."

"She was!"

Noise erupted in the hall, as several rowdy visitors rambled past. They tried the door, but Michael had had the foresight to lock it before beginning his and Pamela's conversation.

There were dozens, perhaps hundreds, of guests in the house. He couldn't count them all. He'd been distracted, alarmed by Alex's dire health, raw and churning over Emily's abandonment.

While he'd been preoccupied, Pamela had proceeded with wedding plans. The current party was a betrothal fete, though his permission to host it hadn't been sought. At a time when he only wanted solitude, his home was teeming with meddlesome people whom he couldn't abide.

Pamela was strutting about as if she were already his countess, as if his mansion—and his money—were already hers. He had no idea why he was being so courteous to her, but she was sixteen and immersed in an intrigue that was far over her head.

"Do you know what I think, Pamela?"

"What?"

She downed her brandy, then poured another. In the few minutes they'd been sequestered, she'd swilled four glasses. She was a lush who put his own drinking habits to shame.

"I don't believe anything happened between us."

"Of course it did."

"Sit down." She didn't move, and he pointed to her chair and shouted, "Sit! Down!"

At his command, she was incensed, but she crossed to the chair, and sniped, "Don't you dare raise your voice to me!"

"Before we're through, you will be lucky if my *voice* is all I raise." Her misplaced bravado had pushed his temper to the limit, and he struggled to control his anger, for he had no doubt that, whatever their shenanigans, Amanda had brought them to fruition. "Were you aware that there's a way to discover if a female has lost her virginity?"

Her gaze narrowed to a vicious squint, her expression growing cruel. "No, I wasn't."

"I've decided I should learn the answer for sure."

"You have my word on it! As I'm about to be your wife, that should be more than sufficient."

"Somehow, your assertions don't allay my reservations."

Prepared to fight it out to the bitter end, she bristled with affront. "Even if I'm still a virgin—and I'm not saying that's the case—we'd have to wed. The story of my ruination is all over London."

"You're correct," he agreed, "but I'd like to discern for myself just how desperate you are to snag me for your husband."

He rang a bell, and an older matron entered.

Pamela scrutinized the woman's plain attire, her aged face, and sneered. "Who is she?"

"She's a midwife. You'll accompany her to your room, where you will lie down and lift your skirt so that she can inspect your privates."

"My . . . my privates?"

"Yes. I've hired her to determine whether or not your maidenhead is intact." He paused, flashing a grim smile. "Unless you'd like to save yourself the embarrassment of being examined and tell me the truth."

"I won't do it," she blustered. "You can't make me."

"I am your guardian. I am your fiancé. I am lord of this manor, and I am about to be your spouse. You will be checked if I have to tie you to the bedposts, myself."

It finally dawned on her that she was trapped, the deceit unveiled, and a theatrical sheen of tears glistened in her eyes.

"How could you accuse me of treachery?" she wailed. "I am the one who was wronged. I sacrificed myself to your male lust. Is this the thanks I am to receive?"

"I'm busy, and I don't have time for your nonsense. Let's finish this, shall we?"

At seeing how he was unaffected by her outburst, she hurled, "Bastard!"

"Sticks and stones, Pamela," he told her. "Sticks and stones."

He walked to the door and opened it. She rose, and they engaged in a staring match she could never win. She hadn't the resolve or patience to best him, and he'd had enough of her antics. She'd cost him Emily, and for that transgression she would never be forgiven. After they wed, she would be ensconced at his most isolated, rural property, where he and Margaret would never have to be around her. Only by separating himself, by sending her far away, could he guarantee that he wouldn't grab her by the throat and choke that infuriating smirk off her pretty face.

Ultimately, she conceded the battle, and she swept by him, but the moment she was in the hall, she raced to the stairs and climbed. He couldn't imagine how she thought she could evade him, and she was merely postponing the inevitable. He wouldn't be dissuaded from his goal. The depth of her perfidy would be revealed.

He turned to the midwife. "I'll have to find her. Wait for us in her bedchamber."

The woman nodded and left him to the dastardly chore of locating Pamela. Fortunately, the upper corridors were empty, the guests having confined their revelry to the lower floor, so he was alone in his methodical search, and he didn't have to invent thorny excuses as to why he was hunting for her.

He reached a landing and stopped, positive that he'd heard Amanda, and he groaned. How did she keep sneaking in? Which servants were admitting her? Would he have to take a strap to somebody before they heeded his admonitions?

He hesitated, anxious to deduce from where her voice was coming, when he realized she was on the balcony that looked out over the garden. When he heard Pamela, too, and that the pair was involved in a heated exchange, he took off at a dead run.

"I'll kill you first," Amanda vowed.

"I'd like to see you try," Pamela retorted. "Now get out of my house."

"Your house? Your house?" Amanda knew she was yelling, that she sounded shrill and deranged, but Pamela had provoked her to irrationality.

"I won't have you sniffing around my husband," Pamela snapped.

"He's not your husband yet," Amanda reminded her, "and if I have anything to say about it, he never will be."

Who could have predicted that Pamela would be bright enough to initiate a betrayal? That she would have had the temerity to stab Amanda in the back?

Amanda's plot to be shed of Emily Barnett had worked fabulously. Barnett had scurried away in a thrice, but Amanda could never have envisaged Pamela's conduct in the aftermath. She'd latched onto Michael like a leech on a thigh.

Pamela was a weak, gullible adolescent who could be bullied and led, who could be patronized and browbeaten. How had she mustered the audacity to carve out her own conclusion? A conclusion that didn't include Amanda in any way, shape, or form?

Amanda wasn't about to lose her place with Michael, and if Pamela presumed she could force Amanda to graciously step aside, then Pamela was a fool.

"Listen to me, you sagging harlot—" Pamela taunted.

"Shut your impertinent mouth, or I will shut it for you!"

"I will not be silent. You are not to consort with Michael!" To emphasize each word, Pamela jabbed a finger into Amanda's chest. "If you so much as speak to him again, if you so much as glance in his direction, it will be the last stupid act you ever perform."

"You dare to threaten me? Me?" Amanda slapped her pompous hand away. "You pathetic little virgin. Don't forget that I know the truth."

"As if I care."

"You will," Amanda declared. "I'll tell Michael what we did, only I'll lie. I'll swear that you blackmailed me. I'll insist that the entire scheme was your idea."

Pamela snickered. "He's already figured out that we tricked him, and he's marrying me anyway. He has no choice. So I repeat: Get out of my house!"

Pamela shoved Amanda so hard that she nearly fell, and Amanda caught herself just before she landed on her rear. When she regained her balance, a blinding rage washed over her.

"Amanda!" Michael called from down the hall, but his appearance couldn't cool her wrath.

She lunged at Pamela, and as Pamela noted her wild stare, her violent countenance, she chuckled merrily and goaded, "Michael is all mine."

"Laugh at me, will you, you deceitful hussy?" Amanda's ire boiled over. She rushed forward and pushed Pamela, smacking into her with bruising strength.

Pamela was at an awkward angle, her bottom resting on the balustrade. The blow sent her flinging backwards, her arms flailing out, and in an instant, she flew over the railing and hurled to the ground two floors below. As she hit the marble stones on the verandah, there was a loud thud.

Amanda gasped and peeked over the edge, stunned to discover that Pamela was still and unmoving, her limbs twisted, her dress askew. Blood seeped from her crushed head.

Guests were walking in the garden, taking the night air, and someone shouted, "What was that? Did you see it?"

There were numerous murmurs; then several people hurried onto the patio to hover over Pamela's body.

"It's Pamela Martin!" a man exclaimed. "I think she's dead."

Amanda lurched into the shadows, shielding herself from view, as Michael raced onto the balcony and peered down to learn what had happened. The crowd was gaping up, trying to ascertain from where Pamela had tumbled, and on espying him lapsed into a shocked silence.

Eventually, a woman pointed at him and hissed, "Murderer! Murderer!"

"Just like your father," another bellowed, "when he killed your mother."

"You Farrows are mad!" a third tossed out. "Every cursed one of you!"

In union, they took up the scathing chorus, and Michael faced them down. For many minutes, he suffered their derision and accusations, letting their insults sluice over him. He was stoic, resigned, and visibly angry, but he didn't respond to the allegations, didn't defend himself or offer an alternate scenario as to what had occurred.

Then, without any explanation, without a question to herself regarding the brutal deed, he turned and went inside. Amanda waited a few seconds, then tiptoed away.

22

"Are we here?" Margaret asked.

Michael looked out the carriage window and surveyed the yard of the coaching inn where they'd stopped. "I believe we are."

"Do you know where their house is located?"

"No. I'll go in and obtain directions."

He gazed at his young traveling companion, relieved that he'd had her accompany him. Considering the losses she'd sustained in the past year, and the changes she'd been through, she was holding up remarkably well.

"Will they be glad to see us?"

"Of course they will," he replied, when he wasn't positive as to what their reception would be.

They were about to arrive at Barnett Manor, unannounced, uninvited, and unexpected. What would Emily say? What would she do?

While she'd never be rude to Margaret, he was fairly sure she would slam the door in his face.

He couldn't describe what bizarre urge had brought

him to Hailsham. Pamela had been buried in a quiet ceremony, but after events had concluded, he and Margaret
had been trapped in the mansion. They'd been unable to
venture out without enduring the scorn and ridicule of
the entire population of London.

When Amanda had pushed Pamela off the balcony,
Margaret had been watching from his bedroom window.
She'd witnessed it all, so Michael had been cleared by
the authorities, but others insisted her story was false.
Everyone was certain that he'd murdered Pamela, and
people were demanding that he be hanged, or that he be
stripped of his title and transported.

He refused to dignify the charges with a response, so
the rumors flew without refutation, and with each passing day, they grew more sordid. Gossip abounded, with
friends and enemies alike spreading outrageous, untrue
tales.

There were even vile fabrications about himself and
Margaret, with perverted claims that he had an unnatural
relationship with her, and thus had coerced her into lying about Pamela's death.

He couldn't abide any of it. The furor too closely resembled the time when his mother had been killed by his
father, when his father had committed suicide. In one
insane instant, Michael had been orphaned and forced to
assume the role of earl. The slew of recent disasters had
stirred a familiar cauldron of detested melancholy. He
was saddened beyond measure, and every despicable
emotion he'd suffered during his parents' calamity had
resurfaced to plague him tenfold.

He'd needed to escape, had needed to take Margaret
away so that she wouldn't overhear the repulsive yarns

that were being bandied. For reasons he couldn't explain or understand, he'd decided to visit Emily in Hailsham.

He felt as if he were on a boat and adrift at sea, that he was about to be swamped by huge waves, and she represented a peculiar type of anchor. He was desperate to speak with her, to ascertain that she was all right. She'd never cashed the bank draft he'd sent, and he was frantic to know why she hadn't. Perhaps she was still too angry, but she couldn't let pride prevent her from using the money to secure her future.

Beyond his desire to inquire about the money, he had to tell her what had actually happened with Pamela. He didn't want anything from her. He would never be so brash as to propose marriage or attempt to inflict himself on her in a more permanent fashion. The last few weeks had proven, once again, that he wasn't fit for polite company, that he should never aspire to a different existence, and he'd accepted that reality.

But she symbolized a better period in his life, when he'd been happy and content, and in his current miserable condition he was yearning to confide in her, was anxious to seek the solace and comfort he attained when he was in her presence.

He had another, more selfish, motive for calling on her. He had to find somewhere for Margaret to go. The girl couldn't live with him, not while such squalid reports were being disseminated, but she'd weathered tremendous adversity, and he couldn't bear the notion of dumping her at an impersonal, distant boarding school, yet he could devise no other option.

Margaret had been great friends with Emily's niece, and Michael hoped he could persuade Emily to let

Margaret stay in Hailsham. At least until matters calmed in the city.

Emily was a kind woman, a generous woman, and despite her low opinion of him, she'd help Margaret. Michael was convinced she would.

"Are you hungry?" he asked Margaret. "Would you like to come in and have something to eat?"

"No, I'm excited to arrive. I'd rather proceed directly to their residence."

He smiled. Though confronted by constant tragedy, she remained the most pleasant and sweet child, and he wished there was a way to keep her with him, but he'd never be that cruel. She had to be sequestered as far away from him as he could manage.

"Give me a minute, and I'll see what I can learn."

"I can hardly wait!"

His appearance had created a stir, and he climbed out to chaos. Boys rushed from the stables to tend the horses, and servants at the inn peeked out the windows to discover who was riding in such a fancy vehicle.

He went in and acquired easy instructions to Barnett Manor, as well as a meat pie for Margaret, and he was prepared to depart when he literally bumped into Reginald Barnett.

By all accounts, it was a small village, but what were the odds?

Michael cringed and resisted the urge to dust off his jacket. The oaf gave him the willies, and Michael couldn't stand Barnett's pompous, pretentious attitude, but then, the sentiment was clearly mutual.

From Barnett's scowl and derisive glare, he disliked Michael as much as or more than Michael disliked him.

"Why are you here, Winchester?" Barnett showed no courtesy, though Michael couldn't blame him. When they'd previously parleyed, Michael had nearly pitched him out in the yard. The shame had to still grate on Barnett's enormous pride.

Michael thought about ignoring the question and the man, but he'd been informed that Emily was living in Barnett's house. "I'm traveling through, and I'd planned on a brief visit to Barnett Manor."

Barnett glanced about, then requested a private room from the innkeeper. They were escorted to one, and as the proprietor closed the door, Barnett spun around.

"So . . . you're sniffing after my cousin. I might have guessed that you would, but since you've dared to impose your eminent self upon us, I must point out a fact you obviously don't know."

"What is that?"

"She's no longer my cousin."

"Don't spew riddles," Michael snapped. "What do you mean?"

"She's my wife."

"Your . . . your wife?"

"Yes."

In all his visions of his meeting Emily, in all the images he'd conjured, the horrid possibility had never entered his mind.

She'd married Reginald Barnett? How could she have?

When she'd been in London, she'd grasped what a villain Barnett was. She'd been ready to survive on the streets rather than subsist under Barnett's roof. What had transpired to change her view?

There was only one answer: It was all Michael's fault.

How could he have failed her so completely? If he'd provided for her, if he'd made sure she'd had the money she
needed for Mary and Rose, she could have forged a different path.

He couldn't believe the appalling news! He simply
couldn't believe it!

Devastated, he wanted to rail and howl, to shake his
fist at the heavens, to bellow, *Why? Why?*

Yet he controlled any outward sign of distress. He
was a master at hiding his emotions, and he'd die before
he'd permit Barnett to realize how grievously the tidings
had wounded him.

"Congratulations," he blandly stated as if the subject
were of no consequence whatsoever. "When was the
ceremony?"

"A few days after she returned. We'd called the banns
earlier in the spring, so the vicar felt it was appropriate
to carry on without calling them again."

Michael would have cut out his tongue so as not to inquire further, but he caught himself saying, "I trust
Emily is happy . . . ?"

"She's back at home, where she always belonged,"
Barnett replied, "and you are not welcome to stop by and
see her."

"As you wish." Now that he'd been advised of her
wedding, Michael was eager to go, but Barnett was keen
to rub it in.

"It's tit for tat, isn't it, Winchester?" Barnett goaded.
"Doesn't it gall you?"

Michael knew he should disregard Barnett and be
off, but the idiot's hostile tone was too provoking, too
infuriating.

"What's that?"

"Can you picture me sawing away between her pretty thighs?" Barnett snickered. "My appetite is voracious, and I have her whenever and wherever the mood strikes me."

Michael was so shocked by the foul comment that he was speechless. What husband would speak so despicably of his new bride? What man would utter such a dastardly remark to another man with whom he was scarcely acquainted?

"You're a swine, Barnett."

The insult had no effect and didn't shut him up as Michael had hoped.

"She's mine," Barnett preened, "and she has to obey me. Would you like me to describe some of the deeds I force her to perform? I give it to her in the mouth. I shove it up her ass. She can't refuse me."

He chortled with glee, and it was such a revolting, nauseating sound that before Michael could pause to reconsider, he punched Barnett as hard as he could. There was a crack, and blood squirted from Barnett's nose.

The knave shrieked as he lurched to the side and covered his face. "Who the hell are you to come in here and assault me?"

"I am the man who loves her, who will love her forever."

"But she isn't yours!" Barnett was cackling with malice. "She'll never be yours!"

Michael grabbed him, shook him like a rag doll, and warned, "I intend to keep track of her."

"Hah! Am I to be frightened?"

"You should be."

"What if you learn that I've harmed her? What will you do? She's my wife, and there's not a person in the kingdom who can gainsay me."

It was true. Whatever ignominy he perpetrated against Emily, it was nobody's business, and no one would interfere. Barnett could murder her, and if he invented a tolerable lie, he'd never be prosecuted.

"If I ever hear that you've hurt her, I'll kill you," Michael vowed. "With my own two hands." In light of recent events, it probably wasn't the wisest threat to level, but Barnett had driven him beyond circumspection.

"I'd like to see you try."

"Believe me, so would I."

Michael pushed Barnett away, and Barnett fell to his knees. He was battered, his eyes blackening, his nose swelling and likely broken, but he was belligerent to the end.

"Bloody rich sod," Barnett hurled.

Michael stared him down, disposed to lean over, to pummel him and pummel him until he was naught but an unrecognizable lump on the floor, but he resisted the violent impulse. The last thing he needed was to be involved in an altercation. He'd never live it down.

He turned and stomped out. The blow he'd delivered had been fierce, had bruised his knuckles, and as he walked to his carriage and climbed in, he was rubbing his hand.

Margaret was smiling and merry, excited to proceed to their destination. "Have you found out where they are?"

"Yes," he responded steadily, determined not to display a hint of his distress, "but I'm sorry. They're gone, visiting relatives. No one is at home."

"Oh."

She was so disheartened that he had to glance away. He couldn't abide her woe, so he quickly added, "Have you ever been to Brighton?"

"No. Father had promised to take us for a holiday, but he never got around to it."

"It's just down the road," he explained. "What if we have a bit of a holiday, ourselves, before we head back to London?"

"Do you mean it?"

"Yes. We can rent a cozy cottage and enjoy the sea air. It will be very fun."

She studied him, shrewdly noting his injured hand. Ultimately, she queried, "Are you all right?"

"Of course, I am."

"Did something bad happen whilst you were inside?"

"No." Eager to reassure her, he scoffed and smiled.

She was very mature for her age, and though she'd deduced that a nefarious incident had occurred, she also realized that she had to accept his insistence that all was fine.

"I think Brighton is a grand idea," she said.

"Let's be off, then. There's no reason to linger."

23

Mary ambled down the quiet country lane toward Barnett Manor, counting her strides and enjoying the smells of the autumn afternoon. Warm sunshine dappled her shoulders, but with the changing season, there was a briskness in the air that hadn't been apparent when they'd first arrived home from their terrible excursion to London.

Occasionally, when she was lonely or bored, she thought about that chaotic episode, about residing in Lord Winchester's house and fornicating with his brother. It was the sole instance in her entire life when she'd dared attempt something rash, something extraordinary, and when she was sitting with the neighbor ladies, chatting and drinking tea, she suffered from the strongest urge to say, "Would you like to know what I *really* did while I was in the city?"

If she ever described her wild fling, she'd likely send her less stalwart acquaintances into a swoon. Much of it seemed preposterous, even to herself, and she frequently wondered if it had happened at all. She had no mementoes, no strands of hair pressed in a locket, no dried flowers tucked away in a book.

Had she actually met Alex Farrow? Had she been madly, passionately, in love with a man to whom she'd hardly spoken?

The whole experience was like a weird dream that, upon awakening, was vague and fuzzy.

She rubbed her stomach, depressed that she'd have to tell and soon. She couldn't let many more weeks pass without acknowledging what she'd done. A woman could conceal a pregnancy for only so long before the secret told itself.

Oh, how could she have been so reckless? So foolish?

Emily's wedding was in two hours, and Mary ought to be inside, helping and getting dressed, but she couldn't feign gladness. She'd tried to talk Emily out of the union, but Emily wouldn't be dissuaded. She was bound and determined to marry Reginald.

The few times Mary had raised the subject, Emily had been adamant. She felt as Mary did, that they shouldn't have left Hailsham, that they shouldn't have strayed so far from their roots. They knew their place and were destined to stay in it.

But how could Emily wed Reginald? Didn't she understand who he was? Couldn't she distinguish his malice and hostility? Mary had struggled to explain what she perceived, but to no avail. For better or worse—mostly worse!—Reginald was about to be Emily's husband.

She tarried, pondering the past, debating the future, and she decided that she had to inform Reginald and Emily that she was having a baby. They had to be apprised before the ceremony. Reginald was so proud of his new position in the community. Once he learned of Mary's scandalous predicament, it was probable that he would evict her as a harlot, and she couldn't continue to avoid the harsh sentence.

Like a felon to the gallows, she started walking. She had to confess, had to discover her fate. There was no reason to put it off, and though the tidings would cast a pall on the festivities, she had to proceed.

Wishing she could lengthen the journey, or never complete it, she took trudging steps. If she prayed fervently enough, could she make herself vanish?

She was at the stile, ready to squeeze through the break in the fence, when she noted the sound of wheels rolling down the lane. She listened, realizing that it wasn't a cart from a nearby farm. It was too lightweight, too fast moving, and there were two horses clomping in a perfect rhythm, indicating they were an expensive, matched pair. This was someone new, someone from outside the area, and she paused, curious as to who would be driving up their road in such a fancy vehicle.

To her utter surprise, the driver slowed, then halted right next to her. The carriage occupant leaned out the window, and she discerned him to be male, for she could smell tobacco on his clothes. She waited for him to speak, but he was strangely silent and staring at her so intently that she could feel his gaze as definitely as if he were touching her.

"Hello, Mary," he finally greeted her.

At hearing that rich baritone voice, she was so rattled that she had to grab for the fence post lest she fall to the grass in an astonished heap. She summoned her courage and curtsied. "Mr. Farrow."

She wasn't about to say anything more, would choke before the beloved name of *Alex* slid from her lips. Her heart was thundering, her mind whirling with questions: Why had he come? What did he want? What did his appearance portend?

The driver climbed down from the box, and there was a creaking of wood and leather as he assisted Alex to the ground. As if Alex was disabled, the servant steadied him, and she frowned. Had he been ill? Had he been injured?

He approached, and she was assailed by his familiar heat and scent.

"What are you doing here?" she asked, which was the sole query that signified.

"I had to see you."

"Well, now you have."

She spun to go, desperate to be away from him, to hide so he wouldn't witness her tears. Anymore, she was so accursedly sentimental, her condition making her fret and stew until she was maudlin. Suddenly, she was simmering with a longing and regret that she'd presumed she'd buried during the frenzied trip home to Hailsham, but evidently, her weeks of reflection hadn't granted her any wisdom.

Absurdly, she was thrilled that he'd sought her out, so ecstatic that she could barely keep from flinging herself into his arms.

She was such an idiot! Had their history taught her nothing?

He was a deceitful, untrustworthy cad, and she locked her fingers in the folds of her skirt so that she wouldn't reach out to him.

"Mary," he called.

Don't stop! Don't turn around! she scolded, but her feet wouldn't obey.

"What?" She whirled to face him.

He advanced, and she detected that he was limping. She braced, refusing to speculate, refusing to inquire as to what had happened. She wouldn't care about him! She wouldn't!

He stared at her again, but he was in turmoil and couldn't begin a conversation, and she wasn't about to help him. He'd caused her so much grief and misery, and she had no compassion to share, couldn't manage simple civility.

Stunning her, he caressed her cheek. As if he was weak and the gesture difficult to accomplish, his hand shook, and she flinched away.

"I'm sorry," he announced. "Can you forgive me?"

"You're . . . you're sorry?" It was the very last comment she'd expected.

"I behaved so badly toward you."

"You're correct. You were an absolute swine."

She didn't want him repentant, couldn't bear his apologies. If he was remorseful, how was she to remain angry? How could she fuel the necessary fire to keep him at bay?

"You were always so kind to me," he said, "so accepting of my faults, yet I used you; I took advantage of you."

"Yes, you did."

"I wish I could travel back in time and change everything. I ought to be whipped for how I treated you."

She was bewildered as to what her response should be. On many previous occasions, she'd allowed herself to fantasize about this confrontation, but in all the mental scenarios she'd concocted—most of them ending in castration!—she'd never envisioned him being contrite.

He craved forgiveness? Fine, he could have it.

"You're forgiven," she snapped. "Now go away and leave me be."

He swayed, as if he was enfeebled, as if he might collapse, and without thinking, she leapt forward and hugged him, taking his weight on her slender shoulders. It occurred to her that they'd immediately fallen into the old rhythm of their relationship. She'd been the strong one, the stable one, and throughout their abbreviated affair, he had relied on her constancy.

"What is it?" she asked. "Are you all right?"

"Might I sit down?" he replied. "It's been a tiring journey from town, and I'm not feeling very well."

"Of course, of course," she soothed, more perplexed than ever about what she wanted. As she led him to the house and into the parlor, as she settled him on the sofa and fetched a stool for his feet, it seemed so natural to be watching over him, once again.

She seated herself, and he murmured, "I couldn't come for you. I meant to, but . . . but . . ."

He was referring to their imprudent elopement plan, but she couldn't discuss it. Her shame was too great. "Don't let's talk about it."

"We have to," he insisted. "When I didn't arrive, what must you have thought? I've been frantic to know."

She wouldn't lie or make it easier for him. "I *thought* that I'd been deluding myself, that a man like you would never marry a woman like me. I was a fool to believe otherwise."

"A man like me . . ." he muttered, and he scoffed. "As if I'm so bloody high-and-mighty! Do you comprehend the type of man I really am, Mary?"

"Yes."

"No, you have no idea. That's why I cherished your company. You saw someone who didn't exist." He sighed. "I'm a drunkard, Mary, a disgusting, pathetic drunkard. I went to war, and I received a nasty scratch on my face, when many of my colleagues perished or lost limbs, and ever since, I've been too spineless to adapt."

"Your habits can be detestable."

Wearily, he chuckled. "You're still being kind, but if you tossed me out on my ear, I'd deserve it."

"I could never throw you out," she pitifully admitted.

"Would you like to hear where I was, and what I was doing, when we were supposed to be eloping?"

"No!" Whatever details he was bent on sharing, she couldn't listen to them.

"I was foxed"—he forged ahead despite her plea that he not—"and I was gambling, and when I'd imbibed to the point where I was incoherent, I was assaulted and robbed by a gang of ruffians. When we should have been merrily winging off to Scotland, I was dying in some criminal's lair, stabbed in the chest and barely able to breathe—"

"Stabbed!"

"—and if Michael hadn't come for me, I can't predict how it would have ended."

"Oh, Alex. . . ." What should she say? She couldn't decide, so she bit down on all the words that were anxious to spill out.

"I've quit drinking, Mary," he vowed. "I swore to

Michael, and I swear to you, that I'll never permit another drop to pass my lips."

"Good. It was killing you."

"I've quit gambling, too. It's over, done."

"I'm so glad."

"I'm determined to turn over a new leaf. I want to show you that I can be the man you assumed I was."

"You won't have to try very hard," she conceded. "I was always convinced that there was a gentleman lurking under the surface."

"In any of my drunken ramblings, did I ever tell you that I love you?"

"No." He'd previously uttered one endearment that she hadn't believed, and at this late juncture, she wasn't sure she was ready for any others.

"Then, I'll tell you now: I love you, Mary Barnett Livingston. Will you marry me?"

"What? Are you mad?"

Mystified by the sudden declaration, she jumped off the couch and marched across the room to dawdle at the window. He'd spewed so many lies. Was this just one more? Or—for once—was he sober and speaking the truth?

How could she be certain? He'd traveled all the way from London. Why would he invest so much time and effort merely to perpetuate another falsehood? Could anyone be that despicable?

Behind her, he rose and walked to her. He nestled himself to her backside, and he cradled her in his arms.

"I've missed you, Mary, so much. I need you. Without you, I'm only half a man."

"Don't say such things to me."

"Why not?"

"Because I doubt you're sincere."

He kissed her hair, her nape. "Considering my treatment of you, that is a perfectly valid and logical concern." He spun her toward him and dug into the pocket of his vest; then he shocked her by slipping a ring onto her finger.

She traced its shape, noting the numerous stones. It had to be a priceless family heirloom, and thus was much too extravagant for a person as modest and ordinary as she deemed herself to be.

On observing her consternation, he advised, "This ring was my mother's favorite piece of jewelry." He guided her thumb across the gems. "It has a gold band, with a sapphire in the middle, encircled by tiny diamonds. Michael gave it to me, so that I could give it to you." He stunned her further by dropping to his knee. "Will you marry me?"

She gasped. "You're serious."

He gazed up at her. "I can provide you with a fine home, Mary. Not anyplace as grand as Michael's, but I enjoy some affluence, so I can support you and your daughter. Let me. Please."

Can I trust him? Will he follow through? The questions screamed at her. She'd been down this road before, but at the last moment, he'd declined to join her, and her broken heart was still healing from that earlier misadventure.

"I'm so confused," she confessed.

"Pardon me for my many sins so that I can prove how much I love you. I want to carry on as the man I was meant to be. For you, Mary. Just for you."

"I'm pregnant," she blurted out, having never intended to confide in him, but it was vital that he be informed so she could assess his opinion of this new fact.

He pulled away, and she could sense him grinning. "Really?"

"Yes."

"I knew it!" he crowed.

"How could you have?"

"I could feel it in my bones."

She waited for him to scoff or deny her statement, but instead, he hugged her tightly and proclaimed, "I hope it's a girl who looks like you."

"You *are* insane," she decreed. There was no other explanation. His injuries had left him deranged.

"You're wrong. I've never been more clear about what I want, and I want you. Have me, Mary. I'll be a father to this child we've made, and we'll build a family together."

"When?" she demanded, recognizing that this was how she could test his earnestness. "If you're resolved to wed me, when would we do it?"

"At once," he responded. "I brought Michael's fastest carriage. We can leave for Scotland as soon as you pack your bags."

"Now?"

"Yes, now. And when we return, and we're not so rushed, we'll have a second ceremony at the cathedral in London. Or if you'd rather, we can hold it here, at your local church."

He stood, his excitement and affection shining through, and she couldn't fathom why he was doing this.

"I'm blind," she declared.

"Yes, you are, but you *see* more than any individual I've ever known. You're also sweet and caring and tolerant. You put up with me when I was at my worst. I want you with me when I'm at my best." He grabbed her shoulders and gave her a firm shake. "Say you'll have me, Mary. I'll spend the rest of my life making you happy. I swear it."

He seemed convinced that it could work out, yet she was trembling with uncertainty. Her wild, impetuous side yearned to clasp his hand, to waltz out and commence a mad dash for Scotland. But her rational, judicious side was terrified that if she totted off with him, he'd change his mind halfway there and abandon her at some coaching inn.

Could she take such a risk? If she relented and went with him, there'd be no going back. If he deserted her, she'd be on her own, and Reginald would never open his door to her. Then again, when she apprised Reginald of her delicate condition, she'd be tossed out anyway.

By accepting Alex, what did she have to lose? Absolutely nothing.

What did she have to gain?

A slow smile spread across her face. She would have a randy, handsome husband. She'd have a home of her own, a father for her children, a family that needed her. She'd have independence and security and . . . she'd have Alex. She'd have Alex forever.

She didn't imagine it would be easy, didn't suppose that there wouldn't be bumps in their path, but wasn't this precisely the sort of escapade she'd always craved? For years, she'd sat docilely by the hearth, listening as others went about their lives, but never actually living her own.

Here was her chance. Here was her destiny.

She reached out and linked their fingers. "Yes, Alex Farrow, I will marry you."

"Do you mean it?"

"Of course, you silly oaf. Do you think I go around accepting marriage proposals every day?"

He let out a whoop that rattled the glass in the windows, and he lifted her up and kissed her. His tongue was in her mouth, his hands in her hair, which vividly triggered memories of the more intriguing aspects of what their marriage would entail. He twirled her around and around until they were both dizzy, but he quickly grew fatigued, and he flopped down on the couch, with her sprawled across his lap.

"I can't believe you agreed," he admitted.

"How could I have refused?"

Like a pair of enamored half-wits, they dawdled and grinned. There were so many details to discuss and arrange, but she couldn't break the wonderful moment.

Finally, he ended it, shifting her so that she was seated next to him, and he said, "I'd like to do something I should have done long ago."

"What is that?"

"Might I meet your daughter?"

A warm glow of assurance swept through her. "I thought you'd never ask."

~ 24 ~

Emily sat at her dressing table, staring at herself in the mirror. She looked ill, as if she'd been sick at her stomach or was about to be. Her hands were so icy that she couldn't pick up the combs to pin her hair.

In less than half an hour, she'd be Mrs. Reginald Barnett. Could she go through with the wedding? How could she not?

At all costs, Mary and Rose had to be safeguarded. She couldn't fail them, as she had when she'd instigated their London catastrophe. She would never again place them in such a precarious position.

Reginald was her past and her future. She comprehended his ways and his habits. Yes, he'd been distraught when she'd initially arrived home, but since then, he'd reverted to his usual demeanor. He could be annoying, he could be patronizing, but he was Reginald. Her dear father had chosen him to be her husband, and she'd been wrong to flout her father's wishes, daft to fight her destiny.

She wasn't the first woman in history to wed a man

she didn't love, and she wouldn't be the last. She wasn't the sole female who'd had to marry to protect her family. She could do this! She could! It was just one day in a lengthy parade of days. She was strong, and she'd persevere.

Reginald's sporty new gig pulled up out front, but she didn't glance at it. He'd been in a dither about the preparations at the church, so he'd gone on ahead and had sent the vehicle back to hurry her along. Well, she had many minutes of freedom remaining before she had to join him, and she wasn't about to rush.

She sighed and gazed out the window. Far out beyond the hills was the city of London. Occasionally, she reflected on her adventure there, on her foiled affair with Michael Farrow.

Did he ever think of her?

After she'd fled, she'd foolishly supposed that he might be sorry for how he'd hurt her, that he might seek her out to apologize.

At other times, she was positive he would furnish her with the money he'd promised, and she'd watched the post for weeks. Waiting. Waiting. To no avail.

If she hadn't been crazed before she'd met him, her constant conviction later on—that he wouldn't fail her—was a glaring illustration of how deranged she'd been after.

How could he abandon her to this cruel fate?

She stood and trudged downstairs. She had to find Mary and Rose, had to proceed to the church. She'd told Mary that she didn't have to attend the ceremony, but Mary had sweetly refused to stay away. No matter how much Mary detested Reginald, she would support Emily throughout the trying ordeal.

It was the only incentive that kept Emily moving forward.

As she reached the foyer, the doors to the parlor were closed, and Rose was on her knees and spying through the keyhole.

"Rose Livingston!" Emily scolded. "What on earth are you doing?"

Rose gestured for silence and whispered, "Mother is inside, with Mr. Farrow."

"Alex Farrow is here?"

"Yes, and Mother is kissing him! Right on the lips!"

"What?"

Emily urged Rose away, then yanked on the doors, and the spectacle was just as Rose had claimed. Alex Farrow was sitting on their sofa and kissing Mary as if there were no tomorrow.

On her entering, they jumped apart. Red-faced and chagrined, Mary stammered and said, "Emily, this may come as a bit of a shock—"

"That's putting it mildly," Emily interjected.

"—but Mr. Farrow, that is, Alex, and I are a bit better acquainted than we ever let on."

"I can see that." Emily wasn't certain of what was happening or what her reaction should be.

She hardly knew Alex Farrow and, other than rumor, had no genuine reason to dislike him, but she'd had her fill of the Quality. No good could be achieved from Mary's having a relationship with him.

Why had she and her sister both been attracted to the Farrow brothers? Was it a defect in their blood? A weakness in their character? Had Mary been carrying on with

Farrow, slipping in and out of his room, as Emily had been with Michael?

The prospect was too humiliating to ponder.

"We're going to be married," Mary declared.

"You're what?"

"We're eloping to Scotland. At once."

"Oh, Mary. . . ." Emily sank into the nearest chair. "Are you sure you should?"

Rose had been eavesdropping, and she peeked in. "Truly, Mother?" she queried. "You're to be married?"

"Yes, Rose." Mary held out her hand. "I want you to meet Mr. Farrow."

Farrow stood, and Mary stood with him. As Mary made introductions, they were joyous and content. Farrow chatted with Rose and politely asked if she would mind terribly if he wed her mother.

Rose—in typical nine-year-old fashion—deemed it very romantic, but she hadn't the maturity necessary to peer down the road and wonder what Mary's future would be like with dissolute, drunken Alex Farrow as her spouse.

Emily was aware of his bad habits, but then again, he'd come for Mary, had sought her out and proposed. Should Emily paint him with the same dark brush with which she'd colored Michael?

Emily was conflicted. Didn't Mary deserve someone to love her? If she and Farrow could build a life together, didn't they merit the chance to try? Who was Emily to interfere with their happiness?

Realizing that his welcome had been a tad cool, Farrow gazed beyond Rose and flashed a tentative smile. His scar was disfiguring, gruesome to view, and Emily kept her focus firmly fixed on his eyes and not his cheek.

"I understand that this is rather sudden," he commenced, "but I care about Mary, and I . . . I . . . love her very much." He blushed, the admission difficult to voice aloud. "I have an income, not like my brother's, of course, but enough to provide for her and Rose. I hope I can have your blessing, Mrs. Barnett."

Emily was awhirl with comments, and she murmured the first that seemed relevant. "I'm not a *Mrs.* Not yet anyway."

As if it were the strangest remark ever, he gaped at her. "You're not married to your cousin?"

"I'm about to be. The wedding starts in a few minutes."

"Are you positive?"

"Believe me, Mr. Farrow, I'm often confused, but I *do* know when my own wedding is scheduled to begin."

"You're not married," he mused; then he frowned at her. "Michael thinks you are."

"He does?"

Upon hearing him refer to Michael, she was so disturbed that she leapt to her feet, not able to decide if she should flee or stay and chat. She'd been so grievously wounded, and she was still so raw, that she couldn't cope with the mere mention of his name.

Farrow said, "He sent you several thousand pounds so you wouldn't have to."

"No, he didn't."

"I swear it, Miss Barnett. But when you never cashed the draft, he grew concerned, and he visited Hailsham to guarantee that you were all right."

"Michael traveled to Hailsham?"

"You didn't know?"

"No."

"He talked with your cousin."

"When?"

"Many weeks ago. Michael had stopped for directions at the coaching inn, and they bumped into each other. Your cousin insisted you'd married him, as the two of you had planned, so Michael returned to London."

"He came for me?"

She collapsed into the chair again. The world seemed to have tipped off its axis. The floor was crooked, the walls askew, and she couldn't find her balance.

He came for me . . . he came for me. . . . The fantastic reality rang through her head.

"Tell me that you're not joking," she demanded, scarcely able to breathe.

"I'm not. They exchanged harsh words, and Michael hit him so hard that he wondered if your cousin's nose was broken."

"Michael hit him?"

"Yes."

Emily vividly recollected the odd afternoon when Reginald had arrived home bruised and battered. He'd contended that he'd had a freak accident, that he'd tripped and fallen. At the memory, she smiled. "I can't say if Michael broke his nose, but it took forever for his black eyes to heal."

Farrow studied Emily, then asked, "You haven't been notified about what transpired in London, have you?"

"You mean with Pamela Martin?"

"That and the rest of it." He looked at Rose and inquired, "Rose, would you excuse us? I need to speak with your aunt."

"Must I go?" she begged, but Mary shooed her out, and once they were alone, Farrow stated, "You're aware of his compromising Pamela."

Emily thought about acting as if she had no special connection to Michael, but she was too disconcerted to lie. "It's why we left London in such a hurry. After what I witnessed, I couldn't bear to remain."

"He did nothing to Pamela," Farrow claimed.

"I was there!" Emily advised. "I saw them!"

"It was all a hoax. Amanda Lambert and Pamela drugged him and undressed him, so it would appear as if Pamela had been ruined."

"To what end?"

"Pamela was eager to marry him, but he would never have agreed, so she trapped him."

Emily was reeling. He hadn't lain with Pamela! He'd journeyed to Hailsham to . . . to . . . what?

"Why?" she probed. "Why was he here?"

"He loves you, Miss Barnett. He always loved you."

Emily glanced at Mary. "Did you know about my affair with him?"

"Yes."

"How could you have?"

"I could smell him on your skin and clothes."

It was Emily's turn to blush. She'd presumed herself discreet, shrewd. Had everyone in Michael's house been cognizant of how thoroughly she'd debased herself?

"You never said anything."

"I figured you'd confide in me when you were ready."

Emily shifted her attention to Farrow. "If Michael *loved* me, he had a funny way of showing it."

"Apparently, my brother hid a few details about our

past. Did he tell you about our parents? Did he explain what our life has been like?"

"Very little." The bulk of her information had been gleaned from servants' whisperings.

"He's a very private person, Miss Barnett, and he needs you. Would you go to him? Would you give him another chance?"

"He doesn't need me," she asserted. "He doesn't need anyone. He was very clear about that fact."

"He does need you!" Farrow countered. "Listen: Michael offered for Pamela—in spite of her duplicity—but then, she and Amanda got in a fight, and Pamela was killed."

Emily gasped. "How?"

"Amanda pushed her off a balcony. Michael wasn't involved, but no one believes him. All of London is convinced that he murdered Pamela just like . . . just like . . . our father murdered our mother."

"They think Michael killed Pamela?"

"Yes."

"But . . . but . . . that's absurd."

"The gossip is outrageous," he said. "It's been terrible."

"How is Michael coping?"

"He pretends to ignore it, but he's devastated. He's carrying on as if nothing happened, as if nothing matters. Why, this weekend, he's interviewing for a new mistress, and he's—"

"He's what?"

"He's interviewing for a . . . well . . . for a . . ."

Emily stood and went to the window. The incident in London had been a sham, concocted by Pamela and Amanda, and Emily had fallen for it.

Michael had sent her money, so that she'd be free of Reginald. He'd visited to check on her welfare. Mr. Farrow maintained that Michael loved her.

She pictured him in town, isolated and surrounded by his enemies, and she cringed. She knew Michael. He was a good man, a generous and kind man. The short summer she'd spent with him had been the sole occasion she'd ever felt truly cherished, truly alive.

What if she'd trusted him? What if she'd stayed? Could they have been happy?

With a ruthless certainty, she recognized that she had to learn the answer.

She walked to the writing desk, grabbed a sheet of paper, and penned a note. Then she handed it to Farrow.

"What's this?" he questioned.

"It's a letter for Reginald," she explained. "He's at the church. Would you deliver it to him? Mary can direct you."

"Of course."

"And please, take my sister and my niece to Scotland. Immediately. You have my most sincere blessing."

"Really?" he and Mary inquired in unison.

"Yes." She moved toward the door.

"Where are you going?" Mary asked.

"I find that I must make a quick trip to London. In case Reginald fusses about his gig, tell him I borrowed it."

She halted, then rushed over and hugged Mary. "I'm so glad for you." She hugged Farrow, too. "I'm delighted that you love my sister. Watch over her for me."

"I will," he vowed.

She started out again, but at the last second, she stopped. "By the way, Mr. Farrow—"

"As I'm about to be your brother, you should probably call me Alex."

She grinned. "Alex, once I arrive in the city, have you any idea where I might purchase a red dress?"

"A red dress?"

"I've heard that red is Michael's favorite color."

"So it is, Emily." Alex laughed. "So it is."

Reginald dawdled at the altar, staring out at the assembled crowd, and he shifted uneasily. It wasn't a large number of people, but those who'd been graced with invitations were the important members of their local society. After waiting his entire life to assume his proper role at Barnett Manor, this was his stellar moment, his shining achievement, and only the richest, most influential neighbors were in attendance.

He scowled at his timepiece, trying to be furtive, but stealth was difficult when so many pairs of eyes were focused on him. It was twenty minutes after eleven. Where was the blasted woman?

The guests were fidgeting, murmuring, and several were peeking at their timepieces, too.

Noise erupted in the vestibule, and everyone stretched and strained to see if she'd entered, but she hadn't. It was a tall, dark-haired gentleman, attired in traveling clothes, and for the briefest instant, Reginald's heart skipped a beat, as he thought the man was the Earl of Winchester. The fellow talked to an usher, then departed, and Reginald discerned that there was a strong resemblance, but it wasn't Winchester.

Reginald snickered. Hah! As if Winchester would dare return to Hailsham!

Winchester had been bested, and Reginald's elation over inflicting such anguish on the exalted snob had almost been worth the pain of being assaulted. Emily would pay for that humiliation, as she would pay for all the others. In a few hours, his wedding night would commence, and he had it planned out. She was about to discover who was her lord and master, who would be her lord and master from now on. She would never escape his clutches.

The usher approached and slipped something to the vicar as the congregation tittered with anticipation.

"What's this?" the vicar queried.

"Evidently, it's a note for Mr. Barnett," the usher replied. "From the bride." Brows shot up as he leaned closer and added, "I'm to inform him that she has the gig, and she'll send it back in a few days."

The vicar was calm, acting as if such interruptions were common. He passed the message to Reginald, then courteously stepped away so as not to read over Reginald's shoulder. Reginald yearned to appear unruffled, but he couldn't manage the vicar's aplomb. Frantically, he ripped at the wax seal.

Reginald, the tidy handwriting began, *did you really think you could keep Michael's visit a secret from me? I'm off to London, to beg his forgiveness. When he hit you, I wish he'd done much more than break your nose. A good thrashing is the least of what you deserve. My apologies to your guests.* She'd signed it with the initial *E.*

Thunderstruck, Reginald scanned the words over and over. He couldn't believe it! The immoral strumpet! How had she found out about Winchester?

Well, in the future, when Winchester tired of her and she came crawling home, Reginald had learned his lesson. He wouldn't let her in! She was an ungrateful wretch! When she huddled on his stoop, when she pleaded for refuge, it would be a cold day in hell before she garnered any sympathy. For all he cared, she could starve in the gutter.

His money, gone! His legacy, gone! Barnett Manor, gone! His jaunty carriage, gone. Because of her and her fickle ways, he'd lost it all.

Blinded by rage and embarrassment, he crumpled the letter and threw it on the floor. Head high, shoulders straight, he marched down the center aisle and out of the church, wondering how he would ever show his face in public again.

His shame would be avenged! When he next crossed paths with her, he would grab her by the throat, and he would squeeze and squeeze until she couldn't breathe. He would hold her down, would press until he choked her to death!

He'd move. That's what he'd do! He'd move far away, where no one knew who he was or what indignities he'd suffered. He'd keep going, to the ends of the earth and beyond. . . .

Grumbling, livid, mortified to his very core, he continued walking.

Amanda sipped on a brandy and gazed out the window of her bedchamber. A chilly autumn wind was blowing, and she shivered. She hadn't dressed yet. Her ruminations were so scattered, her affairs in such disarray, that she rarely went out, so why bother with clothes?

A coach rumbled by, and her pulse thudded with dread. Every sound made her jump as she worried that some thug from Bow Street was about to burst in and arrest her.

Michael hadn't tattled as to what had actually occurred that evening on the balcony, and the silence was driving her mad. Why hadn't he said anything? From the gossip she'd heard, people were positive that he'd shoved Pamela in a fit of temper, and they were gleeful over his plight and salivating over the prospect of a hanging.

She wanted to come forward and offer him a defense, but what was she supposed to say? She wasn't about to tell the truth and implicate herself, and her fury at Pamela surged anew.

The stupid girl! How dare she die! How dare she cause all this trouble!

A rider swiftly approached, the horse's hooves clopping on the cobbles, and she glanced out, stunned to ascertain that it was Michael, strutting up in the middle of the afternoon. He was always welcome—after all, it was his bloody house—but he stopped by at night, when his passions were inflamed, so something bad must have happened.

She studied him from behind the curtains. He was grim, determined, and he briskly dismounted and hastened in without knocking, which propelled her into a dizzying bout of hysterics.

How could such a perfect scheme have gone so awry? All she'd sought was a means to secure her position. Was that too much to ask?

If Pamela was still alive, Amanda would kill her all over again for bringing about so much misery!

As he stomped in, as he climbed the stairs, she braced. Momentarily, he entered her room.

They hadn't communicated since the horrid debacle. After Pamela had fallen, he'd paused, giving Amanda a chance to redeem herself, to step forward and take the blame, but what purpose would have been served by involving herself in the sordid situation?

"Michael, darling, how marvelous. Would you like a brandy, or have you a more tasty treat in mind?" Forcing a smile, she gestured to the bed, trying to look flirtatious but failing. She was a mess. Her hair was loose and uncombed, none of her facial paints had been applied, and she was wearing naught but a comfortable, tattered robe.

"This isn't a social call."

"It isn't?" She feigned obtuseness, anxious to avert whatever dire tidings he was about to share. "I can't imagine why else you'd be here."

"I had to warn you."

"Warn me? About what?"

"You're about to be arrested."

They were the words she'd fretted over for weeks, and now that they'd been uttered, they didn't seem real.

"For what?"

"For Pamela's murder."

"She wasn't *murdered*. The little idiot was drunk. She lost her balance."

"I saw the two of you fighting," he pointed out. "I saw the conclusion."

"The bystanders have described a different scenario, darling, so why rock that boat?"

"Because someone else saw you, too."

Her heart plummeted to the tips of her bare toes. "Who?"

"It hardly matters."

"Maybe not to you, but it certainly does to me."

"She's a very credible witness," he claimed, "and she's been believed."

"By whom?"

"By those who make decisions in these affairs."

"The law?"

He nodded. "They're coming for you, even as we speak."

"It was an accident," she fumed.

"So you say." He shrugged.

"It was an accident!" she repeated, shouting.

As if she hadn't commented, he kept on. "Because I've known you these many years, I'm doing you a favor. Considering the mischief you instigated, I shouldn't, but I am. I want this over."

"At this late juncture, what boon could you possibly render?"

"I'm allowing you a head start, but it's only a few minutes."

"You can't be serious."

"They're about to arrive, Amanda," he gently cautioned. "I've had your carriage readied, and it's out in the alley, but you have to leave. You're out of time."

"I won't," she boasted. "I did nothing wrong, and—as opposed to you—I have nothing to hide."

He shrugged again. "That's definitely your prerogative,

but you should remember that the penalty for murder is hanging."

"Hanging?" As if she could feel the noose tightening, she massaged her throat.

"They think you killed her so that I wouldn't marry her and toss you over."

"Of all the ludicrous, inane notions!" she scoffed. "As if that unpleasant child could have supplanted me!"

A large wagon, with an enclosed bed, lumbered down her street and halted outside. Two men on horseback had accompanied it, and they dismounted to parlay over whether they had the correct residence.

"They're here," he quietly stated.

"Well, I'll simply tell them they've made a mistake."

"Fine, have it your way."

He whirled around to depart, when she panicked. "Where are they planning to take me?"

"To Newgate. To await trial."

"Newgate!" It was the most squalid, most dangerous, prison in the land, and the idea that they would swagger into her home, seize her, and deposit her there was beyond comprehension.

As the riders walked to the door and banged the knocker, her peril finally sunk in and, in desperation, she clasped Michael's arm. "I'm terrified. What should I do?"

"Save yourself. Go. At once."

She assessed him, hoping to encounter a hint of compassion, a glimmer of sympathy, but he stared as if she was a stranger.

"It's because of that accursed governess, isn't it?" she snarled. "You love her. I can see it in your eyes."

He shook off her grip. "I'm not about to discuss her with you. Just let it be."

"How could you betray me like this?"

"I doubt I could convince you otherwise, but I delayed the proceedings as long as I could. Too much of it was beyond my control or authority."

He held out an envelope, and she frowned. "What's in it?"

"Five hundred pounds—to help you get settled—but from then on, you're on your own. Don't ever contact me again."

"But Michael," she wailed, "where should I go?"

"The choice is entirely up to you, and I don't wish to be apprised of your location, though it might be wise to flee the country." He tipped his head. "Good-bye and good luck. You'll need it."

He marched out and down, as the men tromped up. They exchanged curt remarks, then the men hurried on, but as they rushed into her bedchamber, the sole sign that she'd been there was a trace of her expensive perfume.

She raced down the rear stairs and out to the mews, and she leapt into the carriage Michael had arranged. The driver whisked her through town to the docks, where she could purchase fare on the next ship prepared to sail.

How humiliating! How galling! After all she'd accomplished, after all she'd achieved in her rewarding, prosperous life, she would escape England with only the envelope of money and the robe on her back.

25

"Is the first candidate here, Mr. Fitch?"

"Yes, milord."

Michael forced a smile, determined to proceed, and relieved that at least one courageous woman had dared to apply. Apparently, there was still a courtesan in the demimonde who was sufficiently greedy that she could overlook the possibility he was a murderer.

"Is she pretty?"

"Very."

Michael raised a brow. Fitch never had an opinion about his consorts. "Is she wearing a red dress as I requested?"

"An extremely bright shade," Fitch said. "I believe you'll be very pleased."

"Will I?"

"She's a tad out of the ordinary."

"Not my usual cup of tea?"

"Not even close."

"How so?"

"She's very clever, very friendly, well educated—"

"Educated!" Michael scoffed. "Why would I want a mistress who's educated? She won't bore me to death by blathering on about the morning papers or some such, will she?"

"I doubt it," Fitch replied. "She has other matters to occupy her. You'll see what I mean."

"Fitch," he teased, "what's come over you? You're turning into a virtual chatterbox."

"Perhaps I've been spending too much time around you, sir."

"Perhaps."

Michael chuckled but without mirth. Fitch's remark was an offhand reference to the silence in the house. Michael rarely spoke to anyone anymore. What was the point?

He was all alone, and with the scandals he'd endured, he'd quickly discovered how many friends he truly had: none.

Emily had married her cousin. Alex had run off to be a husband and father. Margaret was sequestered at an isolated boarding school, though she would reside with Alex and Mary once they were settled.

Only Michael was left on his own.

At a prior interval in his life, he'd have pretended that he didn't care, but the recent trials had unlocked a reservoir of yearning over which he had no control. He wasted his days pining away for what might have been, and he passed his nights ruing and regretting his terrible choices.

He couldn't step foot outside his door. The rumors were vicious, the stories much more horrendous and graphic than what had actually occurred. Amanda's escaping to Europe was currently the hot topic of conversation, and Michael couldn't bear any of it.

He wanted peace, wanted privacy to carry on as he had before the gaggle of crazed females had descended on him and wreaked their combined havoc.

Previously, he'd suffered through trauma, and he'd learned to cope with the worst. He'd buried his emotions and was gliding along in a void where nothing signified. No one would ever discern how distressed he was. No one would ever guess how he was raging on the inside.

All of London condemned him as a foul, immoral beast, so let them be proved correct.

"Don't keep me in suspense, Fitch. I'm anxious to meet this harlot who has you so fascinated."

"I wouldn't call her a harlot, sir."

"Really?"

"No."

"I would."

"You'd be mistaken."

Fitch was offended on the strumpet's behalf! How hilarious! "Show her in, Mr. Fitch. Show her in. I can hardly wait."

Michael refilled his whiskey and tried to relax in his opulent chair. He gulped the contents, poured another, then gulped that, too, but the potent brew had no effect, which was so frustrating. At a period when he was desperate for oblivion, naught could render him numb.

He listened as Fitch welcomed the woman, as they approached the library, and he tensed, hoping to experience some spark of curiosity, some sizzle of desire, but he was totally uninterested.

Why am I going through with this?

The annoying question taunted him, and he shoved it away. Since Emily had fled, his passion had fled, too. He had no rampant physical drive to be sated, no unbridled need to debase himself with every promiscuous hussy who batted her lashes. If he grew any more chaste, he could join a monastery!

Where had his lust gone? Why couldn't he get it back? He was about to participate in a session of anonymous, nasty sex, which had once been his favorite distraction, yet he couldn't generate any enthusiasm for the endeavor.

The woman crossed the threshold, though she was shielded by the gauze harem curtains he'd had put in place. She was slender, curvaceous, but he didn't feel a glint of titillation. Scolding himself, he bucked up, coaxing himself to act as if he were eager.

"You may enter," he proclaimed, ready for the games to begin, ready to rekindle what was lacking. Maybe a brief, raucous carnal encounter would thaw his frozen, detached self.

"Thank you, my lord and master." As if she were his slave, she bowed obediently; then she rose and slipped through the curtain. He blinked and blinked again.

"Emily?" he murmured.

His pulse pounded with elation, but he ignored his surge of delight. He'd loved her once, beyond all reason, but he'd managed to dispose of the idiotic sentiment, and he refused to have it resurface.

Though he'd never admit it in a thousand years, he'd been crushed by her abandonment, had been terribly wounded by the ease with which she'd deserted him. At his most dreadful hour, she'd forsaken him. His heart was still broken, and it was a pain he was resolved never to suffer again. He had to protect himself at all costs.

Sanity was restored with a vengeance, and he snapped, "What the hell are you doing here?"

"Hello, Michael," she cooed.

Her dress was red, as Fitch had mentioned, but it wasn't so much a dress as a negligee. It had two tiny straps across her shoulders, and it fell to the floor in a crimson wave, the thin fabric outlining every delicious inch of her torso. She had to have been in the house for quite some time, had to have changed in an upstairs bedroom.

He bristled. Who had let her in? How many of his employees had helped her without his consent? Had he any authority in his own home?

A shimmering, shiny vision, she floated toward him, and a flood of panic washed over him where he wondered if he should run out the rear door and continue running. From the minute they'd met, his life had been a string of disasters. Due to his inexplicable fondness for her, he'd made one wrong choice after another, had taken the wrong turn at every fork in the road.

"Go away! Please!" he entreated, alarmed by how ecstatic he was to be with her, but she kept coming, so he called, "Fitch! Mrs. Barnett was just leaving. Would you show her out?"

"I told Fitch to retire for the evening," she said. "He doesn't need to wait up for us."

She was at his chair, and she balanced both hands on the arms. She leaned forward, and her bodice was loose so he could see her breasts—if he was inclined to glance down. Which he wasn't!

They engaged in a staring match, but it was obvious he was losing. Her green eyes were open wide, her ruby lips moist and so close to his own. If he but dared, he could pull her to him, could kiss her senseless, and the notion terrified him.

Around her, he'd never had any willpower, and he didn't know how to fight his attraction. She goaded him to absurd levels of wanting, had him chafing and yearning in ways he couldn't abide.

And she was married! He absolutely would not philander with a new bride. What was she thinking?

"Why have you come?" he probed, bewildered by her arrival.

"Aren't you interviewing for a mistress?"

"Well . . . yes," he stammered, loathe to confess what he was about. She'd left him because he was an indecent animal, and even at this late juncture, he abhorred that he would bolster her dismal opinion.

"Look no further."

Without warning, she climbed onto his lap, her thighs spread, her knees braced on either side of him. She bent down to kiss him on the mouth, but at the last second, he lurched away so that she brushed his cheek instead.

It was a ridiculous moment. She was practically begging to be ravished, but he couldn't oblige her. His heart was too weary to risk another catastrophe. He had to keep her at bay, had to get her off his lap and out the door before he relented and did something stupid.

"Where is your husband?" He gazed at a spot behind her so that he didn't have to stare into her beautiful eyes. "I don't imagine he'll be too thrilled to hear that you're over here prostituting yourself."

"Oh, didn't anyone tell you?"

Don't ask! he admonished. He wouldn't care about her! Yet he found himself questioning, "Tell me what?"

"I never married Reginald." She nibbled his ear, his neck. "That day you were in Hailsham, he was lying."

"You're not married?"

"No."

His spirits soared at the news, but he tamped down his joy. If she was free, if she was single, what was it to him? As he'd long ago accepted, they weren't destined to end up together. So why pine for what could never be?

"I had been curious," he mused, determined not to react. "Thank you for letting me know. Now this *interview* is concluded. As you leave, you may send in the next candidate."

"We're not finished," she declared. "We've scarcely begun."

He watched, horrified, as she slid the strap of her nightgown off her shoulder, and he gulped with dismay. He'd never been able to resist her, and if she removed her clothes, he was in big trouble.

She tugged at the fabric, exposing her bosom, her tantalizing, lush breasts so near, so enticing. He struggled to disregard the temptation, but he failed. He was overwhelmed by her heat, by her smell, and he sucked at the extended tip.

Instantly, he was soothed, his anxiety and distress fading away, and he allowed himself to revel for a bit. She gave him the other, and he indulged again, as she moaned with pleasure, as she lowered her loins to connect with his. The contact was electrifying, and his phallus swelled to an enormous size, vividly reminding him that it had been an eternity since he'd had any carnal relief.

It would be so simple to grab her and ease himself into her tight sheath, but he did nothing, remaining as still as a marble statue, his hands firmly locked at his sides.

"It won't do you any good," he insisted.

"What won't?"

"I will never give you this job, no matter how keen you are to have it."

"Your mind is saying no, but your body is telling me a different story." She reached down and stroked him, and at encountering his rigid cock, she chuckled. "Why don't we see how averse you are to dallying?"

"I'm not averse," he claimed. "I'm perfectly willing to accept whatever is offered. From any female—besides yourself."

"Are you sure about that?"

"Very."

"Let's find out, shall we?"

Before he could prevent her, she was blazing a trail down his chest, pausing at his nipple to nip and bite. She slipped off his lap, knelt on the floor, and plucked at the drawstring of his pants. He observed, dispassionate, detached, as she toyed with the material, as she displayed him for her inspection. Then she leaned down, her glorious hair draped across his thighs, and she commenced at the base of his shaft, working upward until she was at the oozing crown.

She grinned. "Fitch informs me that you haven't had a woman in ages."

"Fitch should mind his own business." He was tense, strained, desperate for her to proceed.

"As far as he knows, you haven't had sex since I left."

"Then obviously, he doesn't know much."

"I wonder how long you can last?"

She glided over the end and sucked him inside. He'd tutored her well, and she performed the naughty exploit as if she were an experienced courtesan. Briefly, he wallowed in ecstasy, but she quickly spurred him to the edge.

He stared down at her, loving her, hating her, elated to have her prostrate before him. He was so ready to spill himself, to seize the moment, but he wouldn't. He couldn't.

He didn't understand why she'd come or what she wanted. Didn't she comprehend that her very presence was torture? He couldn't tolerate having her with him, having her taunt and tease with memories of what might have been.

Pulling away, he set her aside and stomped across the room, fussing with his trousers, tying the string.

His back to her, his emotions in turmoil, he could hear her rising to her feet, could hear her approaching, and he pleaded, "Go home, Emily. Please."

"Sorry, but I no longer have a home to which I can go. I must stay with you."

"Your personal problems aren't any of my affair," he unkindly stated. Once prior, he'd tried to rescue her, and it had been an unmitigated disaster. He wasn't a knight in shining armor and wouldn't pretend to be.

"Isn't that a fine how-do-you-do?" She sounded aggravated, as if *he* was the villain, as if *she* was the aggrieved party. "You've ruined me, and I demand you give me shelter."

"You *demand*?"

He whipped around, only to discover that, without his realizing it, she'd removed her negligee, so she was sinfully, blissfully naked. He was intimately familiar with every magnificent inch of her anatomy, could recall every leisurely exploration he'd undertaken.

How were they to have a rational argument when she was naked?

"Put something on!" he ordered, refusing to gape, refusing to drool, refusing to dream. "Immediately."

"No, I like prancing about in the nude. It suits me."

"It doesn't suit me," he lied.

"You've become such a Puritan."

She advanced on him, each stride bringing her closer, closer, until she pressed herself to him, her fabulous figure flattened to his all the way down. His phallus swelled even further, pushing him to a perilous precipice.

"Why are you doing this?" he inquired.

"Don't you know?"

"I haven't a clue."

"I love you," she asserted.

"No, you don't."

"Yes, I do. I've always loved you."

"You're mad," he scoffed. "Absolutely delusional. What sane woman would presume herself in love with the likes of me? Haven't you heard? I'm a murderer."

She ignored the shocking remark and rose up on tiptoe to kiss him. "You love me, too, Michael," she said. "Show me how much."

He was reeling, his senses igniting with an overload of happiness, which frightened him. Yanking away, he folded his arms around his torso so that his foolish hands couldn't reach out to her. "What will it take to make you go? Money? A house? What? Tell me, and it's yours."

"You thick lummox"—she had a hearty laugh—"I'm not after the things you can buy me."

"What, then?"

"I want *you.*"

"Well, *I* don't want you. As opposed to what you seem to imagine about me, I can't blithely fornicate with you, then send you on your merry way."

"Why not?"

"Because . . . because . . ."

"Because you care about me?" she finished when he couldn't.

"I *cared* about you. In the past. I even loved you, but you left me. You couldn't be bothered to learn the facts. Like everyone else, you thought the worst of me. You didn't give me a chance to explain. You never paused to consider that I might not have hurt you. You merely assumed that I would."

"I was wrong for not trusting you," she murmured. "Can you forgive me?"

Her gentle apology stopped him in his tracks. What should be his response? If she was sorry, how was he to keep his distance? "You're forgiven. Now leave me be. I can't bear this torment."

"Oh, Michael. . . ." She sighed. "Why *do* you suppose I'm here?"

"I told you: I don't know."

"Hazard a guess."

"You must want something from me."

"Yes."

"What?" he queried.

"I have a confession to make."

"Which is . . . ?"

"I don't wish to be your mistress."

"And I'm not about to let you," he concurred, "so we're agreed on that."

"Actually, I want to marry you. Will you have me?"

He gasped. "You want to what?"

"You heard me," she replied, and she repeated, "Will you have me?"

"Me? Have you? No."

"Why not?"

"Last I checked," he pointed out, "the man does the asking—"

"If I waited for you to get around to it," she interrupted, "I'd be a hundred years old."

"—and I don't ever intend to wed. So if that's what you came to discover, you have your answer, and we can end this charade."

"You don't intend to wed? Why?"

He assessed her, trying to decide if she was being cruel or obtuse. She wasn't either, so he couldn't fathom why she'd pretend not to know. "Are you aware of what occurred after you went home?"

"Yes, I've been apprised of every sordid detail. In the process of eloping, Alex raced through Hailsham to fetch my sister, and he spilled all."

"Then, you understand that insanity runs in my family."

"I am beginning to believe it runs in mine, too." As if there were a foul odor in the air, she waved away his declaration. "You didn't kill Pamela."

While Margaret had witnessed the incident and knew

the truth, Emily was the only person besides Alex who hadn't doubted him. Her certainty was a balm to his battered spirit.

"How can you be so sure?"

"You have many faults, Michael, but you're not a killer. You're an extremely kind man, and you have no temper, so you couldn't have lost it in a fit of anger."

"*I* am kind? *I* have no temper?"

"No, you don't, and your bark is much worse than your bite." She kissed him again. "Say yes. Say you'll be my husband."

She was so insistent, her request sounding so genuine, as if she really wanted to marry him. Why would she? Why would she bind herself to him? Her confidence rattled him, nagged at his common sense.

What if . . .

The fascinating prospect slithered by. What if he dared? He ought to call her bluff and consent just to see how fast she'd faint.

"What would you do with me if you had me?" he inquired.

"I'd spend every minute of every day making you happy." She was babbling on as if she'd already reflected, as if she had his entire life planned out. "I would love you, and I would furnish you with a houseful of children who would love you, too."

"Children? What would I do with children?"

"You'd love them back." She rested her palm on his cheek. "You'll never be alone again, Michael. Never. I swear it."

She painted such a pretty picture. Of himself, surrounded by people who cherished him. He'd never thought he wanted to have children, that he was deranged like his parents but his time with Margaret had changed him, had him realizing that he'd missed an important aspect of living, that perhaps he wasn't crazed, after all.

He could envision auburn-haired girls, who looked like Emily, dancing through the parlor, and dark-haired boys, who resembled himself and Alex, wrestling on the rug. Suddenly, he yearned for the dream to be his conclusion.

She snuggled herself to him, and he couldn't prevent his arms from going around her. "Tell me it could be real," he implored. "Tell me it could happen."

"Of course it could happen."

He'd always been on his own, had had to fend for himself. He'd been adrift on a forlorn sea, like a sailor viewing the normal townspeople on the shore. He'd ached to fit in, to be one of them, but he'd convinced himself that he didn't merit an ordinary existence.

She was offering everything he'd ever secretly craved. Could he refuse her? Could he toss her out and walk away? To what? To his quiet house? His isolated world? Was he to putter away into old age, hiding in his drafty mansion, with Fitch his sole companion?

"I want it," he choked out on a tortured breath, the admission wrenched from the innermost part of his being. "I want it all."

"Then you shall have it, my dear man," she promised.

He captured her lips in a torrid kiss, reveling in the taste of her, the feel of her. She was his heaven, she was his earth, and she'd come to him when he was at his lowest ebb. She loved him, when there was no reason she should.

Then and there, he vowed that he would spend the

remainder of his life proving to her that she'd made the right choice. He would never let her down.

He twirled her around and laid her on the couch where she'd first fallen asleep so many months earlier. He stretched out atop her, relishing how her body was pressed so intimately to his.

He was so hard for her, had desired her so desperately, for so long, and he ripped at his pants, anxious to yank them off. She smiled and stopped him.

"Aren't you forgetting something?" she queried.

"What?"

"There's a proposal on the table, and it hasn't been accepted."

"And I told you that the man does the asking."

"So . . . ?"

He was so delighted that he felt as if he might burst with gladness. "Emily Barnett, I love you with my whole heart and soul. Will you marry me?"

She flashed a wise, eloquent look. "There can't be any other women. Only me from this moment on."

"Only you."

"No more drinking."

She couldn't expect him to abandon all his bad habits! "Maybe a brandy after supper?"

"It's negotiable. But there'll be no carousing, no wild parties where you're traipsing around London and I'm worried about you and wondering where you are."

"I'll never be anywhere but by your side. I'll stay so close that you'll grow sick of me. You'll be begging me to leave you in peace."

She laughed at that. "You'll be faithful to me and devoted to our children."

"I can't wait."

"Then in that case, Lord Winchester, yes, I will marry you."

"I'll be the best husband ever."

"I know that you will."

He was so relieved, so thankful that she'd been stubborn enough to grab for what she wanted. If she hadn't risked all, he'd have been alone forever.

She was his, and he was so lucky.

"It seems we've settled our differences," he said. "Now may I remove my trousers?"

"Yes, you may," she answered, grinning, "and don't dawdle. I'm in a bit of a hurry."

Too Tempting to Touch

USA *Today* Bestselling Author

CHERYL HOLT

The paid companion for an aristocratic young woman, Ellen Drake has little opportunity for romance. When Ellen stumbles upon her lady's betrothed engaging in an illicit romp, she spies on the interlude far longer than she should. Alex Marshall is a notorious libertine and the sight of his lovemaking stirs Ellen's imagination with thoughts of a most carnal nature. But as Ellen threatens to reveal Alex's indiscretions to his fiancée, she never imagines that she could fall prey to his infamous charms. The stakes grow higher as their trysts become more heated by the day. And when their affair is finally revealed to all, will their passion finally burn out—or sizzle hotter than ever before?

Visit www.cherylholt.com